"Are yo

The look of a ̶ ̶ ̶ ̶ ̶ ̶ ̶ ̶ ̶ ̶ ̶ on Evan's face had Kelly regretting her words.

"Low blow, Kelly. Why would you ask that?"

She shrugged. "You're a newsman. I just dealt with some pretty awful reporters, and a reporter with no conscience started this problem. Can you blame me?"

"If I asked you to marry me, do you think I would betray you?" His voice lowered to almost a whisper.

It seemed an honest enough question, yet she still couldn't stop her doubt. "Offering marriage could be part of your plan."

He leaned back as if gauging the authenticity of her suggestion. "You're kidding, right?"

"You don't understand how much trusting others in the past has hurt me. Matt and I were doing very well until now."

But a small part of her was beginning to think Evan was that one man she could trust.

Dear Reader,

One of the great perks of fiction writing is I have the opportunity to raise readers' awareness of social issues within an entertaining platform. Most of my fiction is derived from real-life stories. I get huge satisfaction in creating challenges that my heroes and heroines meet head-on with dignity, grace and a good dose of humor to reach that wonderful happily-ever-after.

The Father of Her Son came into being when chatting about the plot with my author friend Heather Graham. After listening to my idea, Heather said, "Did you know that if a woman is raped in the state of New York, gets pregnant and chooses to keep her child, the state will grant the rapist custodial rights to that baby?"

That floored me! You will be glad to know that amendments are currently being tabled to change that law, but that very sad fact is all too true today.

Then I thought of all those stories of politicians who have behaved in ways completely counter to their platforms and I started wondering: What if a nanny was raped by her employer, became pregnant and discovered that this dangerous man could gain joint custody of her baby and effectively control the rest of her life? What would she do? Me? I'd go underground. No one would ever know who the father of my baby was. And so, *The Father of Her Son* was born.

I hope you will enjoy both Kelly Sullivan's and Evan McKenna's journey through this story. I loved writing it. I loved the opportunity to platform a law that is in dire need of change for the rights of women. I hope you enjoy this story. Please visit me at www.kathleenpickering.com and let me know!

I am so grateful that you are out there, dear reader. And thank you for choosing to read *The Father of Her Son.* I am honored to spend this one-on-one time with you.

With love,

Kathleen Pickering

The wink acknowledged more than breakfast. Clearly, Dean had told the senator that the religious experience had more to do with the diner's owner than the meals. All the bucks in the newsroom flirted with Kelly, who managed to fend them off with amazing ease while filling their coffee mugs. To Evan, the woman's aloofness was part of her allure, and she was totally undeserving of the rogue attitude guys like Dean attached to her. Any insinuation that Kelly was available made Evan want to smash a fist into Dean's pointed snout.

Instead, he patted his stomach because sure enough, his late breakfast had been memorable. "Excellent down-home Cajun fare prepared by a cook who'd scare you off the sidewalk as soon as pass him, sir. You'd enjoy the experience."

Buzz laughed, exposing perfect white teeth. "Next time, for sure. For now, let's discuss some important questions I'd like you to ask me on air."

EVAN'S NERVES THRUMMED deep under his controlled exterior. Beneath the hot studio lights, the set was silent except for the exchange between him and Senator Campbell. He'd already exhausted all the carefully choreographed questions Campbell wanted asked. His guest looked completely satisfied sitting across from him in his Brooks Brothers suit, blue shirt and contrasting yellow print tie. With a precious two minutes left, Evan would let the torpedoes fly with some hard-core questions of his own.

"Senator, America has been at war since 2001. How much longer can our country or our economy sustain war, not to mention the loss of America's sons and daughters on foreign soil?"

The momentary lift of an eyebrow on Campbell's face was lost on the viewing world since the camera was on Evan, but he hadn't missed the senator's surprise—or the

the room, Steve occupied a position of favor, chatting with the senator from the right-hand side of his chair.

Evan ignored Dean Porter, whose brown suit and ugly striped tie compounded his lack of professional tact as he lounged in the empty makeup chair to the left of Campbell, as if they were longtime friends. Two other men and a raven-haired beauty who looked to be about thirty were the senator's entourage.

Evan headed straight for Campbell, offering him his hand. "Senator Campbell, sorry I'm late. I was expecting you in half an hour."

"Call me Buzz. No problem at all, Evan. Had an unexpected addition to plans. I thought we'd get an early start, if that's okay with you."

"Sure. I'm just sorry I wasn't here to greet you."

Evan glanced at his boss. He had danced pretty hard to get this early interview with Buzz Campbell—before he announced his candidacy. The look on Steve's face spoke volumes that he was satisfied with Evan's ability to snag breaking news before any other news station. As a senator, Buzz Campbell's impact on the political arena garnered enormous popularity at the grassroots level. That he chose Evan and NCTV to announce his plans for the White House was huge for ratings. Evan tucked that satisfaction away as a perk for negotiating his next raise. Once again, his instinct had landed another first for NCTV morning news.

Out of necessity, Dean vacated the makeup seat next to the senator so Tanya's assistant could touch up Evan's face from the early morning show.

Senator Campbell winked at Evan's reflection in the mirror. "Dean here tells me breakfast at that diner across the way is like a religious experience. Hope you didn't rush on my account."

"Something about having another engagement. Last minute. He's in makeup with Steve and Dean."

"Why Dean?"

She smirked. "He rode the elevator with the senator. Apparently they share the same fraternity. Dean made sure Campbell knew it and has been in the middle of the conversation ever since."

Evan shook his head. Dean was the type of office friend who would stay just that—an office friend. The guy was good at reporting stories, but his overenthusiasm reeked of insincerity. Evan seldom gave the guy much thought unless Dean was in his face for something. He could see Dean tripping over himself to get time with the senator in Evan's absence, despite the fact that Evan had landed the interview.

He pulled his pen from its holder and clicked it a few times. "Is the set ready?"

"Yes. They're waiting for my call."

"Okay. Tell them we'll be down in twenty minutes."

There were five people seated with the senator in the makeup room. Senator Robert "The Buzz" Campbell was holding court with the ease and confidence of a man who knew the effect he had on a crowd. Tanya, the makeup artist, had draped the senator's shoulders and was touching up his complexion, which honestly didn't need much help, under the glare of the white lights. He was average height but built like an athlete. His thick blond hair, summer tan and deep blue eyes exuded those movie star looks that would earn him votes from the female population.

Evan nodded to his silver-haired boss, Steve Fiore. With his hawk eyes, Steve never missed a trick and was, as always, a class act in a navy Armani suit. Steve had won the confidence of the network owners for ten years running, and his self-assurance showed. From the body language in

CHAPTER ONE

THE ATMOSPHERE AROUND the Manhattan newsroom offices at NCTV seemed unusually charged as Evan McKenna pushed through the glass doors on the seventh floor of the Fifth Avenue television station. His assistant, Sarah, paced outside his office, steno pad and file folder in hand.

He'd just come from a quick breakfast across the street at the Neverland Diner, where the proprietor, his friend, a fiery Irish redhead with mesmerizing green eyes and the perfect spray of freckles on her nose, had distracted him a bit longer than expected. He had an important interview scheduled with presidential hopeful Buzz Campbell in an hour but that didn't explain the extracharged air or his assistant's frown. Sarah saw him coming and met him halfway.

"What's up, Sarah?"

She dropped the file into his hands, his favorite pen attached to the steno pad. "He's here already."

"Who?"

"Senator Campbell. I sent you a text, but you didn't answer."

He ran a hand through his collar-length black hair, his aqua eyes flashing regret. Of course he didn't answer. He'd been too preoccupied with Kelly Sullivan to heed the alert. He checked his watch. "He's thirty minutes early. Senators usually keep you waiting."

To Tony Agius and Lisa Russell...
who didn't let life stop the love.

Here's wishing you every happiness!

ABOUT THE AUTHOR

Kathleen Pickering believes stories, like myths of old, are excellent tools for teaching life lessons while entertaining. She loves "happily ever after" but believes her characters have to overcome their life challenges with dignity, grace and a good dose of humor to deserve that special ending. Kathleen draws her characters and stories from real-life situations and finds traveling to research her work an added perk. So beware. If she meets you, you may wind up in one of her novels!

Books by Kathleen Pickering

HARLEQUIN SUPERROMANCE

1754—WHERE IT BEGAN

Other titles by this author available in ebook format.

Recycling programs
for this product may
not exist in your area.

ISBN-13: 978-0-373-71856-6

THE FATHER OF HER SON

Printed in U.S.A.

The Father of Her Son

KATHLEEN PICKERING

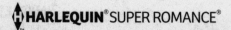

delight at a challenge—that rose in the man's eyes. With camera two recording his answer, Buzz Campbell replied with the face of a concerned father.

"America has no more time for war, Evan. We have to understand the cultural differences driving the forces behind the violence we're trying to subdue. We must understand the people with whom we are at war and make sure American interests are not violating humanitarian interests in those regions. I will work closely with the United Nations to create dialogues and set strategies for conflict transformation on all levels, insuring all interested countries across the globe take part in finding a plan for peace."

Excellent response. Kudos for the senator. Evan let his ease reflect his support for the senator's answer.

"We only have time for one more question, Senator. Given the raw nerve that has been struck by certain politicians and religious groups insisting the government set laws based on religious doctrine, what is your stance on religion influencing government?"

Campbell shook his head. "You know, Evan? Personal interests have always been the motivating factor behind any great society whether right or wrong. While America was founded by God-fearing men and women who used their moral beliefs to fuel our great beginnings, religious doctrine belongs in our hearts, not our politics. I'd like to believe that our leaders will govern our people with wisdom and intelligence—without imposing any religious doctrine that would deny America the freedom of choice. We have to trust that Americans know the difference between right and wrong and will do what is right within this country's fabric of inalienable rights."

The senator's answer raised applause from the set workers, which made both Evan and the senator smile. What a great way to end the segment: with the down-home, middle American approval in the studio reflecting how many viewers would probably respond.

"Thank you for your time, Senator." Evan closed the interview by looking into the camera as he spoke the trailing statement. He didn't have to look at the senator to know he'd just earned the regard of the next president of the country.

THE NEXT MORNING, Evan plowed into Neverland after the show aired, all pumped up from the high ratings the segment with his interview with Buzz Campbell had garnered. He'd done it. He had crawled under the senator's defenses and forced him to answer some hard questions on camera, and America responded favorably.

Best result of the interview, however, was that Buzz Campbell had understood the gift Evan had presented him in his endorsement. Evan had just gotten off the phone with the senator, who had offered his personal cell phone number. If Evan needed quotes in the future, he could contact the senator anytime for his opinion.

Major score as a TV anchor.

Expecting to hear cheers and congratulations from the customers in Neverland, he was immediately struck with… nothing. The big-screen television on the wall—which was always tuned to NCTV—was playing the Robin Williams version of *Peter Pan* instead of the usual midmorning talk show that followed Evan's news program.

Kelly's almost-six-year-old son Matt called to Evan from the family booth, but the boy's eyes quickly returned to the oversize screen, enthralled with the sword battle between Robin Williams and Dustin Hoffman playing the dastardly Hook.

Bewildered, Evan headed for his seat at the counter. Proud of their renewed friendship and Evan's success,

Kelly had painted a gold star on the floor with his name stenciled on it.

Bunny greeted him first. The enthusiasm in her body language was a dead giveaway. Clearly, the manager was embarrassed his show hadn't been viewed.

"Morning, Evan. Ready for some breakfast?"

He motioned to the television. "Didn't you watch the interview?"

She scrunched her shoulders with discomfort. "No. Cable is down. Sorry. How did it go?"

Kelly Sullivan emerged through the kitchen doors. She stopped when his gaze, which he knew was full of questions, captured hers. She wiped her hands on the apron tied to her waste.

"Ah, himself, it is. Good morning, Evan McKenna."

Evan chose to answer Bunny's question, but kept his eyes on Kelly. Her agitation was not lost on him. "The interview was outstanding, Bunny. Actually, impeccable. I hammered the senator with direct questions and his answers probably launched his candidacy in the best light."

Kelly clucked her tongue. "Lies. All of them. I'm sorry, Evan. We watched fairy tales this morning instead of more politics. Really hope you don't mind."

Hell, yes, he minded. He didn't realize how much until he felt this blatant snub. He lowered his voice, not wanting the hurt to show. "You're my friend, Kelly. I told you yesterday how much this interview meant to me. Couldn't you have withheld your political sarcasm long enough to support me for this one important show?"

He inhaled a breath, really wanting to rant, but realized he sounded trite. He shook his head, needing to find a different tack other than personal insult. "Ratings, Kelly. You had a captive audience here. I could have used the help."

He didn't care that Kelly had gone pale, her mouth com-

pressed as if her teeth might draw blood from those luscious lips. Something was very wrong. Kelly knew as well
as he did that her support of NCTV was what brought the
major portion of her regular clientele. Every employee at
NCTV ate at Neverland at least once a week. Half the fun
of eating here was watching themselves, their bosses or
the celebrities they handled through the ranks appear on
the big screen dominating the diner. Fans knew Neverland
was the newsroom's hot spot and the place swelled with
curiosity seekers. Was she giving him a rap on the knuck-
les because he had asked her on a date yesterday for the
seventh—or was it the eighth—time?

"Well, Your Majesty, the television cable line failed last
night. I'm waiting for the repairman. The best I could do
was play a DVD until he arrives."

Now he'd been out of line. Kelly might be brash but she
would never blatantly snub him. If he'd been listening instead of getting insulted, he would have heard Bunny explain the same thing.

He was an idiot. She'd always supported him from the
first time they met seven years ago until his return from a
seven-year assignment in Europe just four months ago. He
had been thrilled to come home and find Kelly now owner
of the diner where she previously worked as a waitress.
She'd transformed the old dinosaur into a retro hot spot
and renamed it. The fact that she was still single added to
his enthusiasm.

But the true shocker had been when she introduced
him to her son, Matt, of whom she was very protective
and curiously tight-lipped about his origins. Her casual
responses to his subtle questions never failed to intrigue
him. His curiosity was always piqued by this voluptuous
Irish siren who occupied more and more of his thoughts.

But something didn't seem right. His usually bold and

funny friend seemed distressed. Her hand had trembled when she pushed a copper tendril off her cheek. Had he upset her that much? He held up a stopping hand, chastened. "Kelly. I'm sorry. I didn't understand."

It took a New York second for her to snap back to her old self. "Indeed, Evan. As pompous an Irishman as ever I've met. So, will it be the usual? Or would you like an order of crow with your coffee?"

CHAPTER TWO

KELLY WOULD BURN in hell. She just knew it. Her excuse
for not airing Evan's interview was true. The cable line
was down. What she omitted, however, was that she had
yanked the cable from the wall specifically to avoid airing
Evan's interview with Senator Robert "The Buzz" Campbell. There was no way she would lay eyes on that bastard
if she could help it. Bunny had caught her yanking the cord
from the wall and had given her grief. Sidestepping her
pointed questions had been tricky enough. Explaining her
motives to Evan would be impossible. Luckily, it looked
like that conversation had been evaded. Bunny kept her
promise and said nothing to Evan.

Damaging the cable was the only way to avoid Evan's
interview and save face with him. Why hadn't she just
burst from the kitchen babbling about how sorry she was
that the TV wouldn't work and how unfortunate for them
to miss his show? Why? Because *that* would have been a
lie, and Kelly Sullivan hated lies.

Lies had short roots that could be plucked from one's
explanation in the face of the truth. Worse, if you were
caught in a lie, no one would ever trust you again. The
nuns at St. Peter's School for Girls in Kinsale, County
Cork, as well as her strict father and fanatically religious
mother had taught her well.

However, what she learned on her own just a few short
years ago—which her parents and the nuns failed to teach

her—was that the truth could also ruin you. With a single word. Like *yes*. Or *no*. Answering yes when a man whom you trusted asked if you thought he was handsome. And then saying, no, when he asked if you'd like him to touch you, only to have him accuse you of lying for speaking the truth then use that handsome body to rape you.

Kelly had learned in the worst possible way what damage the truth could do. While lying was a sin, telling the truth could ruin someone's life. Which was worse? Her only conclusion was to do what she must to keep her world safe. Kelly decided that instead of lying, omitting the truth whenever necessary was a necessary evil. While she would never trust anyone who lied to her, she had certainly perfected the art of portioning out the truth, as God was her witness.

Yes, she would burn in hell, for sure. Evan's look of horror was proof enough.

She sighed. "Don't look so glum, Evan. How will it be if I sweeten your disappointment with a free breakfast?"

His laugh was curt. "Well, of course you'll offer a free meal when I've lost my appetite."

"Well, then, this must be my lucky morning." She poured his coffee, wishing desperately to get back on track with him. "So tell me, did you trounce the senator with all your unbiased nonsense in true fashion?"

This time to her relief, he laughed. "I think you've chastened me enough for my error. Now, let's hear the end of it, if you will."

She threw in their ongoing joke. "Will you try the pancakes, then?"

He reached for her hand, sending all sorts of tingles up her arm, which circled around to the back of her neck. He tugged the slightest bit to bring her face closer to his. She complied, if only to give him a quarter since she did feel bad. His fresh, clean soap scent invaded her nostrils like a clear spring morning.

Evan's voice dropped low and seductive as he said, "No pancakes, Red. I'll take the usual." A grin pulled across her lips.

An older gent chuckled from his seat at the table behind Evan. Everyone knew Kelly teased Evan about pancakes because he'd made it clear he hated them. Their open banter, bordering on flirting had become entertainment for Kelly's patrons. She pulled away, liking her nickname, "Red," but not the way he spoke it as if the word was a secret code for some fantasy he held about her.

Kelly's son, Matt, scrambled onto the stool next to Evan. "Hi, Evan!"

Matt's adoration for Evan tickled her. The kid was beaming. Probably one of the main reasons she rekindled her friendship with Evan was for her son's benefit. Evan's attention to Matt on these workday mornings helped fill in the gap of "guy interaction" that Matt lost when Herby died. The fact that Matt liked Evan alleviated her suspicions about the celebrity anchor's intentions. In the past few months he'd done well in reestablishing the brief friendship that had been severed as soon as it had begun seven years ago.

He mussed the boy's hair as he always did. "Morning, Matt-man. Miss me?"

Matt grabbed Evan's wrists with both hands and Evan lifted him off the seat, which set Matt laughing. "Soon you'll be too big for me to lift you like that, kiddo."

Matt's green eyes, so much like Kelly's own, lit up with joy. "I know. I'll be six on Saturday."

"And those six years will certainly earn you a present."

"Like a Lego set?" Matt was a Lego madman.

Evan shook his head. "You'll have to wait and see."

He tucked his napkin into the neck of his light blue shirt, covering a striped tie of various shades of the same color. His smile assured Kelly that he'd forgiven her the television transgression.

"I'll take my eggs anytime you find fitting, my dear."

Kelly didn't need to write a ticket for Evan. Once Jake spotted him, he knew exactly how to prepare Evan's breakfast. Her television anchor celebrity was a creature of habit. Kelly glanced back into the kitchen and saw Jake already preparing Evan's hash browns and scrambled eggs with Jack cheese and chili peppers.

She left him to answer Matt's relentless questions while she attended to other patrons. As she filled coffee cups and took orders, Kelly congratulated herself one more time for not letting on that Evan's appearance this morning—just as his reappearance four months ago, looking more filled out, worldly wise and more strikingly handsome than ever— had shaken her right down to her well-worn running shoes.

Before his return, she'd almost forgotten about the hunky black-haired, blue-eyed newsman she'd met her first day on the job. She'd spotted him jaywalking across the street during Manhattan morning hour like Moses parting the Red Sea. When he walked through the doors of Herby's diner she'd been so taken by his smile that she poured his cup too full, spilling coffee over the counter.

It was amazing how after seven years, Evan had simply waltzed into Neverland as if a mere day had passed as eager to see her as if he'd never left. He had been quick to explain how the assignment in Paris had turned into a job on the continent. Kelly was surprised to realize she still stewed over his lack of communication over the years and had no desire to hear his excuses. They had struck up a lovely friendship back then that he dropped as abruptly as he had started. Didn't he know that telephones and email were modern-day conveniences that friends used to keep in touch…even seven years ago?

In reality, Evan had only grazed her thoughts while he was away. Too much had happened. Between dropping out of college for Matt's birth, working the diner and those two hard years caring for Herby—the diner's owner and her salvation before he passed away—Kelly didn't have much time for quiet musings. She had taken pains to be sure Evan understood that she had no more to offer him than friendship, a cup of coffee and an occasional free meal. She had a son to raise and protect. A business to run. Owning the diner and the apartment upstairs that she'd inherited from Herby afforded her an independence she never expected.

She had become a mother and businesswoman with intentions of her own, and she meant to stick by them. A distraction like dating, especially with a charming yet intensely career-driven man like Evan McKenna, was simply unwelcome. If she dated at all she'd be better off with a quiet, easy-mannered guy who worked as hard as she did and had no craving for power or fame.

"Penny for your thoughts, Red?"

Evan had been watching her with more attention than usual.

She had been moving at a brisk clip delivering plates and writing up tickets. She hadn't realized her mind was reflecting so easily on her face.

"I'm trying to decide if you should get the fresh bacon or the scraps for the stray dogs out back."

A bearded man next to Matt guffawed.

Her son looked mortified. "Mom!"

Evan drummed his fingers on the counter to a silent beat, exchanging a conspiratorial glance with Matt. Instead of his usual retort, he simply stated, "If you knew what I had planned, you'd give me the whole pig."

She turned to face him, planting fists on hips. "What are you up to, Evan?"

He tapped his breast pocket. "Got something here I'm willing to share to celebrate the interview, despite the fact you missed the show. It all depends on whether you can get a babysitter for Matt."

"Mrs. Walsh will watch me!" Matt seemed to know what Evan had planned.

Reaching into the breast pocket of the impeccable navy suit, Evan slid two tickets across the counter. "Front row seats to *Billy Elliot*."

She couldn't help but grin. He must have overheard her telling Bunny yesterday that *Billy Elliot* was the one Broadway show she wanted to see this season. Temptation tugged, but a clearer head removed its silly hand. Nothing would be sweeter than a few hours' escape into another world, not to mention Evan's grin seemed to be doing silly things to her heart, which to her surprise, puttered a tad faster in her chest.

It didn't matter. Kelly wouldn't accept the offer. Not only was Evan not her type, there was no room in her plans for a relationship. A boyfriend would only distract her from raising her son. Dating would remove her from the diner for which she was eternally grateful and planned to make more successful than Herby could ever imagine. And lastly, what she was least willing to acknowledge, was that she had never dated…anyone.

She met Evan's hopeful gaze with a grin. "Nice try, Evan. Won't happen."

"Oh, Mom." Matt's disappointment was palpable.

"And, I don't appreciate you tangling Matt into your shenanigans."

Evan ignored her. "Look closer. Row One. Center."

She pushed the creamer and sugar toward Evan from

its place by the napkin box. "I said, no. Now, be a nice patron and eat quickly. I have a busy morning ahead of me."

Bunny passed Kelly and stopped when she saw the tickets. Two full plates in hand, she looked from the tickets to Kelly. "*Billy Elliot?* Are you going?"

Kelly laughed out loud at her trusted manager, who had no trouble waiting tables when the morning, lunch or dinner rush began. "No, Bunny. You and Evan both know I do not date."

Bunny nodded once, then flashed Evan a saucy glance. "Right, then. I'll be happy to go with you if she's too lamebrained to go."

If Evan was disappointed that Kelly turned him down—yet again, he didn't show it. This was his eighth try in as many weeks to ask her out. Yet he grinned, shaking his head.

"Well then, ladies. It looks as though you two should take each other. The show starts at nine. The dinner rush should be over by then."

The women exchanged looks. Even though Kelly had sabotaged his interview, Evan still asked her out. Rebuffed again, he was surrendering the tickets. The man was either a fool, a glutton for punishment or uncommonly generous. Something about the playful and confident look in his eyes both intoxicated and unnerved her. For her own security, Kelly needed to be in control when it came to men—but she had to do something. After all, Evan was a *friend*.

"Then you must let me pay for the tickets."

Evan pushed the tickets back and called to Bunny as she planted the overflowing plates before two businessmen at the other end of the counter. "Take your boss out tonight, Bun. She looks like she could use a break."

Wiping her hands on her apron, Bunny rushed back to scoop up the tickets before Kelly could change her mind.

"Absolutely. It's Tuesday. Quiet enough for us both to escape. Thanks, Evan!"

Kelly mustered a smile. "Yes. Thank you, Evan. You are way too kind."

She ducked behind the heat-shield window to catch her best cook's eye from the line of three who ran the morning grill. "Be sure you use the sweetest peppers in his-self's potatoes. He is eating for free this morning."

The burly man, sporting a skull and crossbones earring, winked in return. "They're ready."

Kelly retrieved Evan's plate and refilled his coffee mug.

Evan tapped the deep sea-green granite countertop; the one major extravagance Kelly made when renovating the diner. "You enjoy the show tonight. Don't mind me. I'll just drown my rejection in Jake's free, down-home Louisiana cooking."

She reached under the counter for her ever-present Nikon and snapped a photo of Evan in sheer bliss at Jake's superb cooking. Smiling to herself, she said, "That'll be a keeper."

He swallowed his food. "You certainly are a beautiful sight with a camera for a nose, Kelly Sullivan. I think you missed your calling."

She gestured to the wall of framed photos she'd taken of patrons eating her food. "I think it's time your mug took front and center on the Wall of Fame. Don't you think?"

"Ahh, I thought you'd never offer!"

Matt had grown bored with their conversation and slid off his stool. A booth just outside Kelly's office was designated as the rest station for family and staff. Matt tugged on Evan's jacket and pointed to the booth. "Wanna play with my Lego?"

Evan actually looked disappointed. "Sorry, Matt-man.

I have to get back to the office. How about we'll build a spaceship next time?"

"Okay. I'm gonna start mine now!"

Kelly watched him climb into the booth beneath a large framed photo of her and Matt, taken by holding the camera at arm's length. She smiled. "Again, Evan, thank you for the theater tickets. I hope to repay the gesture one day."

He wiped his plate with a chunk of bread. "Dinner with me on Saturday night will work wonders to assuage my damaged pride." The way one eyebrow arched to complement that crooked, playful smile made her stomach flip-flop.

"But, you know…"

He interrupted before she finished her worn-out declaration of no dating. "It's not a date. It's dinner for Matt for his birthday."

The cable man appeared through the door. Bunny glanced her way before leading the man to the back corner of the building.

Guilt tugged on Kelly like an anchor around her neck as she watched the cable guy disappear into her office. Evan had easily forgiven her for not airing his show this morning, but from his excitement yesterday over snagging that interview with the awful Buzz Campbell, not supporting him had hurt Evan even if the circumstance did appear out of her control. She'd have to make amends this time simply to allay her own guilty feelings.

She swallowed hard. "It's Tuesday, Evan. Do I have to give you an answer now?"

He shrugged. "I am a busy man, Kelly Sullivan. I don't make time for just anyone. I'd appreciate a commitment."

His lips twitched to keep from grinning. She liked that, but at the same time she chafed at pushy men. Kelly chided herself. Evan had been sweet with his continued offers to take her out. Seven years of celibacy was a hard taskmaster. Staring into Evan's smiling eyes made it difficult to drum up reasons to support her stringent decision.

She was a different person from the scared and lonely girl he'd met seven years ago. She had full control of her world now. Yet, she could not deny that if Evan wasn't so headstrong or ambitious, his looks alone could be enough to make her say yes.

Could she handle one dinner with Evan—especially with Matt in the mix? Matt worshipped Evan. He would love the time with him. Or would the dinner give Matt ideas about Evan becoming a part of their private life? She needed more time to stew over the invitation.

"Ask me later, Your Majesty. I need to take one more look at the FBI records to make sure you're not a wanted felon."

He finished the last of his coffee. "Then yes it is, Red. Those records will come up clean. We'll confirm details Saturday morning. Thanks for breakfast."

He eased off the stool and waved to Matt before exiting the diner, whistling.

Bunny sidled up next to her, watching Evan leave. "I told the cable man the cord got caught under the chair wheel. I'm making him shorten the cable line."

Kelly wrapped an arm around her friend for a brief squeeze. "Brilliant solution, Bunny. Thank you."

She shrugged. "Well, your plan of pulling the cable to land a date couldn't have worked any better."

"That was no plan!"

Bunny moved to a table with new customers. "Then why else would you take such a drastic measure to get his undivided attention?"

Kelly left that question unanswered. Better to endure the smile on Bunny's face—which would surely last past lunch—rather than explain the truth. "It's a birthday dinner for Matt. He's going to love it."

Matt heard his name and pulled his attention from his building bricks. "Does Evan know I want a homemade ice-cream cake?"

Bunny burst into laughter.

Kelly headed for the next customer. "No, son, but I'll surely tell him."

CHAPTER THREE

ONE FACT CONSUMED Evan's thoughts as he headed back to the office. Kelly hadn't said no to Saturday night. This was the closest he'd gotten to a yes from her and he high-tailed it out of Neverland before she could reconsider her halfhearted agreement.

When he'd first returned to New York, Steve Fiore said Kelly owned the revamped Neverland diner. Evan's heart did a little twist when he found her ensconced behind the counter, eyes wide at the sight of him.

Yet, Kelly had changed. He'd realized why the minute she introduced him to Matt. Evan had done the math. Matt had been conceived within months after he and Kelly first met, on the first day Herby, the old softie, had hired her.

Kelly wouldn't budge on revealing the paternity of the boy. Honestly, he didn't care. He was more concerned that perhaps some deadbeat needed to be paying child support. If that was the case, he'd be more than happy to hunt down the bastard. Kelly clearly loved her son to distraction, but whatever she went through to get that great kid into her life, the deed had left its mark. Kelly had lost her innocence. She had become cautious while still remaining alluring. Caring, but from the distance of a football field.

Why the hell hadn't he called her while he was gone? Checked up on her?

He knew why. But he didn't even want to go there. Not now that his career launched as he had planned. He swallowed the guilt that he may have hurt her. Back then, he didn't have the time to concentrate on a relationship. Funny how the tables had turned. Now that his career was on solid ground, he was ready to find a wife and begin a family. After all the women he'd dated, his sights continued to zero in on Kelly. No other woman compared. Getting her to date him would help fill the void in his happiness as only a companion could.

Yes, indeed. He was all for second chances. And for finding answers. He wanted to help Kelly as much as he wanted to date her. Someday, he'd unearth Matt's father. If the guy had hurt Kelly in any way, he'd make sure the dude got his comeuppance.

Evan's notoriety in the news world came from his doggedness with a story. If he got wind of possible news, he sniffed out every corner, every fact, every morsel of research until he put flesh on the skeletons he found.

The radar he depended on to alert him to something fishy was pinging intensely over Neverland's cable being out of service. Something didn't add up. Yesterday when he confided in Kelly that Buzz Campbell was his secret interview, she had been holding her precious Nikon camera. When he said Campbell's name the delicate instrument slipped from her hands. Evan managed to catch the camera before it hit the floor, but he hadn't missed the intense shock that had filled those gorgeous green eyes.

Leaving Neverland now, it hit like a jolt that he actually knew nothing about Kelly other than the usual safe, small talk. Irish born. Parents strict Roman Catholics. Her father owned a limousine service, her mother was a homemaker. Two older brothers, married with kids. A sister and another brother, Michael, the priest. Kelly couldn't afford to not work. Raising Matt left no time for dating.

She'd delivered the obvious facts.

All in a tidy little nutshell.

Was there more to the sultry redhead than met the eye? Was she a fugitive from Ireland? A runaway from a marriage? Whatever the secret, his gut prodded him to learn more. All avenues pointed to Matt. Kelly was a pro at keeping topics away from her personal life. Like the enchantress she was, she got folks talking about themselves, leaving little room for self-revelation. And when one did ask questions, as Evan always had, she was quick with that sexy little shrug, pensive look or heart-stopping smile and an evasive answer.

Well, now, Kelly was giving him cause for thought. Her clumsiness after he told her about the senator could very well have been coincidence—slippery fingers, given how quickly she'd been moving around. But something in her face, like mortification or fear, hit the alarm button. His instincts had made him one hell of a good newsman. He'd never ignored them before, and he surely would not now.

He wanted to understand this woman who fascinated him. Only, what if he found bad news? Like an abandoned husband somewhere or that she was a conspirator in some illegal activity with the IRA. For sure, even his own family had problems with that faction. What if she'd kidnapped Matt and he wasn't really hers?

Nah. The kid had her eyes. His gut told him Kelly's trouble was personal; something that made her cautious. Distant. He didn't think what she was hiding would be enough to keep him away. If anything, it triggered his protective inclinations. He hadn't felt like that...ever.

He'd always assumed he'd eventually settle down. His momma didn't raise a fool. He'd watched his parents, who still loved each other after thirty years. That's what Evan wanted in his relationship. Something simple and passionate that could stand the test of time.

Question was, how would he fit simple and passionate into his high-powered, fast-rising career? The job took up all of his time. An anchor newsman was just that: weighted and staying put. Constant interviews. Meetings. Brainstorming ideas with his staff. He had become the face most New Yorkers wanted to watch every morning at eight. Could he honestly become a family man when he had married his job?

Perhaps. If his wife was as busy as he. His thoughts drifted back to Kelly, a rare breed that one. He didn't want to change Kelly one bit. He just wanted to orbit the same world as her and Matt for a while to see if they and he matched.

Evan craved to know what had happened in Kelly's life to produce Matt. He had his suspicions. Given her insistence on remaining independent and self-sufficient, he could only assume she'd been bullied, or overcontrolled. He was pretty sure she would not lie, but would she omit information? Yes, she was certainly capable of editing answers with a tongue as smooth as a leprechaun's. He'd continue to follow his hunches. With time, he'd ferret out the answer.

He punched the elevator button in the lobby. Enough. Pushing Kelly and Matt from his mind, he started thinking about this next interview. Thoughts about Kelly had to be put on the back burner until Friday. Right. Like that was possible.

IT FELT LIKE a bit of hell not going to Neverland for breakfast for the rest of the week. The nature of his job had him on the set early and tying up loose ends afterward, but he'd always managed to shoot over to Kelly's for breakfast before tackling the tasks after the show. This time, he dived directly into the after-show work instead of going to

Neverland. He didn't want to give Kelly a chance to back away from Saturday's plans. He'd gotten this far, and he wasn't about to blow it.

His next show featured a man who fought the courts for custody of his son from his estranged wife. According to his guest, after a whirlwind courtship, he'd married a woman with the best of intentions only to discover, after a year of marriage, that she suffered from dissociative identity disorder—or multiple personalities. After consulting with psychologists, he decided to end the marriage only to have his wife announce she was pregnant. The man stayed on for three more years until he realized that, as the child got older, exposure to his mother's condition would be detrimental for his development—especially since one of the wife's personalities tended toward violence.

Evan had learned that in child custody or children's rights cases, the laws were often too broad to consider more delicate situations. Mothers were widely considered better nurturers for children than the fathers but laws were changing. His interviewee had gained full custody of his son.

Forward thinking, the man had tailored his burgeoning business to accommodate a day care on site for his son and the children of employees. He hired a staff of two preschool instructors. He paid the insurance and offered child care as an incentive to his employees. Not only was he able to bring his son to work but the working mothers on his payroll did, as well. The man's bottom line increased because his employees were happy to be at work. Evan had wanted to feature this heroic dad and introduce alternatives for working parents and employers willing to take the initiative.

What drove Evan's television interviews off the charts were these kinds of economic and social platforms that raised social consciousness. Talk show hosts talked about his topics for days afterward, many times pulling in the same folks he interviewed to follow up. But it was Evan who managed to find and interview these persons of interest first. Evan's keen instinct for a good story kept his boss writing those bonus checks at the end of every quarter. He smiled when Steve knocked on his open office door.

"How about breaking for lunch?"

Evan checked the time in the corner of his computer monitor. Already past noon. "Where are you going?"

Steve shrugged. "Neverland? I'm craving one of Jake's Friday specials."

He needed to dodge the diner just one more day. "Hmm. Sounds great, but I'm putting the finishing touches on Monday's show. I'm not coming in tomorrow."

Steve raised an eyebrow. "Now, that's a first."

Evan met his friend's concerned gaze. Steve came across as wily and distant like a silver fox, but Evan knew better. While Steve was Evan's boss, the men had built a solid friendship during Evan's time abroad. Steve had been an anchor at home, helping with story strategies and getting Evan the support he needed from the network while Evan roamed the continent on behalf of NCTV.

Beneath that austere exterior, Steve had a sense of humor and the heart of a family man. He still loved his wife of thirty-five years, boasted about his three grown kids and was waiting on the birth of his first grandchild.

"What's the look for, Steve?"

"Only a woman could keep you from your desk tomorrow."

Evan grinned. "Well, it is. And, she's in Neverland and I don't want to show up and give her a chance to back out."

Steve slapped the door frame. "Well, I'll be damned. So you groveled and she said yes."

"You betchya, and proud of it."

"Okay, then, how about lunch at Tao?"

Evan powered down his computer, leaving it in lock mode. He didn't like to admit he couldn't trust colleagues not to rifle through his files, but when it came to the ambitions of Dean Porter, anything could happen. He looked at his friend and decided, once again, against airing his concerns. Steve looked relaxed today. NCTV was running smoothly and up for an Emmy. No reason to throw darts at a balloon.

"On second thought, let's go to Neverland. Tao is uptown and I don't have much time. Kelly won't dare mess with our plans with you at the counter."

Steve chuckled. "That's my man. I'd hate to miss Jake's good cooking."

THERE WERE ALWAYS new customers in Neverland. That was what made Manhattan so exciting. But Kelly didn't like the way this particular man watched her while he ate Jake's special corned beef sandwich.

Not that he looked dangerous. Gray suit, navy tie, blue button-down shirt. Well groomed, indeed, but there was something predatory in his smile, which he flashed every time she glanced his way. Better to get it over with and confront the man. She preferred handling clowns like this head-on, rather than finding them lurking around later.

She pointed to his empty glass. "Would you like another New Castle?"

"Sure." He pushed his glass forward as she pulled another beer from the icebox.

She poured. "Everything fine with your meal?"

"Everything, except a few answers."

She frowned, fully expecting a come-on. "What questions?"

He pulled a business card from his pocket. "I'm Jay Doyle. I report for the *New York Sentinel*."

The gossip rag of the city. Good Lord, had someone spoken badly of Neverland? She offered him her most winning smile. "Lovely. What can I do for you?"

"Well, it's a long story, but I was chatting with a former administrative assistant to the senate's newest presidential candidate and your name came up."

Her heart skipped a beat. *Well, here we go.* The devil himself was sitting at her counter with a smile thinking he'd lay a snare. Wouldn't happen on her watch.

Her body relaxed into war mode. "And who, pray tell, would that senator be?"

Doyle pointed to the TV screen above the counter. "Buzz Campbell. I'm sure you heard him throw his hat into the ring during Evan McKenna's show on Monday."

She frowned. "Missed the show, but heard the news. Are you taking a poll or something?"

He was watching her like a hawk. "Of sorts."

She'd handled morons like him before. She just didn't have to bite his bait. "Mr. Doyle, I don't understand."

Doyle laid a hand on the counter, palm down as if planting a root into her world. The action repulsed her. She didn't like this man, at all.

"Well, Ms. Sullivan, it seems this ex-assistant has an ax to grind. Something about sexual harassment."

Years of practice kept the jolt to her gut from showing on her face. "That's unfortunate. I can promise you I do not sexually harass my employees."

He chuckled. "No, but when chatting, this assistant mentioned that the senator had a nanny that abruptly left his employ."

Okay. So he knew. She'd clean up this mess fast. No more dodging questions.

She shared a conspiratorial glance with him. "And, you learned that I was that nanny."

He seemed surprised by her honesty. "Well, yes."

She shook her head as if to say she'd never understand busybodies. She added an extra lilt to her question. "So, Mr. Doyle, at the risk of being rude, why would this be any business of yours?"

He pressed a finger to his lips before speaking. "My contact was given the tedious chore of screening candidates to replace you when you quit on such short notice. Mrs. Campbell had seemed bewildered when you left— she'd thought you were quite content with your job. This assistant suggested that perhaps you'd had a run-in with the senator."

A customer motioned for more coffee at the end of the counter. She released the breath she hadn't known she was holding. "Will you excuse me for a moment?"

Kelly's heart pounded double-time. To regain her calm, she refreshed several coffee mugs, delivered a check and several plates before returning to the reporter. Luckily, Matt was on a playdate and was out of sight. Thank heaven for small favors. This guy was pretty sharp, but so far all he had presented to her were suppositions. One glance at Matt and there would be no question. No one ever considered the possibility before today because no one in her present life knew of her connection to Buzz Campbell. Doyle, however, had targeted the guilty party. If he saw Matt she'd have the war of a lifetime on her hands.

She returned to the reporter as he downed the last of his Newcastle. "So, Mr. Doyle, as you can see, it's lunch hour."

He lifted a hand. "That apple pie looks excellent. I'll have a slice, if you don't mind."

"Not at all. Would you like a dollop of ice cream or whipped cream?"

"Both. And a coffee. Black."

She was tempted to have one of the other waitresses finish serving him, but avoiding him would only encourage the man to persist in his questioning—or worse, return at another time. The fact that he was staying for dessert proved he thought he'd sniffed out a lead. She glanced at Bunny and saw from her friend's expression that she had already assessed the guy as trouble. Kelly shot her a quick grin that confirmed it. As much as her insides quaked, she'd handle this clown and slide him out the door faster than grease off a skillet.

She poured his coffee and watched him shovel a forkful of pie into his mouth. The look on his face as he savored the sweet was priceless. She couldn't help herself. She reached for the ever-present Nikon and snapped a few shots of Jay Doyle enjoying her favorite pie with a goodly amount of whipped cream in the corner of his mouth.

"Hey, what are you doing?" He wiped his mouth with a napkin.

Kelly gestured to the wall covered in photos. "Well, Mr. Doyle. When I spy a customer who is particularly enjoying my food, his or her picture becomes part of Neverland's Wall of Fame."

He grinned. "Nice. I'd like that. I'll bring my wife back to show her."

"You do that, Mr. Doyle. So, let's finish with your questions before I get distracted again. As I said, it's busy in here."

"Sure. Sure." He spooned that last bit of pie into his mouth. "Amazing, this pie," he said as he chewed. "So, it seems this assistant doesn't think she is the only one with a gripe against Buzz Campbell."

Kelly stood with arms crossed. "Is she charging him with harassment?"

"More like sexual assault. She had to fight him off. Only, she's concerned that Campbell's attorneys would pound her into the ground if she accuses him alone. If more women step forward, the charges will have more power."

"What does this have to do with me?"

"My informant knows of other women in Campbell's wake with the same complaint. We were wondering if you were swept into his net, as well."

Doyle's gaze was drilling right through her.

She lowered her voice, grateful that the immediate seats surrounding Doyle at the counter had been vacated. "So you want to know if I was assaulted by the senator. Is that correct?"

"It's the reason I am here, but now that I've had your food, I'll come back for sure."

"I have another question for you."

He drained his coffee mug as if they chatted about the weather. His nonchalance was not lost on Kelly. Actually, it made her blood steam that this man could so blithely discuss female degradation while obviously enjoying his meal.

He placed the cup on the counter as if he'd take a refill. Kelly ignored the gesture.

He asked, "What's your question?"

Instead of pouring, she placed the coffeepot she was holding on the counter between them. "Did Campbell's assistant approach you or did you approach her?"

"Does it matter?"

Kelly let a grin play across her lips. "Motive means everything to me, Mr. Doyle. I'm simply wondering if you really care about this woman's story or if you've been tapped to do a witch hunt by Campbell's opposing party."

The man looked decidedly uncomfortable.

When he didn't answer, she knew. Politics could be such

a dirty business. A rising star under attack by his opponents certainly seemed to be the American model during election years. Only this time, Buzz Campbell's enemies were right on target. The knowledge that Campbell had taken liberties with other women seeped like acid between her ribs, burning her lungs and making her want to cry, all over again. Under any other circumstance, Kelly would have led the cause against the senator—in a heartbeat. Only, now she had a son to protect. Her own shame and/or vindication no longer mattered. Matt's anonymity did. God forbid Campbell learned he'd fathered a son. From the three years she spent caring for his daughters, Kelly knew he'd always wanted a boy. The thought made her want to vomit. Having to battle Buzz Campbell for custody of a child born from his assault would ruin Kelly.

She hated to use the word *rape*. The sound alone slashed her soul like a razor. She'd made a life—a good life—despite the horror of that night and found love for her child like she'd never known. Nothing. Absolutely nothing would destroy the safe and secret world she and Herby, bless his unknowing soul, had created to protect her and Matt from this very moment.

Kelly leaned forward, offering her most conspiratorial voice. "I will tell you how it goes, Mr. Doyle, but please do not repeat it, as my actions are most embarrassing to me. Yes, I was that nanny. Lovely family. Beautiful children, Emily and Mary Kate. But it didn't take me long to realize that I had chosen the wrong career. Caring for someone else's children out in the wilds of Long Island with nary a friend or foe to confide in was more than I could handle. I was desperately lonely. So, I quit. Unfortunately, I left without notice. My actions were not professional. I'm not proud of the fact. For that reason, I prefer that my past ties to the Campbells remain confidential. Can you understand that?"

"You're saying Campbell's kids were difficult, spoiled brats?"

It was easy to become insulted at that remark. Kelly had loved those two young girls like her own. She had developed an affection for their mother, as well. Indignation laced her words. "Absolutely not, Mr. Doyle. You must not have heard me say that they were lovely children."

She leaned closer, tapping her finger on the granite inches from his hand to emphasize her point. "It's important that you understand me very clearly, Mr. Doyle. Given my abrupt departure from the children in my care, it would be nothing but an embarrassment for me. An embarrassment which if advertised could harm my business. I can only hope that after almost seven years, the Campbells hold no complaint against me. If you're looking for a witch hunt, you've come to the wrong place. I have nothing to offer you. You'll have to look elsewhere for a victim."

She had moved so close to him in order to tell her story only to him that he looked as if he had gotten lost in her eyes. For once in a very long time, she was glad for her charm.

"Um…I understand. But why would this assistant name you as one of the senator's targets?"

"Given the time you are citing, I assume you are referring to Helen Thompson." When he didn't answer, Kelly shrugged. "We knew each other. She'd been to the house several times. I remember she was very loyal to Mr. Campbell. If he did indeed assault her, I can only imagine she's feeling betrayed as well as violated. I can understand why she would look for collaboration to support her accusation. I'm sorry, Mr. Doyle. I can't help her or you in this inquiry. But I would appreciate it if you remained discreet about my ties to the Campbells. Now that I understand how devastated I had left Mrs. Campbell, I'd hate to be held accountable for my immaturity. Would you like more coffee?"

That seemed to finish the interview. Knees quaking, Kelly paid little more attention other than a friendly wave as Jay Doyle paid his bill and exited Neverland. She cleared tables, using all her strength to keep her hands from trembling while sending a silent prayer skyward. Holy Saint Michael, she prayed that was the last she'd see of the *Sentinel* reporter.

Shoot. Shoot. Shoot. It was bad enough he had been seated in Evan's favorite stool at the counter. It seemed like a violation of sacred space. Worse, Doyle had hit the truth from which she had carefully erased all connection for so long. She had performed a most uncomfortable two-step to make that man go away but she'd managed. And not one word had been false. Now that he was gone, the urge to throw up what remained of breakfast had her choking back bile.

She filled a glass with cola and sipped slowly to get her wits about her. A turbine of disquiet buzzed in her head. There was no one to whom she could confide her distress, which was rapidly growing into terror that this man would return. She took a moment to absorb the activity and sounds in Neverland. The hum of conversations. Clanking plates and the sizzling grill. The smell of coffee. The ever-present newscasters of NCTV on the screen. The patrons and workers who had become her friends. The city bustling past the windows outside the diner. She released a sigh. Neverland was reality now. The sludge Jay Doyle was trying to unearth was the past. A difficult lesson learned, but most certainly history. All was well in Neverland. Nothing else mattered.

She looked up to see Evan entering the diner with his

boss, his gaze seeking her out. With a single glance at her, concern rose in Evan's eyes. Damn her nerves. He'd read her distress before she had a chance to hide it.

CHAPTER FOUR

STEVE FIORE RUBBED his hands together. "Smells like Friday in here, Kelly. How about serving us up two of Jake's specials?"

Steve's eagerness and his genuinely affable nature helped Kelly shake away her dread. Besides, she'd handled Jay Doyle. There was no need to give his interrogation any further attention. The smile that creased her mouth drained her tension.

"Nothing would please me more, Steve." She gestured to the stool next to Evan's—which he now occupied, his gaze still on her. "Care to sit next to our star patron? I must warn you, he'll chatter your ear to bending."

Evan shook his head. "A man does not chatter, Red. We discuss matters."

Steve was studying Evan's name stenciled on the floor beneath the stool. He gestured to the floor below his own seat. "Where's mine?"

She laughed. "You need your own TV show and must eat here every day to earn that honor."

Steve looked baffled. "But, Evan wouldn't have his own show if it wasn't for me."

Kelly slapped the counter. "Of course. You're right. If you are happy with that perch, I'll stencil your name there tonight."

Satisfied, Steve sat. "I'll get a gold star, as well?"

"Sure, Steve, but you'll have to earn your place on the Wall of Fame."

Steve glanced at the wall holding the fifty or more photos of patrons, all smiling with a mouthful of food. "McKenna isn't up there yet."

"I will be soon," Evan chimed in. "Had my photo op just a few days ago."

Kelly wagged a finger at Evan. "But, you've been absent all week. That photo may have to wait."

"Didn't want to give you a chance to break our date."

Before she could declare that they were not having a *date,* two patrons came up for Evan's autograph, killing the opportunity. At least Steve noticed her consternation. Kelly turned to Jake, who signaled that he had already spotted Evan and Steve's arrival and was preparing their specials.

Moments later, Matt burst through the diner doors like a miniature whirlwind with Jared and his mom, Donna, hot on his heels.

"Mom! We saw the Tyrannosaurus bones at the museum again. I think he got bigger… Evan!"

Matt had been heading for her until he spotted Evan. He and Matt exchanged their knuckle handshake while she invited Jared and Donna to take a booth near the window. She settled them in, catching up on their adventure at the Museum of Natural History until Matt scooted into the booth next to Jared.

"Mom, Evan says we're having birthday dinner tomorrow at his penthouse."

Donna raised an eyebrow and grinned. "Way to score, Kelly."

Kelly scoffed. "Not what you're thinking, Donna. Please don't start any rumors."

Donna gave the TV show host, now deep in conversation with his boss, an appraising glance. "Evan McKenna would be a rumor worth making, my dear."

Kelly met her friend's conspiratorial gaze. The last thing she wanted was uninvited attention over a television personality. "Now, that's enough. Lunch is on me for entertaining Matt this morning."

THE RISING MOUND of clothes littering her bed betrayed Kelly's angst over tonight's dinner with Evan. Something about trespassing into the McKenna inner sanctum sent tendrils of disquiet through her gut—a disquiet she was rapidly translating into a conviction that she had made a mistake. She'd been avoiding Evan for so long that agreeing to see him outside of Neverland seemed like surrender. Despite the fact that she had a son, her experience with men was nonexistent! Her apprehension was turning her stomach into knots.

Matt felt it, too. Despite a birthday party at the diner earlier today, then a romp through FAO Schwartz for Nerf guns, followed by several hours in Central Park playing Nerf gun tag, Matt was practically bouncing off the walls asking her when they were going to leave, as if he was sure she'd change her mind any minute and refuse to go.

She finally reached for her first choice, a soft green Indian tunic dress with an embroidered hem that stopped an inch too high above her knees. She looped a tan leather belt low on her hips and slipped into a pair of matching strappy sandals. She let her hair cascade onto her shoulders, slid silver hoop earrings into each ear, a cuff of bangles on her wrist, and finished her look with a spray of her favorite Christian Dior perfume—one luxury in which she dared to indulge.

Ignoring the pile of clothes on her bed, she dashed from

the room before giving herself a chance to change her mind. "Matt, are you ready?"

He looked up from his latest Lego construction. "Wow, Mom. You look pretty."

The admiration in his young eyes squeezed her heart. "Well, it's your birthday. That's a great reason to dress up."

He jumped from the couch. "Let's go. I hope Evan made an ice-cream cake!"

She reached for her purse and keys, her heart sinking. "Uh-oh. I forgot to tell Evan."

His grin was priceless. "Don't worry, Mom. I told him."

SHE HARDLY NOTICED the taxi ride to the Upper West Side. Matt was full of questions and it wasn't until she chided him that he had to be on his best behavior in Evan's home that he settled down to a round on his game player. As the doorman opened the door to the taxi, she was glad, once again, that she had refused Evan's offer to pick them up. She wanted this evening to be as little like a date as possible.

Matt bolted into the apartment lobby and ran to the elevators. "This place is cool, Mom! Which button do I press?"

"Elevator B."

When the light illuminated, she resisted the urge to hightail it right back out the door. This was crazy. A wave of heat suffused her body, making her palms feel damp. Going to Evan's place was sheer insanity. It didn't help that Bunny had sent her out the door this afternoon with admonitions like, "Take no prisoners," echoing in her wake.

She couldn't believe how awkward she felt—at her age! She was miles out of her league. During the years Evan had been away, she was sure he'd had his fill of women of every kind. She'd not had a single man. She'd never been courted, or wooed. But, tonight was NOT a date. It was a birthday dinner for Matt. Evan was their friend. And honestly, now that Grampy Herby was gone, Kelly was grateful for the male bonding Evan offered her son. It was why she was here in the first place. She would not lose sight of that singular fact.

The elevator doors swooshed open. "Come on, Mom! Which button now?"

Smiling to herself she said, "The one with the letters, PH."

He pressed it and beamed up at her. "Penthouse. Evan is rich, right?"

"Why do you say that?"

"Jared told me."

"Oh, and how does Jared know?"

"He heard his mom talking on her cell phone."

"And, to whom was she telling this priceless information?"

Matt shrugged as if that was a really dumb question. "I don't know, Mom."

The elevator opened onto a black marble landing just outside Evan's door. Creamy yellow Venetian plaster-colored walls were trimmed with wide white moldings. His door, a work in gorgeous carved mahogany stood sentinel guarding the man and his private world.

Kelly felt miles out of her comfort zone. Knowing that Evan lived in opulence like this by his own achievements humbled her to the core. She couldn't help but think this accomplished and excruciatingly handsome man was toying with her and her son. She ran a diner and lived in the two-bedroom apartment above it. They didn't belong here.

She was about to sweep Matt back into the elevator when the door opened. Evan stepped out followed by a waft of air, warm and redolent with the savory smell of garlic and Italian sauce. She looked at his grinning face feeling like the typical deer in headlights.

"Hi, Evan!" Matt scrambled past his host and into the apartment as if he had been given a free pass to an amusement park.

"Hi, Matt…"

Evan answered Matt as an afterthought because his eyes were glued to Kelly. He whistled softly. "You look amazing."

A lightning-fast blush heated her cheeks, ruining her composure. She didn't like the feeling at all. Not now. Not at hello. Not when he looked excellent in a white button-down rolled up at the elbows and a pair of faded denims that sat on his hips as if they were sculpted to his body. She waved away his compliment, wanting him to stop staring while also soaking in the good feeling. "Go on with you now, Evan. I don't always wear sneakers and an apron."

His grin deepened. "You're blushing."

"And you're a blustering fool. Now, will you be inviting me in, or shall I leave Matt to you for the evening?"

EVAN STEPPED BACK, opening the door wider. No way in hell would he permit Kelly to retreat on him now. Not when she looked so hot in that belted green dress and smelled like dessert. And, Holy Mother of God, those legs!

He stepped back, opening the door wider. He grinned when he realized she was grazing his body with her eyes as if enjoying his look. When her eyes met his, her blush deepened.

"Come on in, Red. It won't be a party without you."

She followed his gesture and entered. The soft incense of her perfume shot straight to his groin. What was it about this woman that made her blast his senses like a furnace? The familiar scent didn't have this effect on him in Neverland, where she was steeped in her own territory and surrounded with patrons and friends. She eased past him as if trying to avoid a sidewinder. He'd have to tread slowly and carefully to put her at ease.

"Don't worry. I won't bite. Promise."

"Of course, you won't." The temperature rising up her neck betrayed how foolish she felt.

He tilted his head into her line of vision. "Kelly, I am honored that you and Matt are here. I don't want to do anything to make you uncomfortable. Please, feel welcome."

She glanced into the apartment, where Matt seemed to have vanished. "I appreciate you saying that, Evan. Matt can use a male figure in his world."

"I get that. I was an only child, too. My dad was a huge influence."

She frowned. "You never told me you were an only child."

"Really? How did we never get to that topic?"

She chuckled. "Because you always have your nose in my business."

He gestured to the table beneath a huge framed mirror. "You can put your bag here if you'd like."

He could sense that she was starting to calm when she lifted her face and inhaled. "I smell spaghetti sauce."

"My boss's family recipe. I'm hopeful this Irishman meets Steve's Italian standards."

"I'm sure Matt told you spaghetti is his favorite meal."

"That and ice-cream cake. This newsman listens." He tapped his ear to punctuate his promise.

Matt charged back toward them from somewhere in the open expanse, his face animated with delight. "Mom! Evan has a basketball hoop. Inside!"

Kelly appraised Evan's home. He liked the way she smiled as she took in the mahogany entrance, the sprawling floors reflecting the same deep, polished timber as the door.

Her gaze rested on the huge, deep blue jewel-toned Oriental rug that delineated the living room. There were overstuffed caramel-colored couches, matching ottomans and inlaid antique tables with carved wooden elephants flanking the couches.

"Your home certainly is welcoming, Evan."

He enjoyed his home. He'd taken pains to ensure that despite its modern decor, his home offered warmth and comfort—from the art-deco reading lights perched on each table to the "floating" mahogany wall unit that divided the living room from the open kitchen. The unit was stacked with books, unusual pottery and knickknacks from his travels. He'd placed the dining room by the floor-to-ceiling windows to give the effect of bringing outdoors inside.

He'd set a table on the balcony with place settings for three. Potted trees along the balustrade brought the park in the distance up to Evan's living space. Candles dotted the table, though they had yet to be lit in the waning light. He felt a surge of pride as Kelly appraised his home. What struck him more was that he liked the way she looked in his place. Kelly against the backdrop of his belongings sent his senses thrumming.

Kelly frowned. "I don't see a basketball hoop, Matt. For goodness' sake, were you snooping?"

Evan pointed to an area blocked by another floating wall. Over its top, she would be able to see that the ceiling rose to a second level.

"It's over there," he said. "Come on. I'll show you."

Kelly followed him around the wall. A large open game area held a regulation pool table, an antique table with two chairs set for a chess game, a Ping-Pong table and yes, the rest of the room was laid out to accommodate a half court, regulation-height basketball hoop.

At the far end of the room, a detached staircase led up to a loft that housed his master bedroom suite backlit with more windows. Evan gestured toward the stairs.

"The stairs lead to my room. That hallway at the foot of the stairs goes to guest bedrooms. Would you like a tour?"

Kelly's jaw dropped. "You live here? Alone?"

He shrugged. "I bought it when I took the home job. Do you like it?"

She smiled. "It's wonderful. You're a lucky man."

Matt tugged on Evan's hand. "What's that?" He pointed to the pinball machine.

"Wow," Kelly said.

Evan grinned. "That is an original Flash Gordon pinball machine. Ever play one?"

Matt's wide-eyed look held awe. "I don't know what it is."

Evan crossed the distance to the pinball machine in a few strides. "Come on, Matt-man. I'll set you up. The sounds are great. You can play while I finish making your birthday supper."

Evan pinched a handful of quarters from a bowl on the table next to another overstuffed lounge chair. He tugged the ottoman over to the machine.

Matt scrambled onto the ottoman, looking into the pinball machine as if he'd discovered a secret world. "Wow! What does it do?"

Evan dropped a quarter into the slot. The machine lit up. Bells sounded and a dastardly but hilarious, "Ah, ha, ha!" resounded.

Matt yelled with delight. "How do you play?"

Evan showed Matt how to launch the silver ball and manipulate the flippers on the sides of the table. The ma-

chine dinged and pinged with lights flashing every time
the ball hit a bumper beneath the glass. It didn't take long
for Matt to become completely absorbed with the game—
especially with that large bowl of quarters on hand. The
boy was grinning from ear to ear.

"Oh, man. This is the best birthday, ever!"

Satisfied that Matt was entertained for the moment,
Evan gestured toward the kitchen, where a pot of water
boiled on the stove. "Kelly, would you like a glass of
wine?"

With a longing look at the pinball machine, she said,
"I've never played."

Chuckling, he led her to a chair at the black granite
counter. "I'll make sure you get a turn." He circled to the
work side of the counter. He poured a glass of Cabernet to
match his. "Anything for you, Kelly. When are you going
to figure that out?"

He regretted his words the moment they left his mouth.
Kelly stiffened in her seat, her glass stopping in midair.

She pointed a finger at him. "Now, Sir Smooth, save
the suave words for your lady friends."

Oh, well. Now he had to save face. He held up a stopping hand. "Sorry. I can't help myself with your hair down
like that."

She lowered her voice to a whisper. "If it wasn't Matt's
birthday, we would not be here. Now behave!"

He tapped his glass to hers. "Mea culpa."

Well, he'd pay in spades. Just watching her lift the glass
to those luscious lips was payback enough. *Damn.* He'd
love to be that glass.

Before taking another sip she gave him her sternest
look. "No tomfoolery here now, Evan McKenna. You
promised."

He sipped his wine if only to do something with his

mouth other than try to kiss her, and nearly groaned when she let the flavor of her wine swirl on her tongue before swallowing.

"Mmm. This is delicious."

I'll bet you are. If he was going to make this night a success he had to get his head out of the bedroom, or the living room floor, or the dining room table. He held up the bottle. "It's a good year."

"Oh, yes? And which year is that?"

"The year we met."

She almost choked.

He reached over to pat her back. "Did I have that bad an effect on you?"

She held a hand to her throat. "That year was rather awful for me. I'd say the following year was a better time."

"Why do you say that?"

She frowned. "Well, it doesn't matter. That year began a prestigious career for you. So I'm happy to toast to a fine year." She lifted her glass.

He studied her from across the counter. There she was dodging information, one more time. "Yes, there was that."

She smiled sweetly. "Is there anything I can do to help with the meal?"

She looked uncomfortable again and it pained him that she felt she had to be so protective. He shook his head. "You serve folks every day. I want you to relax and enjoy yourself."

Behind them the pinball machine dinged wildly. Matt jumped up and down on the ottoman. "Score!"

"Easy on the furniture, son."

"Okay." Without even looking at Kelly, he slipped another quarter into the machine and began playing again.

"Don't worry. I bought the furniture to handle my rowdiest friends. Matt can do no harm in here. Let him be free."

Kelly smiled. "That's nice. Thank you. He doesn't get much room in the apartment."

"Well, you and Matt are welcome here anytime."

"I'll be sure to call first. Wouldn't want to interrupt a hot date."

He laughed. Boy, did she have the wrong idea. "Not much worry there."

She slanted him a sideways glance. "Oh, please. Your reputation precedes you."

"Lies. All of them."

"Hmm. I seem to remember some political, fund-raising auction and you were the main prize for a dinner date."

"Oh, don't remind me of that hellish night."

She chuckled. "If I remember correctly, three women pooled their money and you ended up taking them all out. Even I bought the tabloids to read about your escapades."

He slapped his chest. "Tell me you didn't."

"I didn't. But, I was tempted."

He leaned closer. "And what about you?"

"I never…"

"Yes?"

There it was again. Their easy conversation stalled midway by Kelly's refusal to speak her mind. What would it take to make her trust him?

She sipped her wine. "I never discuss my private life."

He laughed. "Touché."

He'd have to try another way to penetrate her defenses. Instead, he tasted the sauce. Not bad. He turned the burner off. Dropped fresh pasta into the boiling water. "Just five minutes and we can eat."

He stirred the pasta in the pot, wanting very much to stir another proverbial pot. Taking a shot at the hard questions with Kelly would certainly quash any flirting he had on his mind.

He added more wine to her glass. "So tell me, Kelly. Who is your best friend?"

She frowned. "Bunny, I'd say."

"No, she is your employee."

"Well, she has also grown to be my friend."

He sipped his wine. "As luck would have it." He took another tack. "Then tell me this. Is she your confidante? Someone you can trust?"

"No. Herby was the closest person to me and now he's gone."

The pinball machine sounded. "Bwaa, ha, ha!" Matt's laughter pulled their attention to him.

Across the counter, Evan could sense Kelly's defenses rising, as he expected. He found it hard to believe that someone as personable as Kelly didn't allow anyone except a kindly old gent into her inner sanctuary.

She turned her attention back to him. "Why do you ask, Evan?"

He poured the steaming pasta into a colander in the sink then shook the extra water from the noodles. He placed a pasta bowl next to the sink.

"You seemed distressed yesterday afternoon when Steve and I arrived at Neverland. You did a fine job of distracting Steve, my dear, but not me. I was wondering if you have anyone to talk to when something bothers you."

She managed a smile. "Not much bothers me, Evan."

He shook his head. "You don't fool me, Kelly Sullivan. Something rattled your cage yesterday, and I saw it. As your friend, I want you to know, I'm here if you ever need me."

He was talking as he worked, pouring the pasta into the serving bowl, ladling the sauce over the top, pulling the Parmesan cheese from the refrigerator and slicing a chunk into the hand grater.

Kelly placed her goblet on the counter, pulling herself up on the stool like a Valkyrie. "I appreciate the offer, Evan, but let me be honest with you."

Uh-oh. Would she unleash her Irish ire even before Matt had his cake? "Okay. Shoot."

"You are a newsman. A very clever, crafty and intelligent researcher who surpasses his counterparts in every way."

He didn't expect the compliment. "Why, thank you, Red."

She shook her head. "I am not done."

He met her fiery gaze. "Oh."

"You have been snooping for answers about my life since you returned. I like my privacy. If I wanted to share things with you or anyone, I would have. Sometimes you're a tad too big for your britches—even if they do fit you to a fine turn."

He burst out laughing at that. "Well I've never been shot down and built up so effectively in one delivery."

She nodded once. "The pleasure is mine."

He wanted to thank her for the pleasure of just watching her get all heated up defending herself. He loved the way her chest heaved beneath the gauzy green dress with the embroidery that matched the dye and traced the V-neck of the dress right into her delightful cleavage. That, along with the jangle of her bracelets mixed with her bravado and unabashed ease in standing her ground with him, all turned him on something fierce. He tore his eyes from the daring in her emerald-green gaze and pulled garlic bread from the warming drawer beneath the oven. He tossed the salad with his favorite homemade balsamic dressing, if only to give himself time to regroup. This intoxicating woman was having an even more profound effect on him simply by sitting in his kitchen.

She settled back down into her seat, as if ready to move on from the topic. "You are quite the chef."

He tapped his wineglass to hers. "There is so much you don't know about me, Ms. Sullivan. Hopefully, we'll change that."

He lifted his focus to the game room. "Yo, Matt-man. Help me serve dinner."

"Almost done!" Matt was becoming a pinball wizard in his own right, working the flippers as if he had been born in the sixties.

Evan laughed. "I think I've created a monster."

Kelly sipped her wine. "I suppose we've all created a few of those in our time, now, Evan. Haven't we?"

CHAPTER FIVE

WHEN THE PHONE rang at five-thirty Monday morning, Kelly was already up preparing lunch for Matt's first day of school. She reached for the phone frowning. Either someone was in distress or calling long-distance. Those long-distance calls usually left *her* distressed. She wasn't happy when she read the caller ID. She considered not answering, but Mum would chase her down until they finally spoke. She might as well take the call. Matt still slept.

"Top of the morning to ya, Kelly m' love!"

Kelly scrunched her face. "And a fine morning it is, Mum. What a surprise to hear from you so early."

"It's almost noon here. I knew you'd be up being the businesswoman you are. Have you found yourself a husband yet?"

She rolled her eyes at the familiar question. "Saints be praised, no. Neverland is all mine, and I don't have to share it with anyone."

"You've always been a peculiar child."

"Mum, did you call me just to air your insults?"

"I'm only well meaning. You know that."

What would Mum say if she knew about her six-year-old grandson? Keeping Matt's existence unknown to her family had been easy since none of them ever ventured farther than the Kinsale county line. As far as Matt was concerned, Grampy Herby had been his grandfather, and his death had closed that door. He was too young to con-

sider anything else. Although they were few and far between, Kelly was vigilant in never taking long-distance
calls when Matt was within earshot. Of all of her careful
planning and covering her tracks, this was the trickiest
tightrope she walked.

"So, what can I do for you today, Mum? How is Da?"

"He's just fine. I'm calling to tell you that Michael has
moved to New York. He left yesterday. Have ye heard
from him?"

A lump caught in her throat. "Michael?"

"Yes! They've assigned him as pastor of a lovely parish
in Brooklyn. I know he'll be busy, but he wants to see you
as soon as possible. Being near his baby sister was part of
his reason for going to the States."

The floor shifted beneath her feet. *Oh, my God!* She
dropped onto the stool at the counter. With her brother
living a train ride away, she would be busted in no time.

"Kelly? Are you there?"

"Yes. Of course. That is wonderful news. How can I
find him?"

"His new parish is called The Church of The Little
Flower, after Saint Theresa. Isn't that lovely?"

"He will be wonderful for the congregation, I'm sure. Is
it a large church?" Lord, she would begin babbling soon,
but staunch Catholic that her mother was, anything to do
with the church was exciting conversation. Kelly asked
nonsense so she could get her wits about her.

"It's a good size, he tells me. He showed me a photo
before he left. The church is lovely. Beautiful windows."

"I have to call him. Do you know his phone number?"
She scribbled the number on a notepad. "I'll contact him
as soon as I can. This is quite a surprise."

Mum chuckled. "I knew you'd be happy. I'll be going

now. Your Da will be wanting his lunch. Will you call me to tell me how your reunion goes?"

"Of course!" Her heart was about to pound out of her chest.

"That's a good daughter."

"Big hug and kiss to all. Bye, Mum."

She hung up way too fast, but she couldn't help it. *What was she going to do?* She sat, head in hands in the predawn light thinking her world was about to cave in around her head. How would she explain Matt to Michael, let alone Michael to Matt? Well, when the time came she'd be honest and matter-of-fact. If he was old enough to tackle a first day of school, he'd be old enough to wrap his brain around the idea that they had family in a foreign country. She'd figure out the details later.

She lifted her head. She'd dealt with worse. Offense made the best defense she'd always heard. As she finished packing Matt's lunch, a plan started forming in her mind. Good Catholic girl that she was, she just might have to make a visit to church.

LUCKILY, MATT'S SCHOOL was within walking distance and the morning was sunny and warm. He looked like a little man in his light blue Henley and chino shorts. He gripped the straps of his new Urban Hero backpack with enough nervous energy to make Kelly glad to be accompanying the small troupe of kids and their mothers. Actually, nothing would have stopped her from this momentous occasion in her son's life. If all of New York clamored for breakfast at Neverland, she'd send them away, or make them wait. Life would always go on, but these precious moments were meant to be cherished.

She walked with Donna while Matt and Jared chattered with their friends. When they arrived at the school with kids swarming everywhere, Matt froze in place. Kelly hugged him hard as the teachers began rounding up the kids.

"You'll have a great day today, Matt. I'll be right here waiting for you at two-thirty."

Matt watched the other kids lining up as if deciding whether or not it was a good idea to join them. Kelly leaned over. "Remember when we checked out your classroom last week? I can't wait to hear about all the fun things you do when I see you later."

Jared tugged on his shirt. "C'mon, dude!"

Jared's enthusiasm seemed to cinch Matt's resolve. "Okay, Mom. See you later!"

Kelly stared at the doorway he disappeared through, amazed at the mixture of pride and abandonment she felt that her baby was stepping out into the world without her. He'd probably fare better than she would, worrying about him all day.

She and Donna headed back for Neverland.

"So, I've been dying to ask you. How did your date go Saturday night with Evan?"

The absurdity of the question made her laugh. "Matt's birthday dinner was great fun. Did you know Evan has half of a basketball court in his game room?"

Donna chuckled. "Okay, avoid the question."

"It was no date, Donna, but it was really nice of Evan to go to all that effort for Matt. He's a good friend."

Do you have anyone to confide in? Evan's question flooded her mind. Was it only two nights ago that he had made the evening so very comfortable for both her and Matt? The thought of having him for a confidant reached deeper than she had imagined, but then again, he was a man used to adjusting the world to get what he wanted. She pushed the thought of Evan from her mind and was glad when they reached Neverland. "So, I'll see you back at school around two-fifteen, Donna?"

"Okay! I'm headed downtown. Jeff and I are celebrating our anniversary this weekend. I have to find a gift."

Anniversary. A husband. Time spent together. She wondered if she'd ever know what that was like. She tied on her apron and approached the nearest customers to take their orders.

MICHAEL HAD CALLED twice but she hadn't answered the phone. She couldn't until she had the chance to put her plan into action. She'd had to wait until Saturday. Now, she passed through the front doors of the Church of the Little Flower. As she worked her way down the center aisle, she was struck by the cool air wafting through the shadowed vestibule, the smell of incense, beeswax and summer flowers that were bunched in bouquets along the altar. With one phone call to the rectory, Kelly learned that the pastor and the only other priest in the rectory listened to Confession on Saturday afternoons.

The only problem, Kelly thought as she watched the two confessionals with the little red lights glowing above the priests' doors, was to discern which cubicle held her brother. If Kelly was going to pull off her plan, she at least needed the ear of the correct priest.

An elderly woman exited from behind the curtain of the closest confessional. Kelly approached her.

"Excuse me. I'd like to speak with Pastor Sullivan. Do you know where he is?"

The woman indicated the confessional from which she came. "He's in there, my dear." She patted Kelly's arm and headed for the kneeling bench before a small altar in an alcove.

Kelly stared at the vacant cubicle adjacent to the closed

door where her brother sat. She hadn't seen Michael in eight years and had spoken to him maybe that many times throughout the years because he had been so involved in the seminary and the two other parishes where he'd been assigned. He had no idea Kelly was in his church. Her knees almost buckled as she stepped closer. Inhaling a deep, fortifying breath, she pulled the curtain closed behind her, knelt and waited for her brother to open the small door to listen to her anonymously through the darkened screen.

She waited, her pulse pounding, until finally the door slid open.

"Good afternoon."

She smiled at the sound of his gentle voice. She spoke quietly, imagining herself as a regular Brooklyn girl and hid her accent as best she could. "Bless me, Father, for I have sinned. It has been several years since my last confession and I need your help."

"Several years is a long time."

"I know, Father, but I didn't know how to handle my situation." She worked to keep from falling into her lilt since her brother's accent was so very predominant.

"How can I help you, lass?"

She hesitated. She'd never told anyone her secret. Now she was about to reveal it to her brother, a family member, the kiss of death—even if she was in disguise.

"You can feel free to speak. I will not judge you."

Tears filled her eyes. "I have a son out of wedlock. He just turned six and my family does not know he exists."

Father Michael remained silent for a moment. "And this boy's father?"

She shook her head, even though her brother could not see. "He does not know about the boy."

"And why would you not tell him?"

The memory of that awful night flooded her. It was as if the dam of tears she held back for all these years poured from her at the sound of her brother's concerned voice. "Because, Michael, the man raped me. I couldn't get far enough away from him! I didn't know I was pregnant until I was long gone."

Oh, God, she used the hated *R* word and it cut into her heart like a razor blade. Blinded by her own tears, it was too late before she realized she'd returned to her native accent and her brother was charging from the confessional and reaching for her from behind the curtain.

"Kelly!"

He pulled her into his arms, holding her so tightly she could hardly breathe. She laid her head against his chest and sobbed, the cool fabric of his vestments soothing her hot skin. Each hiccupping breath released the pain and horror she'd tamped down for all those years in order to continue putting one foot in front of the other.

"What are you doing coming to confession like that? Why didn't you call me?"

Kelly couldn't stop crying, so Michael led her from the side door of the church to the garden behind the rectory. They sat together on a bench beneath an ancient oak tree. Becoming reduced to a weeping fool was not part of her original plan.

With her brother's strong arm around her shoulder, those huge blue eyes watching her as if she'd crumble any moment, she sucked in the Sullivan courage and managed to smile at Michael through her tears.

"Well, I never thought that the first time I finally told my story I'd turn in to a blubbering schoolgirl."

Michael tucked a finger beneath her chin and lifted her gaze to meet his. His handsome face framed with a mop of auburn hair was so familiar.

"So, I have the honor of being the first to hear that there is an addition to our family?"

She nodded. "Mum and Da are so closed minded. I couldn't tell them and bring shame to my Matthew."

He smiled. "So, he's named for the apostle who began life as an outcast. You are deep, Kelly, my girl."

"He's a wonderful boy."

He grabbed her hands. "Truly, you were raped?"

She sucked in a huge breath. "Yes, Michael, but please don't ask me for details, because I won't tell you. I had every intention of putting Matt up for adoption, but at the last moment, I couldn't. He is my life."

"Now, how shall we tell the family of your blessed news?"

She pulled away. "We won't! Not yet, at least. I'm not ready."

"That is wrong, Kelly."

The anger that she had used all these years to shield her secret erupted. "Michael, I confessed this so-called sin to you, a priest, in God's confessional. You are under oath to God and the Church to keep my secret."

His eyes narrowed. "Why, you conniving little sister! Holding me to my vows is irreverent and untrustworthy."

She frowned. "Perhaps, but it is Church doctrine, and I need the security of your silence."

"And this is the greeting I get after not seeing you since you were nineteen." He pulled her to her feet. "Did you become more mule-headed while growing into a beautiful woman?"

Just like her brother to add sugar to a dose of truth. "Michael, I would never have told anyone in our family about Matthew, especially now that I have become an American citizen, but you've come to my side of the world. Now that you are here, I see Matt cannot be kept secret from our family for much longer, but I must rely on your discretion. When I'm ready to tell our folks, I'll need your help, but not until I am ready. I will not tolerate anyone treating my son unkindly."

He exhaled a long breath. "I understand. Kelly, I can't tell you how upset I am that you carried this burden alone for all these years. Why didn't you call me?"

Again, Evan's words rushed in... *Do you have someone to confide in?* She closed her eyes to dispel the image of him in her mind. "My situation was so complicated. I feared if I spoke one word the entire story would tumble out. No one can know who Matt's father is."

"Kelly, do you think I am daft? You came here as a nanny and now own a diner. I can already guess."

A jolt of panic stole her breath. She swallowed hard. "Still. Don't ask. I will not tell you, Michael. I have to protect my son. New York laws don't protect rape victims from their assailant if they become pregnant and keep the child. If he were to file suit, I would have to give him joint custody—at best!"

Michael glanced toward the church. "I can leave Peter to hear confession. Let's go inside to talk. I'll make you some tea."

"I can't, Michael. I have to get back to work."

"Well, then, are you free tonight?"

"No. Give me a few days and I'll bring Matt to meet you. I want to tell him about you first. Okay?"

He hugged her again. "Kelly, I wish you would have trusted me sooner. I hate to think how difficult this ordeal must have been for you."

"The Lord has provided for me, Michael. He sent me to Herby George who was my shining light during the dark hours. Now I have Neverland, a roof over my head and the love of a beautiful child. I am blessed."

"Herbert George should be sainted."

She smiled. "Aye."

"And, your new citizenship? Another secret?"

"Not so much. My American friends know."

"Oh, but we in Ireland don't deserve such courtesy?"

"I'm sorry, Michael. I've become so used to keeping my own counsel."

"To hide the child."

"Yes."

Michael watched her for a long, silent moment. She could see him struggling with the rising anger she knew all too well, against the man who raped her, but what Michael needed to understand was that even now, that man could be a danger.

"Michael, please. You must trust me that silence is the safest road for me."

"I'd like to get my hands on that…"

She squeezed his arm. "No, Michael. The devil will get his due. We need only carry on with our lives as quietly as possible." She managed a smile. "Wait until you see Matthew. He is a marvelous boy. And, Neverland. I've done a splendid job of making my mark in Manhattan—no matter how small. I'll even let you eat for free."

"You are amazing, Kelly."

His compliment warmed her heart. "And without a man, which Mum seemed to think was impossible. I am proud of my accomplishments."

"And so you should be. Now, for your sins you must say two rosaries, come back here next Friday, do the stations of the cross and then recite ten novenas to make up for your irreverent confession."

She laughed and hugged her brother. "I have missed you, Michael!"

"When will you come back?"

She bit her lip as she tried to figure out a way to break the news to Matt. "This is going to be tricky. Matt thinks Herby George was his only relative."

"You've lied to the child?"

"No! I simply omitted information."

He frowned. "I'm thinking you might be due for another round in the confessional."

"Believe me, the good Lord knows all my faults."

"Sounds to me like you've carved out some rules of your own to get by."

"They've gotten me this far, Michael. Don't be judging me now."

"As if my judgment would matter. So, when?"

She tapped a finger to her lips. "Friday? For dinner?"

He turned to escort her from the garden. "That will do. We have a lot of time to catch up on. Come early so you can do those stations of the cross."

CHAPTER SIX

EVAN'S EARLY ARRIVAL at Neverland the next day took her by surprise. She slid a coffee cup across the counter, ignoring his self-important grin.

"Sunday morning, Evan? Thought you'd sleep in."

"Not when I promised Matt to take you both to the zoo."

"What?"

Evan glanced at Matt on the stool to his left, which now had Steve Fiore's name stenciled on the floor below. "You didn't tell her?"

Matt had the good sense to look reticent. He squeezed one eye shut as he looked at Kelly. "Well, if I told her she might say no, and I wanna go."

Kelly's eyes widened. "Dishonesty is not the answer, young man."

He held up open hands. "I wasn't dishonest. I just didn't say anything!"

Kelly almost fell over. Matt was now using her own tools as a way to obtain his goal. She was downright mortified. Her motive had been self-preservation.

Evan sipped his coffee as if completely innocent of the impending train wreck. Going to the zoo was a bad idea. It would be their second time out together in a "family" setting in a week. She didn't want to give either Evan or Matt the wrong idea.

"Evan, I know you mean well…"

He held up a stopping hand. "My limo will be arriving

in fifteen minutes. Instead of telling me the usual reasons, how about you run upstairs, get into some play clothes and let's go. I hear the monkeys are especially funny at lunchtime."

The absurdity of his statement made her chuckle. "And why is that?"

He shrugged. "I have no idea. I just made that up."

Matt leaned over the counter. "Come on, Mom! We'll have fun. They even have two gorillas!"

Evan pounded his chest. "We can play Tarzan and Jane."

Bunny sidled next to Kelly. "I'll go if she says no."

Two women at the table adjacent to the counter said, "We'll go, too."

Bunny nudged Kelly's arm. "Take your son to the zoo. He had a wonderful first week at school. Celebrate a little."

Matt folded his hands as if praying. "Please, Mom? Please? Please? Please?"

As much as her gut said no, she could not resist the barrage of possibilities. Most of all, Evan's question, *Do you have someone to confide in?* She sure would like to bounce some ideas off another adult on how to approach Matt's introduction to her brother. A man's perspective just might help.

"Well, I suppose it's not every day we get to ride in a limousine to the zoo."

Evan clapped his hands. "Excellent, Red. I'll make sure the monkeys don't eat all your peanuts."

She grinned. "It's not the monkeys that concern me."

"Hold on there. I'm your friend. Remember?"

She took off her apron. "Just making a point, Evan Mc-Kenna. Now give me ten minutes and I'll be right down."

AN HOUR LATER, with a bag of peanuts in hand and wearing a turquoise T-shirt, denim skirt and strappy sandals,

Kelly realized she couldn't remember the last time she'd impulsively taken a day off to play. She pushed her sunglasses onto her nose against the noontime glare to watch Evan and Matt imitate the elephants. She had been studying the zoo map, wanting to see the gorillas, snow leopard and lemurs before they finished their tour.

She laughed out loud. She'd actually mapped out an agenda for her own amusement. How long had it been since she'd done that?

Evan looked over. "What's so funny, Red?"

She shook her head. "Oh, nothing. You two are more amusing than the wildlife."

He grinned. "Really?"

Why was it that he could make everything she said sound like a come-on? Maybe because a hunk like him had women throwing themselves at him all the time, and he was used to flirting. "Oh, sure. I can't wait to compare you to the gorilla next. Should be a perfect fit."

He grinned. "If only they had mules here."

"Hey, if you are comparing me…"

"Oh, never you, lass. You're as malleable as marshmallow fluff."

"Now I'm insulted!"

His laughter was disarming. "Kelly, I've never met a more independent or resilient woman than you. Now, how about some lunch before we tackle the rest of the zoo?"

Matt jumped up and down. "I want a hot dog, French fries and a root beer."

"Done."

Evan reached for Kelly's hand, and the gesture was clearly impulsive because he let his hand drop at the surprise she felt fill her face.

Instead he ruffled Matt's hair. "There's a concession stand down this path. One hot dog, coming up."

He fell into step beside her while Matt ran ahead, then tracked back to them. "I hope you are enjoying yourself as much as I am."

"Actually, I didn't realize how much I needed to take a day off. I have to admit you had a good idea."

"I find it comfortable being with you. I like this." The sweeping gesture of his hands indicated the three of them and their surroundings.

"Well, I don't want you or Matt getting the wrong impression."

He frowned. "Don't tell me you are going to launch…"

She held up a hand. "Don't get me wrong. I appreciate your friendship. More than you can imagine."

"But we can only be friends because you don't date?"

"Yes."

"Kelly, you really do not have to reiterate that fact every time we meet. I heard you the first, second, third and the millionth time. I get it. But I like you. I like Matt. I'm hoping we can be friends. And friends spend time with each other. Can you tolerate that?"

They reached the concession stand. Oblivious to their conversation, Matt pointed to the picture of an ice-cream cone plastered on a poster near the ordering window.

"Can I get one, Mom?"

She paused to read the brief menu on the board. "Let's eat our lunch first and see how we feel afterward."

Evan nudged her. "Does the same answer apply to my question?"

She laughed. "No, Evan. I can answer you right off. I am happy to be your friend. Thank you for understanding." She chuckled. "I can tell you that my gal friends will be green with envy."

"So will the guys in the newsroom."

"Really?"

He looked dismayed at her surprise. "Kelly, your male patrons think you are a hotter item than, oh, say, your Friday Special."

She laughed. "Given how much you like that Reuben sandwich, I'm flattered." When she was with Evan, she laughed often. She liked that.

Matt had ordered his hot dog, Evan seconded the order. She asked for a knish with mustard and a bottled water. Kelly was acutely aware that Evan watched her as she spoke. Goodness, his grin was like a physical touch. She could see how women fell for him and sent a grateful prayer skyward that she had already set the boundaries between them. The last thing she wanted was to be another notch on his bedpost.

They stayed at the zoo until closing time at five-thirty. Traffic back into Manhattan wasn't too bad for a Sunday. Matt turned on the small television in the limo and promptly fell asleep, sprawled on the cushions along the side lounge. Kelly and Evan sat on either side of the back-seat. Despite the arm's length between them, no matter how much she tried, Kelly could not ignore the pull Evan's body had on hers. Never mind how good Evan looked in a business suit during the week—now in jeans and a black T-shirt with sleeves pulled across well-formed biceps, his dark hair pushed back and almost too long on his neck, the scent of his skin rising on the air between them, Kelly had to swallow a few times to reel herself in. His strong hand lay palm down on his thigh. She couldn't even look at his hand without remembering that he had reached for hers earlier—and how nice it would have been to slide her hand into his, just once.

Evan had become quiet, staring out the window. His profile, strong and kind and appealing, tugged at her as well, especially because he appeared so relaxed. He had been wonderful with Matt today, matching that small boy's energy moment for moment. The proof lay in the fact that Matt lay sleeping when usually he'd still be bouncing around the limo. If Evan wasn't such an ambitious man, one who took conquering the world as a sport and winning hearts as a hobby, she might actually consider him as a keeper one day. But no. She already knew what happened at the hands of a man who knew no boundaries.

While as a lover, she could never truly relax with Evan, as a friend it was abundantly clear that she could rely on him. He'd already proven himself in that arena with Matt and his constant presence. She was okay with accepting the man's limitations. Besides, by the time she was ready to date, she'd want a nice simple man with a good sense of humor and a strong heart, with eyes only for her. She could wait for that day because in the meantime she had so much more to do.

CAUGHT IN HIS own thoughts about how perfectly the afternoon had passed with Kelly and Matt, it took a moment before the heat of Kelly's stare penetrated Evan's awareness. The way her brow, lightly dusted with freckles, furrowed in concentration betrayed how she was battling with thoughts of her own. Wouldn't it be great if she was rethinking her stance on their friendship-only status? He liked the fit of Kelly and Matt in his world. He hadn't realized how much he missed creating his own family life until spending time with these two. He smiled when he realized she was unaware that she was staring at him.

He turned his full focus on her. "Penny for your thoughts, Red?"

Ever the body language reader, he didn't miss the fact that she took time to clear her throat, which meant that she was stealing a precious moment to regroup.

She leaned toward him. "Actually, I wanted to ask your advice about something."

He turned his body to face her. "If I can help, I will."

She leaned back, but kept her voice low. "I have a brother who is a priest."

He smiled. "I know. You've told me."

She looked at her hands. "That's right. I forgot. Well, it seems Michael has found himself shepherding a new flock of parishioners in Brooklyn."

"That's terrific, Kelly. You must be happy to have family here."

She released a sigh. "Yes, and no."

"What do you mean?"

Kelly glanced at Matt to reassure herself he was asleep. "Until yesterday, Michael did not know about Matt. No one in Ireland does. And worse, Matt knows nothing about my family."

A soft whistle escaped his lips. "My God, Kelly. How did you pull that one off?"

She shrugged. "It's probably been the hardest thing I've ever done. Until recently, we had Herby George. Everyone else who knows me lives in Ireland. The distance makes it easier. Having Matt out of wedlock, I knew my parents would never accept him. I decided not to expose my son or myself to their disapproval. I keep communications with Ireland short and sweet."

Along with the barrage of questions that rose in his mind, a swell of new respect for this woman's indomitable spirit filled him. He hoped she could see admiration reflected in his eyes. The questions could wait. He didn't want to raise Kelly's defenses with an interrogation.

She tilted her head, as if trying to read him. "Why are you shaking your head?"

He wanted to reach for her, but refrained. Instead he

pressed his back against the limo wall. "Because you truly amaze me, Kelly. You are like a lioness with her cub. I'd love to do a news piece on you."

Horror rose in her eyes. "Never, Evan! Don't even think something like that."

He held up his hand. "Easy, girl. It's just a statement of my admiration for you."

She settled back into her seat. "Okay."

He watched her struggle, as if she wanted to say something. "Kelly. When it comes to you, I feel like that gorilla in the zoo pounding my chest to protect you."

"I am more than capable of caring for my son and myself."

He had to smile at her Irish ire. "Don't I know it! But, hear me out. Please believe me when I say that you can rely on me. I want nothing more than to be a steel-vaulted, sealed-at-the-lips trusted friend." He leaned closer. "Everyone needs a friend, Kelly. I am here for you."

She managed a smile. "Okay, then. Thank you, Evan."

He squeezed her hand, enjoying the soft silk of her skin. "So, how can I help you?"

"Michael insists on meeting Matt. It's time. When I tell Matt about Michael and his grandparents in Ireland, he's going to have so many questions. I'm not sure how to handle them."

Evan hadn't released her hand, and she hadn't pulled away. He liked that. He curled his fingers through hers. He liked the warmth of her hand in his, the delicate yet capable fingers heating beneath the press of his own.

"You will answer his questions with the same bravery and truth you've used as a single parent to get you both this far."

"Matt thinks his only family was Herby George."

He waited until she lifted her green eyes to meet his.

"You can be honest with him. Tell him your parents are difficult, sometimes unkind. And that you two lived your quiet life surrounded with people who supported you."

She slowly nodded. "I see your point."

He watched her closely as he delivered his next thought. "What about Matt's father? Is there family around who could complicate matters?"

Evan didn't miss the internal flinch Kelly immediately suppressed before she pulled her hand from his, which sent his radar pinging, all over again. When she didn't respond, he added. "Is your brother receptive to meeting Matt?"

Here, her smile became genuine. "He nearly horse-whipped me for keeping Matt secret from him. He's demanding I do penance for my sin of omission." She laughed out loud. "They will get along famously."

She inhaled a deep breath. "So, should Matt speak any of this to you, I trust you will handle your response with the same wisdom you just shared with me?"

"It depends, my friend."

"On what?"

"Dinner. Tomorrow night. You can't say no."

"That sounds suspiciously like a date."

He shook his head. "Not at all. If I ask another woman, she'll think I have designs on her. I don't have time for dating. You and I already set our friendship on solid footing. I know I'm safe with you."

She frowned. "Safe with me? Why does that suddenly sound as if I have no sex appeal?"

His grin turned devilish. "Sex appeal you have, Kelly Sullivan, but it's your mind that turns me on."

The limo pulled up to Neverland. Still grinning from Evan's tease, Kelly gently shook Matt's shoulder. "Wake up, buddy. We're home."

"Here, let me." Evan leaned to scoop Matt into his arms.

Matt awoke and to his delight, Evan tossed him over his shoulder like a sack of laundry.

The smile on Kelly's face had Evan thinking he'd like to do this more often. Matt was a great kid and seeing Kelly relax like this was worth the price of admission. He loved the way one corner of her mouth turned up, punctuating the one dimple in her right cheek. She was about to open the door to the apartment when something across the street caught her eye, making that smile disappear like water on a hot skillet.

She clenched Evan's arm. "My God, Evan. That man is taking our picture."

Across the street, a man pointed a camera with a telephoto lens in their direction. When the photographer realized Kelly saw him, he lowered the camera and began walking briskly down the street.

Kelly said, "And that's an expensive lens. I don't like this."

Evan's jaw dropped when Kelly bolted after the man. "Hey, you! Stop!"

"Kelly, wait!" He bundled Matt back into the limousine. "Stay here, buddy. I'll be right back."

He shot after Kelly, who was chasing the photographer with the stride of an athlete, her gorgeous red hair streaming like fire as she ran. The photographer disappeared around the corner with Kelly hot on his heels. Evan picked up his pace.

He found her standing on the corner of Madison Avenue and Fifty-First Street, bewildered and with tears in her eyes.

"Kelly, what are you doing? He was probably some fan of the news show."

Her fists were clenched. Tears started falling. "You don't understand!"

"Well, try me, for God's sake. Chasing after someone because he took your picture is insane."

Her scathing look would have felled a weaker man. "So you think."

She headed back toward Neverland, leaving him in her wake.

"Kelly, wait."

When he caught up to her, she asked, "What did you do with Matt?"

"He's in the limo. He's okay." He grabbed her arm. "Kelly, talk to me."

She jerked from his grasp and kept walking. "No. I knew it was a mistake to spend time with you. The last thing I need is a celebrity in my life."

He felt like he'd been sucker punched. Suddenly this was his fault? "Well, then, what do you need? This is crazy. Are you wanted by the police?"

Her laugh was like a knife edge. "I want to be left alone, Evan. Is that too much to ask?"

His gut reaction was to walk away from Kelly right there and then. He didn't deserve her anger or how easily she shut him out. Something didn't add up with her behavior, and honestly, he didn't need a woman with a hidden past to complicate his life. Yet, the abject fear filling those usually laughing eyes, her creased brow and tearstained cheeks walloped his heart like a hammer hitting hot iron on an anvil. Kelly had a secret and it could very possibly be her undoing. He wanted to help. He wasn't going anywhere.

He kept up with her brisk pace back to Neverland without uttering a word. When they reached the limo, he opened the door. "Come on, Matt-man. Looks like playtime is over."

CHAPTER SEVEN

KELLY COULDN'T GET Evan from her mind as she tucked Matt into his antique wrought-iron bed that had once been Herby's. Everything had gone so beautifully today before that cursed photographer set off her paranoia. Now Evan probably thought she was a lunatic, especially blaming him for the incident because of his celebrity. She strongly suspected Jay Doyle sent the man. Looked like she'd be offering Evan another free breakfast to make amends.

Matt's favorite bedside lamp, the figure of Urban Hero with a cowboy hat for a lampshade, cast a small circle of light in the darkened room. Matt gave Kelly a concerned look. "Mom, why did you chase that man?"

Kelly scrunched her nose. "That was pretty dumb of me, wasn't it?"

He nodded. "Yeah. Did he steal something?"

She pushed a lock of hair from his forehead. "No, honey. He was taking our picture and I don't think anyone should do that without our permission."

"Why would he take our picture?"

"Probably because we were with Evan. He is famous, you know."

Matt yawned. "Yeah. But now you're mad at him."

"What makes you say that?"

"I saw his face. He looked sad, like I feel when you tell me I did something wrong."

Her eyebrows shot up. "Well, I'll make sure he's okay

in the morning. Now, go to sleep. Tomorrow is a big day."
She kissed him on the cheek and reveled in the bear hug
he gave her. "Love you, Matthew Sullivan."

His spoke sleepily. "Love you, too, Mom."

She switched off his lamp just as her cell phone began
ringing. Evan's number flashed on the screen. She closed
Matt's door before answering.

"Evan?" She made her way into the small kitchen and
put the kettle on for a cup of tea.

"Hey, Red. Can you talk?"

"Yes."

"I just want to remind you that before you lost your
cool with me today, you promised to have dinner with me
tomorrow night."

She laughed, despite her hesitations about speaking with
him. "You have some cheek, Evan!"

He had sounded contrite, but when he replied her laughter seemed to take the tension from his voice. "Look, I
have to accept that you have your reasons for getting upset
with that photographer. It all just took me by surprise.
And honestly, I was concerned for your safety. Makes me
kinda nuts when someone I care for might be getting herself into trouble."

She wanted to be vexed with him, but Matt's words
echoed in her ear. "Matt wants me to make sure I didn't
hurt your feelings."

He chuckled. "Now, he's my hero."

She didn't respond. She was too busy trying to decide
what she would do about his invitation.

"So, I'll pick you up at seven-thirty?" At her prolonged
silence he added, "Red?"

She sighed. She was caving. After seven years, she was
caving. "Okay. But, it's not a date."

"Nope. No date. Just friends having dinner."

"Okay. Seven-thirty. And Evan?"

His voice dropped. "Yes?"

"I'm sorry I lost my cool with you."

"No problem. You just made up for it by saying yes."

BY EIGHT O'CLOCK the next evening, Evan had escorted
Kelly through the doors of one of the oldest historic res-
taurants in Manhattan. The low ceilings were reminiscent
of colonial times, with dark paneling and snowy linens
on the tables. It reminded her of the well-tended ancient
buildings found in Dublin and the countryside around it
that she loved so much.

While totally enchanted, she couldn't help feel like she'd
been shot from a cannon. Bunny had insisted on dressing
her. She now walked beside Evan wearing a black dress
and heels she bought a year ago on a whim. Her hair was
down and slightly wild from hair products. She'd applied
makeup with a nervous hand. Now, with her arm circled
around Evan's, she felt a little breathless.

She had never in her life been on a date. She had no
idea how to act and had to keep reminding herself this
was no date.

Evan wore a pair of excellently fitted gray pants, slim
belt and a tapered white shirt open at the neck beneath a
black raw silk blazer. His blue eyes flashed with interest
when he looked at her, as if trying to measure her reaction
to his choice of restaurant.

Maybe it was the enticement of being alone with him,
but Evan looked incredibly appealing right now. His broad
shoulders, his open, expressive face with the crooked smile
that hinted of his sense of humor had her wishing nothing
regrettable hung between them. The smell of his cologne
and the warmth of his body as she walked next to him

intensified the feel of his strong arm. All these triggers mingled to make this man seem irresistible.

Ugh! Not good thoughts for a woman committed to celibacy. Evan seemed like a modern-day troubadour or some sophisticated artsy type with his debonair style. The ease of his steps and his confident manner hinted that she could depend on him. Over and over again. Which she had, until she lost her temper with him yesterday.

She was glad when he pulled out the chair that faced her toward the room. She didn't think her knees were going to hold out much longer.

He sat next to her, instead of across the table, as she expected. His leg brushed hers under the table. She moved hers away.

"So, are you pleased with this place?"

She smiled. "Oh, yes. I feel like we're in Dublin."

He opened his menu. "There's that smile. I'm glad."

She rolled her eyes. "Have I been so ornery?"

He closed the menu to insure he had her full attention. "I'd say you are a woman with a lot of concerns. Sometimes they get the better of you."

Her mouth snapped shut. That was the last reply she expected to hear. And darn it all if it wasn't the truth.

He looked amused. "I've struck you dumb. This is a first."

She laughed. "Don't you dare be telling a soul!"

EVAN SCANNED HIS menu and glanced at Kelly. Watching her bite that lightly glossed lower lip as she read, he drew on every ounce of strength not to claim her mouth in a searing kiss to match the fire burning in his gut. From the moment she had stepped from her room in that curve-hugging black sheath—which looked both sexy and sophisticated on her incredible body—he felt the earth move beneath his feet. And he hadn't been able to find solid footing since. When she'd sauntered toward him with an easy stride in a pair of mile-high stilettos he never expected she'd wear, his heart pounded so hard in his chest he thought he'd have heart failure.

If Kelly only knew the power she held just by walking up to him. He'd never felt anything like this for a woman before. Sure, he'd had more than his share of dates. Most of his affairs ended once he discovered a selfish or calculating side, or worse, a complete lack of depth. He could understand how Kelly would be wary of a man with the same traits. His designs on her surprised even him. He was ready to settle down, but every time he laid eyes on Kelly it hammered home how much he was ready to settle down with *her*.

Kelly was different. Earthy. Honest. Driven by a moral code that matched his own, and she was *hot.* Hot enough to make him second-guess whether she was real. Before they had left her apartment, the light in those dazzling green eyes, the rising color on her cheeks, the glistening gold hoops in her ears and the way her hair cascaded about her shoulders, all had him thinking that he'd never survive the car ride downtown without touching her.

He'd whistled softly and she actually wagged a finger at him, admonishing him to behave. He laughed, knowing right then and there that he was lost. All the same, he was determined to keep their dinner nice and relaxed. He'd deposit her at home tonight feeling like she'd been out with her best buddy.

Riiiiight.

"What are you smiling about?"

Kelly had her head tilted in a beguiling way. He wanted to slide his hand beneath that sheaf of hair and feel the soft skin of her neck. He cleared his throat.

"I was thinking I will have to buy Matt a Lego set for softening you up toward me."

Kelly arched an eyebrow in reply. "Really? Don't you go bribing my son, now. I'll put you both in a time-out."

The raised eyebrow made him smile. "You don't realize the effect you have on a man."

"Oh, be gone with you. There goes that flirting again."

He frowned. "Don't you understand how attractive you are?"

"I have red hair and freckles…everywhere."

"Yeah, and I could play connect-the-dots all day long."

She laughed. "Time to change the subject, my friend."

That's right. *Friends.* "Okay. To what?"

She tapped a finger to her mouth. "You told me your parents were immigrants. What brought them over?"

Now that answer would sour any of his amorous thoughts. "Patrick, my mother's brother, died due to circumstances with the IRA."

"Was he a sympathizer?"

"No. He worked for the government as an IRA liaison to negotiate for a cease-fire. The Brits refused talks. Patrick got targeted as misrepresenting the IRA and was killed." Evan expelled a breath. "From what Mom tells me, Patrick died trying to end fighting among his people."

"How awful."

"Unfortunately, the militants started threatening Mom's family. She and my dad had just married. They decided to start a new life here."

"Looks like they fared well."

He grinned. "How do you like living here?"

She shrugged. "It's my life now. Matt is my life."

He gave her what he hoped was an encouraging smile. "And it looks like you, too, have fared well."

Two days later, Kelly's world unraveled.

Neverland was in the middle of its midmorning rush when Bunny received a phone call from her sister. Bunny reached for the remote and switched from NCTV to their competitor. It took seconds for the patrons, the waitstaff and Kelly herself to stop everything they were doing to listen to the newspaper reporter, Jay Doyle, airing his case against Presidential hopeful Buzz Campbell, accusing him of being a womanizer.

Doyle sat with Campbell's disgruntled employee, Helen Thompson. It looked as though they just finished airing a segment on her sexual harassment case.

Doyle continued, "From the years she spent working closely with the senator, Ms. Thompson believes she is not the only woman he accosted."

Behind him, half a dozen photos of Matt plastered the video monitors, including the photos taken of Evan carrying Matt over his shoulder after they got out of the limo. Close-ups of Matt's face were set beside childhood photos of Buzz Campbell.

"In an interview with Mrs. Campbell, she showed me these photos of Senator Campbell as a child. Kelly Sullivan was once the Campbell's nanny, who abruptly left their employ and now has a son who looks suspiciously like the senator."

The news anchor said, "That is a damaging assumption. Aren't you concerned about a lawsuit for slander?"

Doyle shook his head like a man delivering a death sentence. "I am so confident of the facts that a lawsuit would only prove the validity of my statements."

Neverland became silent as a morgue. Kelly raced for the remote and snapped off the television. She turned to Bunny, feeling like she was about to puke.

"I need an attorney now!"

The place erupted in muffled conversation. Her patrons, some of them long-standing customers, stared at her with open shock.

Kelly's throat was closing. She couldn't breathe. Bunny pushed her toward the kitchen, but a woman sitting at the counter reached for Kelly's arm. "Is he telling the truth?"

Kelly glanced around the diner. The woman was asking the same thing as every questioning gaze in the room. Kelly had protected herself from this possibility for so long that admitting the truth would be like peeling the skin from her body. Now wasn't the time to change direction. "I cannot believe that man singled me out and tied me to the senator."

Bunny added, "Any child with blond hair and blue eyes could resemble a dozen other children. This guy is off his rocker."

Like a man on a mission, Evan barreled through Neverland's doors. He ignored everyone in his way until he reached Kelly. From the look on his face, he'd seen the interview.

"Where's Matt?"

It took a moment for the meaning behind his question to register. "Oh, Lord. He's at school."

He grabbed her hand. "Let's go!"

THE SIGHT OF reporters already thronged outside the school had Kelly grasping Evan's hand once more.

"How did they get here so fast?"

Evan shook his head. "Reporters get wind of these stories hours before they air."

A few news vans lined the street with their antennae hoisted for transmission. Evan squeezed her fingers, sending her a silent look of encouragement.

He offered a fifty-dollar bill to the taxi driver. "If you'd be so kind as to drive around the block and wait on the next street, we'll be ready in a few minutes."

The guy palmed the bill. "Sure."

Evan turned to Kelly. "You are going to be barraged with questions. Don't say a word. If anything, plaster a look of outrage on your face."

His words penetrated the panic constricting her chest. Despite the few times she had formulated a game plan should Matt's identity surface, she hadn't truly prepared herself for the reality of the situation. She hadn't prepared herself for the emotional crush that she just might have to confront her rapist and fight him for her child. This terror had her fight-or-flight response on full alert. She recalled her helplessness against the full force of Campbell's power, and fear seeped right down to her bones. For the first time in her independent life she was grateful for Evan's presence and his savvy in dealing with the media. His steady head helped cement her resolve to get through this ordeal intact. The determination in his eyes replaced her panic with anger at Doyle's violation of her personal life.

She inhaled a breath, ready for the gauntlet. "You have yet to see angry, Evan."

"Good! Let's go."

Once outside the taxi, Evan pulled her past reporters shoving microphones in her face and shouting questions. She had no problem saying nothing. She'd never said anything before and wasn't inclined to do so now. Behind her she heard one female reporter saying, "And NCTV morning show host, Evan McKenna, is escorting Kelly Sullivan into her son's school."

Oh, dear. Evan's friendship would certainly be tested now.

Kelly had phoned the school's headmistress en route. Matt jumped from his seat in her office when they entered.

"Hi, Mom! Hi, Evan!"

Kelly's heart squeezed at the joy in his innocent face. He had no idea how his world would change in the next few hours. She exchanged looks with the headmistress. "Thank you for having him ready. If it's okay, I'll call you later with details. We really must get moving."

"Don't worry, Ms. Sullivan. Happy to help in any way we can."

"Where are we going?" Matt looked from Kelly to Evan.

Evan raised his hand for their secret handshake. "Hey, Matt-man! We're going to play a little hooky today. I have a surprise."

"Really? Can we, Mom?" He looked at Kelly with hopeful eyes.

While her knees felt like they'd buckle beneath her if Matt saw the reporters outside the school, she hadn't come this far protecting her son to fall apart now. "That's why we're here, honey."

Evan turned his winning smile on the headmistress. "We sure could use a back door if you have one."

She returned the smile. "We have children of celebrities at our school. If you'll follow me, I'll take you through to the building next door. It has a private garage."

"Excellent. We'll need one additional favor, if you don't mind?"

"Yes?"

"I have a taxi waiting on the next street. The driver is a guy wearing a Yankees baseball cap. If you could direct him to the garage, that would be a big help."

A young secretary rose from her desk and headed for the door. "I can do that for you, Mr. McKenna."

"Thank you." Kelly and Evan spoke at the same time. Kelly prodded Matt forward in the headmistress's wake. "Time to go, buddy."

NOT UNTIL MATT was in Evan's penthouse absorbed in the pinball machine with the buzzing, bells and the macabre laughter did Evan lead Kelly to the overstuffed couch in the living room. He sat next to her, his close proximity more daunting than Kelly wanted to admit. She wondered if he sat so close with the intention to intimidate her. She wouldn't give him the chance.

She held up a hand. "Don't ask."

"That's not an option, Kelly. Were you the Campbell's nanny?"

She met the interrogation in his eyes directly. Had she brought this moment upon herself by speaking the truth to her brother? It was hard enough revealing her secret once, but to say it again—especially to a newsman? Jay Doyle was proof enough of what a reporter would do for a story. Could she depend on Evan to hold her best interest in mind over a newsworthy scandal? Difficult as it was to reveal her past to Michael under a church vow, telling her story to Evan could be like broadcasting her personal life to the world and bringing the wrath of Senator Robert Buzz Campbell right to her door. Then again, Doyle had already done that. Now it was time for damage control. Evan had asked her to trust him. Bringing him into her confidence would be the ultimate test of his loyalty.

She released the breath she held. "Jay Doyle came into Neverland two weeks ago to ask me the very same question."

"And you said yes. Hence, the snooping and the photographer. So, can I assume the rest of Doyle's accusations are fact?"

She couldn't just blurt out the facts. She glanced over to where Matt played pinball. "Young towheaded boys can look like a multitude of people. I plan to sue Mr. Doyle for his accusation."

Evan shook his head. "That is not an answer, Kelly. Talk to me. If Campbell reacts the way I think he will, he's going to demand a DNA test to prove his innocence. Then it won't matter if you tell me the truth or not."

She watched Evan for a long moment. While she felt her defenses rising to protect her and Matt from the cruel and ugly world divined by Buzz Campbell, a part of her understood she needed help in keeping Matt safe. Somehow, her son had to disappear off the media radar. No one could make that happen better than Evan.

She pulled at nonexistent lint on her jeans.

Evan leaned forward. Lowering his voice, he said, "Kelly. Please. This situation will do nothing but escalate. I want to help."

She met his gaze, her chest tightening with fear. Her worst nightmare was turning into real life, and so much was at stake: Matt's innocent world, her reputation, their privacy and the absolute worst—the very real chance that Buzz Campbell might try to take Matt from her. There was no more room for dalliance here. She had to commit.

She released another heated breath. "Buzz Campbell will not be able to prove his innocence with a DNA test."

To his credit, Evan didn't react. He studied her, as if gauging a fine balance. Very softly he asked, "Were you lovers?"

Her cheeks heated, but she would not look away. She struggled to keep her voice low because, God help her, she wanted to scream.

"He raped me, Evan. I packed my bags and left the next morning after giving Madeline Campbell some inane excuse for quitting. The bastard took my virginity. I had never, I repeat, *never* dated a man before he touched me. I was twenty and came from a very strict family. If Herbert

George hadn't taken me in, I don't know what would have happened to us, because I could not go home."

She closed her eyes to keep from having to meet his gaze. There, she'd said it. Now she fought tears. She'd already shed enough of them with Michael and had no intention of crying in front of Evan, especially because losing her composure now would draw Matt's attention. She had yet to tell her son about his uncle Michael, let alone the fact that some strange man might try to claim him as his son.

Saints alive. How was she going to protect Matthew now? Unshed tears pressed against her closed lids.

The feel of Evan's fingers wrapping around her hand startled her. She opened her eyes to see tamped-down anger in his eyes.

"Why didn't you have Buzz arrested?"

She leaned back into the cushions, the sense of helplessness and guilt from that night feeling real, yet so foreign. She had come so far since then, but the scar still ran deep.

Across the room, Matt jumped up and down as the pinball machine hit yet another jackpot. Her heart ached, thinking about the onslaught this little boy was about to face.

"Kelly?"

She released a breath. "The senator told me it was my fault that he assaulted me. He said I seduced him by walking around his house with a body like mine and caring for his children as if I was their mother and his lover. He threatened to have me deported if I told anyone what, in his words, 'I made him do.' I left the next day with so much fear, guilt and shame that for the longest time, I believed him."

He frowned. "Did you seduce him?"

"Of course not! How can you ask?"

"Then why did you believe him, Kelly? Why didn't you fight him?"

Damn it all, she couldn't stop the tears sneaking silently down her cheek. She swiped at them, angry with her own weakness and angry that she could not explain how vulnerable she felt in those terrifying moments. When she realized Campbell was assaulting her, shock and panic became twin emotions. She had tried to fight him off, but he was too strong, too fast, and he had hurt her. While Campbell had pumped into her, uncaring of her pain, her mother's words echoed in her head that her body would get her into trouble one day. Although innocent, Campbell's accusations that she seduced him continued to haunt her because her body had betrayed her and she carried the shame. She could never explain that to Evan.

She swallowed hard. "A part of me believed him, Evan. There's more to it, but I really cannot talk about it. Besides, Buzz was so handsome and kind. Charismatic, really. I developed a crush on him as would any impressionable young woman. I suppose you'd call it hero worship. But, Evan, I can assure you, I never said, did, dressed or acted in any way to entice him other than be attentive when he spoke and return his smiles, the same way I respond to everyone."

YES, SHE DID respond to everyone with attention and smiles. That was one of the most attractive traits Evan admired about Kelly, but it never occurred to him to rape her over her friendly nature.

Seeing Kelly humiliated at the hands of Buzz Campbell shot the senator to number one on Evan's scum-of-the-earth hit list. Campbell was going down. Evan would make him accountable for his actions and, if humanly possible, have the slimeball thrown in jail.

And, to think Evan had been about to publicly endorse

KATHLEEN PICKERING 93

the senator as a presidential candidate. The thought of how the man carried on his duplicitous life made Evan's stomach heave. For all intents and purposes, Campbell appeared as a family man with unquestionable moral character. His wife and children adored him. On national television, Madeline Campbell spoke with nothing but love and admiration about their twenty-year marriage. Now the senator would be lucky if Evan didn't knock those pearly whites down his throat the next time they met.

He seethed inside as he offered Kelly his steady and calm attention. He didn't want to make her too skittish to trust him, and understood how much fortitude it had taken her to confide as much as she had, because he was sure there was more. While he had suspected a secret lay behind Matt's parentage, he never thought that Kelly had been raped. She was too congenial, welcoming and, damn it all, kind, to be carrying a soul-rending burden that would bring most people to their knees and destroy their lives.

Watching her sit with legs tucked beneath her, red hair falling about her shoulders, eyes misted with tears, his caveman urge to protect this woman surged into overload. The ferocity of his anger against Kelly's violation squeezed his chest stronger than any outrage he'd ever felt. But, before he gunned for Campbell, he had to set a strategy in place. And he needed Kelly's compliance.

"Evan! Can I play basketball?"

Matt's question broke his internal tirade. He smiled at Matt, who looked as if he'd grown tired of the pinball machine and found the basketball.

"Sure, champ! Give me a few more minutes with your mom, and I'll play some hoops with you."

Matt dribbled the ball as best he could, focused on the hoop towering above him and shot—not even coming close. Chasing after the ball would keep him busy awhile longer.

He looked at Kelly. "He's a great kid."

She shook her head. "He's about to get walloped, and I don't know how to protect him."

"We'll get you through this."

She leaned forward, desperation lighting her eyes. "Evan, you don't understand. New York State law does not protect a mother or a child born from rape if the assailant files for custody rights. My biggest fear is that Buzz Campbell will come after Matt, and I'll have to comply!"

Evan was shocked. "That can't be true."

She dropped her voice to a whisper. "Oh, it is. I did my homework. The law says that unless my situation fit a certain stereotype of what the courts consider rape, especially since I raised Matt instead of seeking an abortion or putting him up for adoption, my accusation becomes suspicious. I would be viewed as a wronged lover seeking revenge instead of a victim of assault. Why do you think I've stayed off the radar for all these years?"

Evan immediately wanted to make Kelly's case a television issue. He'd succeeded in helping underdogs caught in the machine of big business or the whims of powerful people by airing their cases in the news. If he could convince Kelly to speak out, she could earn public support against Campbell while raising awareness against this damaging lack of legal support for victimized women.

"Kelly…"

"No, Evan. I know what you are going to say. I will not go public." The desperation catching in her voice almost made her choke. "Can you imagine what that little boy will feel when he comprehends that he was the product of a violent crime? I can't drag Matt through a scandal. I just want Buzz Campbell to go away. Quietly."

"You know that's not going to happen."

She bit her lower lip. "I know. I've always understood the futility of my chances against a powerful politician. Again, why I kept a low profile."

Evan's mind raced as he tried to imagine Kelly's utter sense of helplessness and shame wondering how she would survive, let alone create an income and raise a child while constantly looking over her shoulder for someone to swoop down and take her son.

He tamped down his desire to pulverize Campbell for being the animal he was. Instead he focused. What did Kelly need? Protection. An alibi. Another story to throw the snooping media off her scent. How could he help? Well, hell. He'd met Kelly for the first time on the heels of her attack. She probably didn't even know she was pregnant when she poured his first coffee. That thought wrenched his gut.

The answer came to him in a flood. He reached for Kelly's hands. She didn't resist. He saw that through her unhappiness she welcomed the warmth of his touch.

"I know one step we can take to strengthen your position."

A glimmer of hope lit her face. "What is that?"

"Marry me."

She pulled her hands from his, wrapping her arms tightly around her torso. "Don't be crazy, Evan. Marriage is not a solution."

Suddenly this idea seemed all too perfect. He lowered his voice. "No, Kelly, listen. Do you think Buzz Campbell wants an illegitimate son marring his candidacy?"

She frowned. "No, but I know he always wanted a son."

He shook his head. "Enough to jeopardize his bid for the White House?"

He saw the light of his reasoning taking hold. "Probably not."

"So what if I approach Campbell and offer to make this scandal go away if I claim Matt as mine and marry you? I'll make him promise not to ask for a DNA test. He can go his way, and we can go ours."

Suddenly the idea of marrying Kelly sat perfectly with him. His family and friends might think he was crazy, but he'd been with enough women to know that no woman he'd ever met or ever would meet could compare with Kelly. She'd already proven her courage and strength. He was already smitten by her kindness, compassion and humor, and God help them both, she was so damned sexy and smelled so good that keeping his hands off her was a constant trial. Throw in the fact that he was saving the day in the mix, and she'd fall in love with him in no time.

He was willing to take the chance.

"No matter what you decide, Kelly, I can and will do everything in my power to protect you. I'm not bragging or anything, but I can raise one helluva case on national television to gain support for you. If you become my wife it strengthens my position."

This time she reached for his hand. "Evan McKenna, that is the kindest proposal I have ever heard." She grinned. "Actually, it is the only proposal I've ever heard, but please, stop now. First of all, when I marry, it will be for love and the desire to spend the rest of my life with a man. Secondly, I will never agree to my story becoming public any more than it has." She shook her head. "You are talking about a marriage of convenience. That would only complicate matters and prove to be very inconvenient for both of us."

He laughed. The fact that Kelly could make jokes at a critical moment was yet another of her endearing qualities. Oh, yeah. Evan felt love for this woman. He wouldn't have made the marriage proposal if he thought otherwise. But, she was nowhere close to accepting the fact that his love could be true.

He leaned close enough to get a whiff of her perfume, then even closer, as if sharing a secret. He could feel her body heat. "Even Matt likes me. The three of us can go to Van Cleef's in the morning and choose your dream engagement ring. I will get down on one knee and slide the ring on your hand right there in the store. We can elope and then revisit the state of our marriage after we've secured Matt's protection."

Shocked, she shook her head and chuckled. "You silly man. Your gorilla nature is showing. I have never had a 'dream' engagement ring. The thought of getting married has rarely entered my mind."

He stood up. Wow. Low blow. Here he was seriously making her a marriage proposal and she was treating him like some dude flirting with her at the Neverland counter.

"Don't you even want to think about it?"

She laughed. "Don't tell me you are serious?"

He shrugged. "Well, I am. Chances are your life is going to get pretty complicated very soon. You have my protection, but marriage and two parents make a strong argument in Matt's defense. Besides, I have feelings for you that we haven't had the chance to explore. Think about it."

He strode toward the basketball hoop. Damn it all if he sat there a moment longer, he'd be begging her to marry him. Kelly's rejection burned his pride, yet he wondered if she was too deeply scarred by Buzz Campbell to ever trust another man. Maybe he was a little too close to Kelly's world not to see clearly how, in time, the offer of marriage might not bring the results he craved with her. Technically, she was no longer a virgin, but emotionally, she'd never even had the chance to date, let alone have a lover. He'd have his work cut out for him to make her feel safe enough to become emotionally involved with him.

Was awakening her to the power of love a task he was willing to tackle?

Matt saw him coming. "Show me how to do a slam dunk."

"Sure, Matt-man. Pass the ball. I'll show you."

Evan took a few steps while dribbling the ball and jumped for the hoop, imagining the ball was a baby grand piano coming down on Buzz Campbell's head.

Slam!

He made a low pass of the ball to Matt. When the boy gripped it with both hands, Evan lifted him up close to the rim. "Shoot!"

Matt tossed the ball and made the hoop. He yelled with delight. Evan put him back on his feet and started performing some kind of chicken dance. Matt followed. They slapped each other a high five.

Evan glanced at Kelly. She watched them, a smile plastered on her face, but he could see that in her mind, she was miles away. God, she was beautiful. And strong. And perfect for him. Yeah. He'd take that chance on love with her. He'd probably have more success once she finally vanquished the one obstacle that had kept her defenses up for all these years: Senator Robert "The Buzz" Campbell.

Evan knew exactly how to cut the man off at the knees. What was it going to take to convince this stubborn beauty that speaking out against Campbell was her only possible solution? Until she stated her case, she'd be deluged by reporters, religious groups, women's rights groups—and who knew who else would take up a banner the minute she stepped foot into Neverland.

Uh-oh. Neverland.

"Hey, Red!"

She'd already risen from the couch and was heading toward the game room. "Yes, Evan?"

He waited until she stood in the middle of the half-court to toss the basketball at her. To her credit, she caught it.

"Where are you and Matt staying tonight?"

"We'll go home, of course."

Evan shook his head. "Think about the reporters we dodged this morning. You are a target until someone gets a story."

"Mom's gonna be on TV?"

"Not if I can help it, honey," Kelly said, sending Evan a look that said, *now it's starting.*

Evan winced. "Hey, are you guys hungry? We can order lunch and have it delivered."

"Pizza? Can we get Caruso's, Mom?"

Kelly frowned. "I don't think I can eat." She handed Matt the basketball.

"Let me get some menus," Evan insisted. "Maybe you'll change your mind."

Matt grabbed a handful of quarters and climbed on the ottoman to play pinball again. Kelly followed Evan to the kitchen.

"You don't think it's safe for us to go home?"

He turned his body to face her, speaking quietly. "No, I don't. You and I both know that Buzz Campbell already has heard about Doyle's interview. He's seen your photo, he's seen Matt's. With Helen Thompson's accusations, Doyle is building quite a formidable case here. Buzz has major damage control on his hands."

"I can't leave town. I have Neverland."

"I know that. You and Matt should stay here."

Kelly shook her head. "Impossible. I have to work."

"You can't go home with Matt."

"Well, I can't leave him here."

"If the good senator can't make you disappear, he'll try to make everything look correct in the public eye. He'll demand DNA testing. He'll try to smear you, cite you as unfit or a liar, and depending on what his attorneys tell him, he may sue you for custody. If you think I asked you tough questions earlier, you have yet to run the gauntlet. The man was a marine, Kelly. He doesn't back down."

KELLY SAT ON the closest chair. Of course. She knew all this. "I'm in for the battle of my life."

He pulled menus from the drawer and splayed them on the counter, as if on autopilot. "You have to keep your son out of reach. Stay here. No one can get past my doorman."

The way Evan said *your son* convinced her that he considered Matt off-limits to the senator. "Thank you for saying that, Evan."

"What?"

"Calling Matt my son."

He reached for her. Very tentatively, he wrapped his arms around her. "And a fine son he is. With a mother like a warrior princess."

Kelly stiffened in his arms, but when she felt the warmth of his concern to match his words, she melted against him, sorely needing the comfort of strong arms. She laid her cheek against his chest. He rested his chin against the crown of her head as if he'd done it a thousand times. Wow. He was tall. And, goodness. He felt warm and familiar. His masculine scent suffused her senses like much-needed air.

A brief impulse almost had her wrapping her arms around his waist. Instead, she tucked her palms between them on his chest.

She whispered, "It's been Matt and me against the world from the start. I hated the senator for what he did to me, but I've loved Matt since I felt the first flutter in my belly.

All my plans to put him up for adoption fell away, and I never looked back."

He caressed her head, and she could not remember when she felt more safe. Within the sanctuary of his arms, she opened the floodgate a bit wider.

"When Campbell violated me, he stole my right to choose whether I wanted to become pregnant, let alone have sex. I don't want Buzz Campbell anywhere near my baby. I can't imagine the confusion Matt will suffer if he learns that he is a child born of rape and has to acknowledge that ogre as his father."

Evan held her at arm's length, meeting her gaze with as much conviction as she felt. "Then, we declare war."

She stepped away from him, once again her own counsel. Evan kept saying, *we*. When it came to surmounting challenges, her world had been, *I*. A few days ago, Evan had offered friendship and trust. Moments ago he offered marriage. She blew him off as if he'd been kidding because she couldn't consider that he'd been sincere. If he was sincere, then she'd have to examine her own feelings. Right now, she was upset. She needed to think clearly—and on her own.

While Evan's overpowering personality and take-charge attitude could be a welcome escape from facing Campbell alone, those very traits overrode her comfort level. Evan's aggressive career and unwillingness to take *no* for an answer reminded her startlingly of Buzz Campbell. Yet, Evan was different. He possessed a kindness that was unmistakably genuine and his moral standard matched her own. Yet, could he truly be trusted? He had already pushed her to go public with her story. He seemed to have no intention of letting that topic drop. A thread of suspicion had her wondering how much of Evan's motives were geared more toward uncovering a news story than toward standing by her.

She chided herself. How unflattering to indulge mistrust when Evan had been nothing but spot-on in all his help. Despite her concerns, she very much appreciated that she wasn't alone with this Doyle debacle, but she had to make the decisions. Listening to Evan's advice didn't make her weak. He gave her food for thought. She sat back in the chair.

"Okay, so I can't take Matt back to Neverland for a while. I can take him to Michael, but first they have to meet, and Matt would have to get comfortable with him before I left him."

Evan shook his head. "No, Kelly. We're talking now. Tonight. Tomorrow. Just stay here. There are two guest rooms down the hall. I won't even know you are here."

"What about Neverland?"

He shrugged. "You can go. They don't need DNA from you."

"There is no way I can take him back to school, either."

"I know. This is going to be tricky."

"What do you suggest?"

He grabbed the menus. "We order lunch. Then, we fortify our forces."

She tilted her head at his grin. "What do you mean?"

"We call my mother."

CHAPTER EIGHT

No sooner was pizza delivered than Kelly's cell phone rang. She didn't recognize the number but the area code was Brooklyn. It could only be one person. She answered.

"Kelly, it's Michael."

"Hello, Michael." She waved a reassuring hand at Evan's questioning gaze and gestured that she'd take the call on the balcony. Once outside, she leaned against the balustrade soaking in the view over tree-lined Central Park. "I guess you've seen the news."

"Looks like the good Lord brought me here in time to help." His brotherly concern sounded so familiar. She realized how glad she was to finally have family on her side of the ocean.

"Michael, please don't breathe a word of this to the family."

"Do you think this event will make international headlines?"

She closed her eyes at the thought. "God, I hope not."

"How can I help?"

"I'm not sure. I'm with a friend right now. He's offered to let us stay here. We have to keep Matt away from Senator Campbell."

Michael was silent a moment. "I am not having very kind thoughts about that man."

She laughed. "Believe me, Michael, I know the feeling."

"I'd prefer you come here."

"I already thought of that but Evan's penthouse is close to Neverland and the closest thing to a fortified castle as I can get."

"You've never heard of the church as sanctuary?"

She sighed at the hurt in his voice. Men. Ever the protectors. "Michael, can you come into Manhattan? Evan is asking his mother to help. I sure could use some brotherly support, and it is time for Matthew to meet you."

He didn't hesitate. "When?"

"Tomorrow? I have to arrange the schedule at Neverland to give myself some time off."

"I'll be there after noon mass."

A wave of relief filled her. Big brother would come to the rescue without a hint of reprimand. "I'll wait for you at Neverland."

He questioned, "So, who is the Evan with whom you are planning to stay the night?"

Kelly chuckled. "Evan McKenna. He's a friend, Michael. The television morning show host for NCTV?"

"Ah. Well, at least he is Irish. Are you dating him, lass?"

"No, Michael. I don't date. I have a son to raise. You can see the arrangements for yourself tomorrow."

"Ah. I see. Well, then. Till tomorrow. And, Kelly?"

"Yes?"

"You are not alone. Ever."

She pressed a hand to her heart. Her response was choking her throat. "I know it, Michael. Thank you."

Evan and Matt were hatching some plan for playing manhunt through the penthouse after lunch. Evan had removed his suit jacket and loosened his tie. His ability to make a crisis seem like an everyday event was not lost on her. A wave of warmth filled her. Men like Evan and Michael restored her belief that not all males were heartless. That said, she'd never lose sight of the fact that even these men—while willing to help her—would handle her situation differently if she gave them the reins. Handing over her control would never happen, but she wasn't fool enough to refuse the help they offered.

"Everything okay?" Evan asked.

She nodded once. "It was my brother."

Matt's eyes went wide. "You have a brother?"

His question was pure curiosity, as if it wouldn't even occur to him that Kelly had withheld information. She sat down next to Matt and shot a quick glance at Evan, who leaned back from the counter as if giving her space to speak.

She smiled at Matt. "As a matter of fact, I do."

"Where is he?"

"He used to live in Ireland. He just moved to Brooklyn. He's a priest."

Matt's eyes grew wide. "Like Father Benjamin at church?"

"Exactly. Only my brother is called Father Michael. He is coming to meet you tomorrow. You can call him Uncle Michael."

Matt nodded. "Okay." He opened the box of pizza. "We saved you two pieces, Mom. Want one?"

"Sure!"

Kelly met Evan's amused gaze. How about that? Here she had wasted time in angst over telling Matt about her family, and he was more interested in feeding her pizza. She took a bite shaking her head. "Will wonders never cease?"

Evan polished off his last bite of pizza. "Let's hope the next question is as easy."

Kelly devoured her slice, unaware she had been so hungry, while Evan told Matt about his upcoming show. Tomorrow he'd be interviewing the lead actor in the latest

Urban Hero movie. When he promised Matt that he'd bring him to the "green" room to meet the actor if they could convince his mother to give him tomorrow off from school, Kelly shot to full alert.

She gave Evan a look that said, *are-you-crazy?* "I thought being visible wasn't a good idea."

"Well, I've been giving it some thought. Matt could sit with me during the show. He can ask Urban Hero the questions every kid would want to ask him. It would be a great interview."

"Absolutely not!"

"Why, Mom? I wanna meet Urban Hero!" Matt sounded awestruck at the chance few kids would get.

Kelly closed her eyes to compose herself against the jolt of anger that rocked her. Evan had no right to make plans with Matt without her permission. Making this offer, then forcing her to say no, made her look like the bad guy between them. Evan had taken this tactic twice already. First the theater, then the zoo. It was time she eliminated this poor choice of persuasion immediately.

"Matt, honey. I'm going to ask you to go play for a few minutes while I have a private discussion with Evan."

Matt slipped from his stool. He gave Evan a sympathetic look, as if he knew all too well what her tone of voice meant. "Can I turn on the TV?"

Evan pointed to the coffee table. "The remote is over there. Push the red button at the top."

When Matt left the room, Evan leaned toward her. "Kelly, I called my mother while you were outside. She can't get here until tomorrow afternoon. You can't take Matt to Neverland, and we can't leave him alone. I thought taking him to work was the best solution."

She saw the wisdom behind his thinking, but didn't like

that Evan hadn't consulted her first. "So, my thoughts on the subject don't matter?"

"Oh." At least he had the wisdom to look contrite. "I'm used to getting things done. My mistake. Apologies."

"That's the third time you've used that little maneuver to manipulate me. I don't like it."

He held up both hands as if he was going to object, then he frowned. "Really?"

"Don't play dumb with me, Evan. You know exactly what you are doing. And let me add, it is not one of your endearing qualities."

He grinned. "Do I have endearing qualities?"

She almost burst out laughing, not expecting him to change the subject. She tapped her chest. "I know you mean well, but please don't forget. I'm in charge. My son. My life. My responsibility. If you have any more brilliant ideas, please check with me first before discussing them with Matt."

He nodded once. "Understood."

It was on the tip of her tongue to say that she was grateful that he was looking out for their interests, but no. This take-charge approach was exactly what concerned her about men like Evan. They bulldozed their way through the days, manipulating situations to conform to their needs, even if done with the best of intentions—and charm. Luckily for Evan, he caught on and apologized. This time.

"So, what do you think? Can I take him with me tomorrow?"

She sighed. "Let me explain my objections to your idea."

"I'm sure I know them, but shoot."

Why did Evan look so damn appealing leaning back in his seat giving her his full attention? Mentally, she shook off the feeling. "I've kept Matt low-key for his entire life. I'm not comfortable with his face plastered on television."

"Yes, but you were hiding him from Campbell. Now his anonymity is impossible."

She shook her head, disquiet squeezing her heart at the thought of Campbell pulling strings to take Matt from her. "He has goons who do his bidding. Matt could be abducted."

"No way, Kelly. Won't happen. I can promise you Campbell is scrambling to find a way to make this story as untrue as possible. Matt will be safe with me. You have to go to Neverland tomorrow if only to show the world that you're not hiding from the senator. Once my mom gets here, she'll watch Matt for you." He grinned. "She's a formidable woman. You two will get along."

"Let me think about it."

He stood. "Okay. I'll show you your rooms."

"I didn't agree to stay."

"But you will, because you know it's the best solution."

He tried to take her hand, but she pulled away. "You are awfully sure of yourself."

The concern in his eyes touched her heart. "In truth, I don't trust anyone else to keep you safe. This building is like a vault. It's perfect."

"But I have to go home to get clothes and sleeping gear. Someone might follow me back."

He shrugged. "That's bound to happen. They still won't gain access."

She glanced at her watch. Two o'clock. "Okay. I'll call Bunny and see if she can stay through the dinner shift."

He led her across the game room to the hallway she'd seen before. "I'll work from here for the rest of the afternoon. Why don't you take a few hours? I'll call my driver. I think once you see how many sharks are in that pool out there, you'll be glad you agreed. I specifically bought this place for its privacy."

Matt ran up behind them. "Where are you guys going?"

Kelly took Matt's hand. "We're going to have a sleepover tonight with Evan. He's showing me our rooms."

"Cool! Does that mean I can go to work with him in the morning?"

NOT ONLY WERE reporters camped outside of Neverland, but along the counter and seated at tables, as well. Kelly first stopped when they swarmed her exiting Evan's car; now she entered the diner and stopped to make the same sweeping declaration she spoke to the reporters outside.

"Lovely to see you all, but I have no story for you. If you are eating, then you are welcome to stay. Enjoy the menu and tell your friends about Neverland. Otherwise, please leave. You're crowding the dining room."

Her statement did nothing to stop the barrage of questions. She was grateful that Jake muscled his way through the group to lead her toward the kitchen. One reporter said, "Miss Sullivan, were you Buzz Campbell's lover?"

Her heart jolted at the revolting thought. The outrage must have reflected on her face because camera shutters clicked like mousetraps snapping shut. Her feet planted firmly, she turned to the speaker of the offending question. Jake tugged her arm as if understanding what she was about to do. He shook his head, but she ignored him.

"I will make one statement, and please, be very clear on my answer because I will say nothing further. Never, and I repeat, *never* were Senator Campbell and I lovers. That is absolutely ridiculous. Now, please, either enjoy a meal or go home."

When the volley of questions began about Matt, Jake

pulled her through the kitchen to the back hall leading up to her apartment.

"You okay, Kelly?"

She laid a hand on his shoulder. "I'm going to need help from all of you. I'm keeping Matt out of sight for a while. If Bunny gets a free minute, please send her up with the schedule."

Her burly cook gave her a look of reassurance. "We'll do whatever you need."

She managed a smile. "Thanks."

"And, hey…"

She met the sparkle in his eyes. "Yes?"

"There's an upside to all of this…mess."

"Oh, yes?"

"Business is booming."

She had to laugh. "Can you handle the load?"

He grinned. "Piece of cake."

She took the stairs two at a time. Damn it all. Evan was right about the sharks. Well, it was small consolation that maybe she could make a profit from them.

SHE RETURNED TO Evan's penthouse after rush hour. Matt threw the door open to greet her. The savory aroma of garlic and tomatoes wafted around them in a homey hug. She'd been so busy packing and getting everything in order at Neverland that she'd forgotten about food and now realized how hungry she was.

"Mom! I made meatballs! Evan showed me how."

She wheeled the carry-on with Matt's clothes through the door, a small satchel of gear for herself hooked through the handle.

"Is that what smells so good?" She handed the gear off to him. "Would you take these to our rooms, honey? Thanks."

She found Evan in the kitchen already pouring her a glass of wine. He'd changed from his work clothes into a gray T-shirt and jean shorts with surfer flip-flops on his feet. The concern on his face offered a safety net she hadn't felt in a long time.

"So, how was the shark tank?"

She took the proffered glass of wine and clinked it to his. "Daunting. You were right."

"Can I get that in writing?"

She chuckled. "Don't push it, Evan. I'm sorry to tell you they're camped outside your building now."

"I expected as much."

She cleared her throat to ask the question haunting her for the past few hours. "Are you helping us for the ratings?"

The look of absolute disgust on his face had her regretting her words.

"Low blow, Kelly. Why would you ask that?"

She shrugged. "You're a newsman. I just dealt with some pretty awful reporters, and a reporter with no conscience started this problem. Can you blame me?"

He placed his glass of wine on the counter, his voice lowered to a whisper. "If I asked you to marry me, do you think I would betray you?"

She felt her face scrunch. "Offering marriage could be part of your plan."

He leaned back as if gauging the authenticity of her suggestion. "You're kidding, right?"

Her hand jumped to the lump forming in her throat. "You don't understand how much trusting others in the past has hurt me. Matt and I were doing very well until now."

"Didn't you trust Herby?"

She swallowed the lump. "Yes."

He picked up his glass and toasted her. "Well, now you can add me to your very short list."

"Please. No insult intended."

He shook his head. "I'm trying to imagine what it must be like to be in your shoes or I'd be pissed as hell at you."

She sipped her wine, letting the fragrant bouquet of the dark liquid soothe her senses. "Thank you, Evan. Truly. I appreciate what you are doing for us more than I can express."

He dropped spaghetti noodles into the boiling water, reminding her of the last time he cooked for them just a short time ago.

"Well, then, why don't you just kick off those shoes and relax awhile. Let's enjoy a nice dinner." He turned to look at her. "Think you can do that?"

She managed a smile. "Aye. Especially if you are cooking."

He held up a finger as Matt climbed into the seat by the counter. "Your son prepared dinner. I'm just the sous-chef."

"I can be a cook like Jake when I grow up!"

Kelly laughed and pulled Matt into a bear hug. She inhaled the sweet essence of his young skin, realizing there wouldn't be too many more years when he'd let her hug him like this. "You can be anything you want, Matthew Sullivan."

He pulled away. "Can I go to work with Evan tomorrow? Please, Mom?"

Kelly inhaled a fortifying breath. She truly did not want to stay hidden from Neverland and look like Doyle's accusations were true. She most certainly could not take Matt to school or Neverland until she could explain the situation to him—which God help her, she had no clue how to do. The next best solution was leaving him in Evan's care for the day. Yet, making her son a celebrity in the face of scandal was unacceptable.

She had an idea.

"What if Matt wears an Urban costume with the mask and doesn't have to give his name?"

Matt's eyes lit up. "Cool!"

Evan reached for his cell phone. "That's a great idea. I'll call Sarah. Maybe she can pick one up before work."

THREE HOURS LATER, Evan watched Kelly emerge onto the balcony, where he sat at the table overlooking the city skyline, the bottle of wine and an empty glass for Kelly waiting on the table. From the fatigue creasing her brow, she'd had a long day.

He stood and pulled the seat next to him away from the table. "Join me for one more glass of wine before bed."

"Okay, but only one more."

He grinned. "Don't worry, Red. I'm not trying to get you drunk."

She laughed. "After today's brouhaha, a good snort of Irish whiskey would do the trick."

He gestured to the bar just within the glass walls. "I'll be happy to pour."

"No, no, Evan. The wine is perfect."

He poured her wine as she settled into her seat. The breeze raised her perfume on the air and he inhaled thinking he could breathe her scent for the rest of his life. It didn't help that throughout the day, during dinner and even during their heart-to-heart about his overprotective self, that sense of intimacy rose between them that he'd become acutely aware was missing from his life. Kelly and Matt made an instant family for him. He liked it. No, loved it, and could easily imagine having a brood of his own with this sassy redheaded siren.

It had stung him pretty hard when Kelly asked if he was helping her and Matt for news ratings. Especially because he had indeed considered how his close proximity could offer viewers an intimate view of how Kelly struggled with reliving her rape while trying to protect Matt from learning the painful truth behind his parentage. She'd actually been pretty perceptive about his intentions, but what she didn't know was that he had already decided that there would be no story from him unless she permitted it.

Steve Fiore would not like that one bit.

Despite his decision to respect her privacy, Evan still had every intention of persuading Kelly to go public. That is what stung. Although he knew exactly how to help her, his method would appear to her as nothing but a betrayal of her confidence in exchange for breaking news. Somehow, he had to convince Kelly that telling her story was her best defense.

He sipped his wine. This was an issue they needed to tackle. Lord knew they didn't have much longer than tomorrow at the latest to make a decision. He glanced at Kelly. Lost in her own thoughts, those beautiful green eyes gazed into the night.

"Matt get to sleep okay?"

She smiled, and his heart skipped a beat. "He climbed under the covers to sleep well for tomorrow's show—which he proudly told me were your instructions."

"Is that good?"

She chuckled. "You are good for him, Evan. Thank you, again."

He leaned closer. "And you? Am I good for you?"

She met his gaze, her face softly lit by the candles on the table. "You are a good man."

The mirth in her voice seemed to permeate his skin. What was it about this woman that affected him right down to the bone?

He sat back in his seat. "That's not what I asked you. Kelly Sullivan, you are a pro at dodging direct questions."

A momentary look of surprise colored her face. "I haven't the slightest idea of what you mean."

"Oh, yes you do, Red. I couldn't believe it took me so long to figure you out. The day you almost dropped your camera in Neverland was the first inkling I got that there was something between you and Campbell. I would have let it go but you didn't air my interview the next day. You set my investigative radar pinging something steady."

"You are a newsman. Your instincts are excellent."

Still, she had not denied her evasion tactics. He pressed on. "You get folks to talk about themselves while revealing little to nothing about yourself. You are a clever woman."

She slanted him a suspicious gaze. "I'm not sure if I should take that as a compliment or not."

"A compliment. A talent. The perfect tool when it's you against hundreds of patrons a week, eh?"

"I'm sure plenty of service providers do the same."

"True."

"Isn't a woman allowed to keep her privacy?"

He turned his body to face her. "Keep your privacy, but let *someone* in."

She looked surprised. "Why involve others in my affairs?"

"Because friends care. They help each other."

She exhaled a breath as if taking time to reach a decision. "Okay, what do you want to know?"

He shrugged. "Oh, I don't know. Do you ever think about being in love?"

"That's rather direct. Don't you think?"

"Well, I'm curious."

She inhaled a breath before meeting his gaze. "I told you yesterday. I never had a boyfriend."

Reminding him of that truth was like taking a sledgehammer to the chest a second time. Campbell stole her innocence. Never gave her a chance to flirt, discover the give-and-take of building a relationship, or give herself over to a man of her own free will. His inner caveman wanted to do some heavy damage to a certain senator once again. He leaned closer. "Do you want one?"

A fleeting desire lit her eyes before it disappeared. "Maybe someday."

He nodded slowly. "That's good, Red. You are a beautiful woman with a strong heart. A man would be honored to have the chance to earn your love."

She scoffed. "I'll attract a man because he'll eat free for the rest of his life."

He leaned toward her one more time. He couldn't help himself. He wanted to pull her into his lap and kiss her until she was drunk on his mouth instead of that silly supposition.

"Oh, no, Kelly. If you were mine, I'd open every door possible to give you what your heart desires. You've already proven that you are capable of caring for others."

Her look became guarded. "Don't you be trying to soften me up, now."

He let his fingers rest on the top of her hand, which was splayed on the arm of the chair. "What I would like to do is kiss you."

She placed her glass on the table. "Evan…"

He sat back, palms up. "Okay. Don't let me chase you away. I'll stop."

"It's not that you aren't attractive, mind you. I just…"

"What, Kelly?"

She met his gaze with determination. "I have reservations. Powerful men like you overwhelm me. I think I'm more suited for a gentle, unassuming, hardworking man who would consider me an equal."

"I consider you very much my equal, Kelly. Never be mistaken about that point."

"Yes, but you are aggressive."

"Hey, I may have aspirations, but I'm not like Buzz Campbell."

She hesitated. "No...not really."

He frowned. "So, you'd prefer some softy like Herby?"

Her smile was sad. "He was the kindest man I have ever known."

"Yeah, but he didn't ask you for anything. He cared for you as if you were a daughter. I'm talking about a lover, Kelly. What do you want from a *lover?*"

Her pained expression twisted his heart. He didn't want to hurt her. He wanted to understand her. He needed to see what his chances were with this elusive woman. Part of him had to accept that maybe, just maybe, Kelly may have been hurt so badly that she would never be willing to give him the intimacy he required in a mate—and he wasn't simply talking about sex.

She settled back into her chair as if preparing for battle. She tilted her pretty head. "Let me ask you the same question."

He grinned to mask his rising frustration. "See? There you go again. Turning the question around so you don't have to answer."

The small smile that crossed her lips had him thinking about what he'd like to do to her—soft and slow, until she yielded.

"Caught me. I guess asking questions comes as second nature."

He grew serious. "Could you trust me, Kelly? I mean, really trust me enough to know that I would never hurt you?"

She rested her hand on his. "Since you returned, you

have made it very easy to trust you. I just do not want to be involved with anyone right now." She shook her head. "Especially, right now."

He took her hand. "Okay, I understand. But, I want to go on record here. I was expressing an interest in dating you way before Campbell came into view." He grinned. "The more I know you, the more I want to date you, for… oh, I don't know, like forever."

She managed a chuckle. "This is exactly the type of steamrolling that aggressive men do. I don't like it."

He interlaced his fingers with hers. "I know you care for me, Red. And, I know what I want in a woman. You have it all."

She frowned. "We've hardly even held hands."

He looked down at their entwined fingers. "We're holding hands now."

She gently pulled her hand from his and stood. "It's time for me to go to bed, but know this, Evan McKenna. I don't shrink from problems. If I did, I would have attached to someone years ago. When I marry, it will be for love and no other reason."

He'd done it. Chased her away, one more time. He drained his glass, defeated—for the moment. "I know exactly what you mean, Red. Sleep tight. I won't mention it again."

KELLY LAY IN bed, her heart pummeling inside her rib cage. Her conversation with Evan left her breathless. He wanted to know what type of lover she wanted? The last thing she'd admit was that on those scattered, lonely nights when the thought of a lover occupied her mind, the man in whose arms she imagined herself wrapped was always Evan.

When he had entered her life as a newly recruited newsman in that brief period before she discovered she was pregnant, he left an impression of a fun and trustworthy man that she'd never forgotten. Then he ran off and became as important as he promised he would be. While her life changed forever, he became a powerful man. The exact kind that she mistrusted.

Yet, she had to admit Evan was different. His consideration for her and Matt was genuine. He was funny. Thoughtful. Was definitely easy on the eyes and he understood her Irish heritage. All pluses. If she hadn't trusted him she wouldn't be sleeping on these soft sheets in his masculine guest room right now, with Matt tucked soundly asleep in the next room.

So what was it that made her keep denying him?

Control. Could she learn to love a man and keep her hands on the wheel of her own future? She'd never seen it in her mother's relationship. She didn't want the disparity of power that existed between her parents. She saw Madeline Campbell adjust her life to accommodate Buzz. And Evan had attempted to manipulate her into accepting his plans.

It was so much easier to remain single than to take the chance and find out how she'd handle a man. The thought made her shudder. She had managed to desensitize her emotions around Campbell's assault, so didn't think she was hesitant about dating because of the rape. No, it was more because she had yet to see a relationship in which the woman's needs were considered as important as her husband's.

Only, there was a catch about the rape that kept her on guard. The reason was a little more involved than anyone might suspect. Kelly understood that the average man did not employ rape as a means of seducing a woman. She actually looked forward to being courted one day. Kelly's problem stemmed from the fact that while Campbell was busy satisfying his own lust with her body, he had driven her to an orgasm. She had actually experienced the thrill of intercourse against her will. Campbell had not hesitated to point out that fact after he was through. It was his way of convincing himself, and her, that she'd enjoyed his assault as much as he had. He had accused her of seducing him and said her orgasm was proof that she got what she wanted.

Campbell's accusation had compounded her shame. She could not convince herself that he was totally wrong. All the time he was on top of her, she hated him, yet succumbed to a sensation that had turned her pained whimpers into unbidden moans through her tears. She'd never quite tackled her guilt over that one.

She had experienced her first and only orgasm at the price of assault. Heaven and hell in one awful moment. So, if she were to become lovers with Evan and experience an orgasm under mutual attraction, would she lose herself to him completely? Fall in love and give over her power? Like her mother? Is that how relationships worked?

Not for her. She'd rather stay single.

Kelly fell into a fitful sleep clenching her jaw while tears stained her pillow.

CHAPTER NINE

JUST BEFORE SUNRISE, Evan's town car pulled into the parking garage at the news station. He sat in the front with his driver. Matt sat between Kelly and Sarah, who had arrived at his penthouse early to deliver the very cool Urban Hero costume that Matt now wore. He held the black, pullover mask in his hand as if it was the most important item he'd ever possessed. Sarah had done her job well by finding the perfect costume. If she kept performing top-notch with such a great disposition, he'd be sure to give her a bonus with her raise come the holidays.

Kelly and Evan had decided that the best way to keep Matt anonymous was to drive directly to the news building and ensconce Matt in Evan's office until showtime. Kelly would walk across the street to Neverland from the garage entrance behind the news building. It would give her enough lead time before any reporters spotted her and figured out where Matt was.

Kelly seemed more subdued than usual this morning. They hadn't had a chance to talk, what with Sarah arriving so early and Matt bouncing around the penthouse like the silver ball in the pinball machine. Both Evan's mother and Kelly's brother were due to arrive after lunch. The group would meet up at the penthouse and plan their next strategy.

Evan was looking forward to meeting Father Michael Sullivan. No doubt he'd learn more about Kelly by watching her with her brother. He was also curious to see how territorial the good priest would be about his sister. And the dynamic with his mother would prove interesting, as well. He hadn't said much to her about Kelly except that she was someone special to him. Knowing his mother's well-meaning but conniving Irish nature, once she saw what Evan appreciated in Kelly, she'd be matchmaking for a winter wedding. The fun part would be watching Kelly stop Julie McKenna's plans dead in her tracks. One Irish woman matching wits with another would be worth any price of admission.

But right now, guilt tugged at him. He wanted to know what had made Kelly unhappy this morning. His gut twisted with the thought that his aggressive self the night before might be making her regret staying with him. Add to that, he fully understood that Buzz Campbell was no fool—no one understood that better than Kelly. He was probably already gunning for Matt. The fact that Kelly trusted Evan enough to allow the boy into his charge spoke volumes about her faith in him.

He wouldn't take that trust lightly.

As the car pulled up to the entrance, Kelly kissed Matt on the top of the head.

"You stay close to Evan and do what Sarah tells you. Okay? Be nothing but the perfect gentleman today."

The excitement in his face made her laugh. "Mom, I'm gonna meet Urban Hero!"

She squeezed his shoulders. "With that costume, the audience won't be able to tell who is the real Urban Hero. I'll be watching the show from Neverland and cheering you on."

The driver opened the door and Matt was the first to scramble out.

Sarah gave Kelly a reassuring look. "I have two younger brothers. I'll take good care of him."

Kelly shook the younger woman's hand. "I am sure that he is in the most competent care. I am directly across the street if you need me."

Matt ran toward the lower lobby doors. "See ya, Mom!"

"Hey, Matt-man, hold up a second. I want to say good-bye to your mother."

Matt practically skidded to a halt at Evan's words. Sarah walked over and waited with him by the entrance.

It pained him that Kelly looked exhausted—beautiful, but clearly the weight of all of this sneaking around had caused some unsettling sleep. He waited until she looked at him. "Are you okay?"

She shrugged. "I'm not very comfortable with our plan here. I hate to let Matt out of my sight."

Evan reached for her hand, glad that she didn't resist. "He'll be fine. Right now, I'm more concerned about you. Can you handle the crowd at Neverland?"

Her small grin didn't fool him for a second. "Just another day at work."

He pulled her into a hug. "This will all come out right, Kelly. You'll see."

She broke free from his embrace yet he sensed her hesitation. "There's no room for any other alternative, Evan."

He tapped her chin. "On that we agree, Red."

"Let's go, Evan!" Matt was jumping up and down.

Evan kissed her cheek. "Text me when you leave Neverland."

She headed from the garage. "As soon as Michael arrives, we'll come over."

DEAN LEANED AGAINST the doorjamb of Evan's office, surprise on his face. "Well, who do we have here?"

Matt looked up from his game player with expectation, but frowned, as if disappointed the new visitor wasn't Urban Hero.

Evan looked up, closing the file on the latest legal research he was investigating on Kelly's behalf. "Morning, Dean. You're in early."

Dean pointed to Matt. "Isn't he the Neverland kid?"

The Neverland kid? Not, Kelly's son? Dean knew Kelly from Neverland, ate her food and flirted with her just like all the other guys in the newsroom. His word choice revealed everything. With those three words, Dean had betrayed the fact that Kelly and Matt were nothing but a story to him. Why did Evan feel the sudden urge to stuff the moron down the mail chute?

Then again, Evan had to check his anger. If he wasn't emotionally invested in Kelly and Matt, he'd have the same vulturelike eye for a story. He had to admit that Dean's moniker for Matt would make a great lead-in if the media got hold of it. He could see the headlines: Senator's Lost Boy Found in Neverland.

Like a bank vault door slamming shut to protect this particular boy, Evan wanted all attention off him. He decided he wouldn't admit Matt's identity to Dean even if he did know. "This young man is an Urban Hero aficionado. He's on the show with me this morning."

"Looks like you're up to your hairline in the Campbell debacle, Evan."

"And it looks like you've got your sniffer in the wrong can, Dean." Evan stood, which got Matt's attention. "Come on, champ. Time to make sure we're beautiful for the cameras."

Matt jumped from his seat. He held up his empty juice box. "I finished my juice."

Evan deposited the empty container into his wastebas-

ket, then slid his research file beneath his show notes. He
wouldn't leave anything for prying eyes, especially since
Sarah would be with them instead of manning her desk.
He'd lock his door, but wanted everything to seem status quo.

"Can I put my mask on now?"

"Sure!" That was a great idea. Evan didn't like the way
Dean was staring at Matt as if the man hadn't eaten in a
week and Matt was prime rib cooked rare. Dean's gaze
cemented Evan's resolve. Story be damned. He'd do anything to protect this boy.

As he led Matt past Dean, the boy waved. "Hey, mister.
I'm gonna be on TV!"

Dean gave Evan a knowing look over the boy's head.
"Oh, I'll bet you are."

KELLY LAUGHED OUT loud with the rest of the patrons watching Matt do his best imitation of Urban Hero for Evan and
the actor without the slightest hint of inhibition. Oh, to be
so innocent! Her heart swelled watching her baby charm
the camera. He took his Marvello comic characters seriously and everyone could see that fact. She was grateful
that Matt liked wearing the mask. As much as she would
love to see his face, she never wanted Buzz Campbell to
lay eyes on him. Ever.

There would be no quieting Matt this afternoon. Being
on Evan's show was by far the most exciting event in his
young life. Once again, Evan had made an impression on
Matt which way surpassed expectation. She wondered how
Matt would remember this day once he was grown-up and
all of this was behind them.

A commercial break sent her attention back to her patrons. For a fleeting moment it seemed that all was back
to normal in Neverland with everyone chattering about her

son and smiling, while the entire diner was unaware that the charming boy inside the costume was Matt. No sooner did a sigh of relief leave her lungs when two men pushed through the diner doors. Steely faced with conservative suits, not looking the least bit interested in a meal, they surveyed the room until one man's gaze locked with hers. The other closed the distance toward her as if she was the only person in the diner.

"Miss Sullivan?"

"Who is asking?"

He pulled an envelope from his breast pocket. "This is a court order issued on behalf of Senator Robert Campbell."

Her breath caught in her throat. She didn't reach for the envelope. "What is this about?"

"Proof of paternity. You have twenty-four hours to respond. The senator wants this issue resolved immediately."

Refusing to accept the envelope, her voice dropped despite her fury. "For your information, gentlemen, I don't quite give a fig what the senator wants. Please leave before I call the police."

He laid the envelope across the top of the coffeepot she held. "We are the police, ma'am, and you've just been served."

On Evan's penthouse balcony, the formalities of everyone's introductions were quickly dropped once the court order had been passed around the table. This crisis had removed any chance these four would remain as strangers and united the group in seeking one important result: justice for Kelly Ann Sullivan and her son, Matthew.

Kelly sat next to her brother beneath the shade of an awning that was rolled out against the afternoon sun. If Kelly hadn't mentioned to Evan's mother that Michael was a priest, no one would have guessed. Michael wore his hair a bit longer than the average priest. His lanky physique was clad in black plaid shorts and a white polo shirt. His feet sported a new pair of running shoes. Kelly didn't know how he did it, but the warm peat scent of Ireland's hills seemed to arise with his body heat. She wondered if his indulgence in smoking a pipe a night had gotten into his clothing.

Beautiful Julie McKenna had the foresight to bring two of Evan's nephews with her. The boys now played a raucous round of basketball in the game room, giving the adults the freedom to discuss this touchy subject without Matt listening. Julie sat next to her son on the opposite side of the table from Kelly. Her light blue eyes matched both the formfitting turquoise sundress and strappy, flat sandals on her feet. She wore her long dark hair loose which complemented the healthy glow of her skin—a testimony to her efforts to maintain good health.

To play with the boys, Evan had changed from work clothes into basketball shorts and a tank top. He now lounged as if careless, though the muscle jumping in his jaw betrayed his concern for the topic they were about to discuss.

Evan's housekeeper had served coffee and pastries. A welcoming breeze cooled the warm air. With the boys occupied, Evan opened the file before him. He gave Kelly a meaningful glance.

"I've helped so many people in difficult situations but I never quite understood how the deck gets stacked against a woman who becomes pregnant from an assault."

Father Michael frowned. "I'm sure shame keeps many women from coming forward for help."

Evan shook his head. "It's worse than that, Michael. New York State law is abysmal in protecting women in this situation."

Hearing Evan voice what she already knew sent a wave of gratitude through Kelly. "Now you understand one of the reasons I kept my secret."

Evan met her gaze. "You are an amazing woman, Kelly. I admired you before, but after what I've learned I am humbled by your strength."

Julie leaned forward. "I don't understand."

Kelly couldn't believe she could finally relive her trauma out loud without shame or secrecy. "I lost control of my life for a while after I left the Campbell's. The chaos of emotions and shame had me reeling. I couldn't quite believe that what had happened actually did. I was too afraid of Buzz Campbell to press charges. When I realized that a baby was made, I panicked. I went to a center for women for advice."

"What did you learn?" The concern in the other woman's face offered encouragement.

"That the state would support me financially if I either aborted the baby or gave him up for adoption."

Michael's voice reflected his surprise. "And if you kept the baby?"

Kelly's lips pressed together to tamp down her long-buried anger. "The courts would not consider the incident a rape. I would receive no protection to keep the father away nor any monetary aid."

"That's outrageous!"

Evan added, "What's worse, and why Kelly is so adamant about Matt's identity staying secret, is that rape is *not* included on the very short list of reasons accepted by the court to terminate a man's claim to paternity."

"What?" Julie and Michael responded at the same time.

A press of unshed tears threatened to fall. Kelly swiped at one that escaped down her cheek. Heaven help her, this was the first time she had supporters fighting for her, and against Buzz Campbell. Herby George never knew she'd been raped. He had protected her and Matt as a father would. But these three sitting with her were raising the banner on her behalf without judgment or revulsion. She swallowed the flood of emotions rising in her throat.

"Evan is correct. In this state, a rapist may claim custody rights if a child is born from the attack and the mother chooses to keep the babe."

Julie sat back in her chair. "So, Senator Campbell is well within his right to demand this DNA test."

Kelly spoke softly. "And could most probably succeed in taking Matt from me because of his political position and the fact that I am a single mother."

Michael slammed a fist on the table. "We will not permit that to happen."

"I don't know how we can stop him, Michael."

"I do."

They all looked at Evan. The determination in his face had Kelly raising her guard. She knew what he was going to say, but asked anyway. "What do you suggest, Evan?"

"Go public with your story, Kelly. It's the only way to…"

"No." The word escaped her lips before he even finished his sentence. "I love my son. I don't care who the father was. For all anyone knows I received an anonymous donation from a sperm bank. But if Matthew came to understand that he was produced from violence, I cannot imagine what emotional effect that information would have on him. I will not expose him to such scandal."

Evan pressed on. "Kelly, your son is too young to understand what assault means. We can handle how Matt receives this information until he is older. Right now, all he needs to understand is that you love him more than life. That fact is clear to everyone, especially to that little boy."

"Can you edit the jibes from children in the school yard? Or from strangers in the grocery store who recognize us from television? Or from the slur campaign Buzz Campbell will surely launch? No. Matt will hear cruel words. I will not entertain the idea."

Alarms had started pounding in her head. Was Evan insisting on this point of attack because the newsman in him wanted the latest story sensation to be his? Her heart sank when he confirmed her suspicion.

"Kelly, I can do this story to your advantage. I don't want someone who doesn't care for you handling this delicate situation. I know how to redirect people's outrage away from you personally and toward the lack of proper legal protection."

Her heart squeezed. "So my plight becomes your personal, public campaign? Perhaps a tool to bring down the all-powerful senator and gain high ratings, as well?"

The outrage reflecting in his eyes acknowledged her accusation. "Your story has nothing to do with me. We are talking about fighting for your son in an arena *I* know how to fight in. Jay Doyle has made your case all too public. Not me."

Michael reached for Kelly's hand. "I think your friend is right, Kelly. Perhaps we should mount a campaign in your defense."

"I can't!"

"Kelly, look at me," Evan said.

The demand in his voice grated on her nerves. Part of her understood his position, but she had experienced the dark underbelly that Buzz Campbell hid so well from the public eye. Fighting him was useless. She didn't like the fact that Evan was pushing her. She hated this most of all and refused to look at him as she spoke.

"Evan, I do not believe public support would sway a

judge influenced by Senator Campbell or his party. We have no chance of winning."

"We can fight," Michael said. He was siding with Evan. Not good.

She held up a stopping hand. "Look, I've done my homework. Any other man would have taken weeks to obtain a court order for a paternity test. Campbell accomplished the task within twenty-four hours. In order for him to have done so, he either has deep pockets or presented reasons as to why I would be an unfit mother for Matthew. I'm telling you now. We cannot fight Robert Campbell and win."

Julie leaned forward. "But what about the senator's assistant? The one who started this entire investigation? If that reporter Doyle is gathering evidence that Campbell is a womanizer, our conniving senator could, for all intents and purposes, be thrown in jail."

Kelly shook her head. "I disagree. There are politicians who had women die at their hands and were acquitted. I will fight Campbell, but privately. I want none of it in the press. I want the story to disappear from public view. I'm sure the senator would welcome the offer."

"In a perfect world, that might happen, Kelly, but not now. We don't have control of the story. It's in Doyle's hands and Campbell's hands. That's why I want to take control. I can work with both men to turn the story away from you and Matt." Promise simmered in Evan's words.

"That sounds reasonable," Michael added.

"Maybe I should take Matt and go home to Ireland."

Julie sighed. "Campbell can have you extradited."

"I have another idea," Evan announced.

Kelly looked at him. "What is that?"

He shrugged. "We can say we had a one-night stand seven years ago before I left and Matt is my son. Campbell would buy into this story. He'd drop the paternity suit and sue Doyle and his assistant for libel."

Julie's eyes widened. "You cannot do that, Evan."

He grinned. "Oh, I surely am willing."

"That would be a bold-faced lie, Evan. Totally unacceptable," Kelly added.

Michael chuckled. "I like the idea."

Never looking more serious in his life, Evan added, "Your brother could perform our wedding."

"Wedding? Have you gone daft?" Kelly's heart practically stopped in her chest.

Michael laughed out loud. "Oh, my Kelly. Wouldn't Mum love that if she heard you'd finally married!"

"Your jokes are not funny, Michael!"

Evan feigned hurt. "Marrying me would be a joke?"

His question left Kelly with her mouth agape. Would marrying Evan be a joke? Indeed not. The thought sent a frisson of heat right to her core. The romantic woman lying dormant inside her stirred. No doubt Evan was appealing in so very many ways. His looks alone would be worth waking up to in the morning. But he was neither claiming to be in love with her, nor settled enough in his career to offer stability. He was offering marriage as a solution to her problem and to add fodder for a blockbuster news story. The pang of mistrust that squeezed her chest took her breath away.

"We'll not consider marriage in this equation, thank you very much, gentlemen."

Kelly couldn't help but notice the relief in Julie's eyes. Clearly, Evan's mother rejected Evan's motives, as well. Kelly had noticed that Julie, after almost forty years of marriage, wore her wedding ring with the ease and comfort of a contented lover. She would not condone her son's reasons for offering marriage without passion and love.

Evan appeared oblivious to his mother's reaction. "Kelly, as a woman married to me, I could protect you. I know Campbell would welcome the solution."

Frustration heated her face. She glanced at Julie, who had become uncomfortably silent. Kelly knew she herself would be upset if, as an adult, Matt offered to marry a woman to rescue her when there was no love between them. What was it with these men who thought they could so blithely choreograph a woman's future? Her attraction to this man was rapidly being replaced with insult.

"You must be joking, Evan."

He shrugged. "Honestly, I am not. But, if you don't like that idea as much as I do, then we have no choice but to take my first suggestion."

The circling argument was making her weary. "Which is?"

"Come on my show and do an interview."

The boys barreled through the door onto the balcony. The older cousin asked, "Can we have ice cream, Uncle Evan?"

"Sure. Alicia will serve you."

"Can we watch a movie?"

"If you bring your bowls back to the kitchen when you're finished."

Inside, Alicia was already opening the freezer, which attracted the boys' attention.

Kelly inhaled a fortifying breath. "I should speak to an attorney. I want to settle this quietly."

Michael returned his coffee cup to its saucer. "Kelly, I think Evan is right on this one point. Senator Campbell is no longer in a position to let these accusations die quietly. He has been publicly accused. He has to admit fault or defend himself at your expense. There can be no quiet solution."

Kelly wanted to scream. Nothing made her feel more helpless than to be pushed into a situation in which she knew she couldn't win. In her mind, Buzz Campbell was the giant wielding a huge club and they were mere Lilliputians scurrying around his feet. She would not budge on this one point.

"Make me a solemn promise, Evan."

"What's that?"

"No part of my ordeal goes on the air."

The look in Evan's eyes said he wanted to pull her into his arms and soothe her. "Kelly, you have to trust me. There is no way around the uncomfortable truth. To win this one, you really must go public with your story."

Julie expelled a breath. "Kelly, when Evan was a young boy, his uncle—my brother—was killed in Dublin. He was a negotiator for the IRA and was assassinated."

"Evan told me. How awful."

"Condolences," Michael added.

Julie shot a heated look at Evan. "We McKennas feel strongly about fighting for what is right. Quite honestly, I'm a bit shocked my son is willing to publicly lie on your behalf." She turned her gaze on Kelly. "You must be a remarkable woman."

"I will not tolerate lies. So you have no worries there, Mrs. McKenna."

She smiled. "Please, call me Julie. I am glad to hear you are adamant about telling the truth."

Julie patted her son's arm. "While Evan's noble gesture of marriage will protect your safe little world, it would also let a criminal go free to assault other women in the future. Whereas, if you stand and fight, especially with Evan backing you, you have an excellent chance of putting the senator behind bars where he belongs." She tilted her head in question. "Which choice will give you a peaceful sleep each night for the rest of your life?"

The pressure of tears started again. Kelly understood Julie completely. She had wrestled with her own cowardice for years after not pressing charges against Campbell. But as Matt grew older and the memory of Campbell grew more distant, she didn't care anymore about the assault. She wanted to live for her baby. Protect him. Let him grow to be a strong, honest man who could contribute to his world. She released a sigh that pained her right down to her soul.

"It's not about me, Julie. Or the senator. It's about protecting my son, who is innocent."

Evan held up a hand. "Protecting a child's best interest is one thing the law in this state does recognize. If we can get Campbell prosecuted for a crime, we can prove it is in Matt's best interest to revoke Campbell's right to custody."

"You said you could steer the story away from Matt and me? Can we try that approach first?"

He nodded once. "I'll call Doyle."

She bit her lip. "I have only one problem with Doyle."

"What is that?"

"When we spoke in Neverland, he made it pretty clear he's politically motivated to bring Campbell down. I don't think he cares who gets hurt in the process."

"Okay. I'll encourage Doyle to get other women to speak up."

Michael scoffed. "But they've already fingered Matt. I don't think any newsman would take the spotlight from that prime story."

"It'll be tricky. I will do my best."

Michael looked at Kelly. "If Evan can engineer this situation in a direction away from Matt, will you work with him?"

"I don't want to be on camera."

Evan closed the file. "We'll start without including you, but I can't promise that you will remain off the air. You just might have to speak up, Red. Do you understand?"

Her stomach burned. There seemed to be no way around this nightmare. "Only as a very last resort. And, I want to see your strategy in writing before I agree."

"I'll take that. In the meantime, I'll have my attorney stall this DNA testing. The good senator can cool his heels on this court order until we get a story mounted."

CHAPTER TEN

KELLY AND EVAN sat at the kitchen island finishing a cup of cappuccino and sharing a huge serving of tiramasu she'd brought from Neverland. Matt had been in bed for about thirty minutes. Michael had departed with a big hug and a mutual promise to see each other soon. Julie and the boys exited after an early dinner. Julie agreed to return in the morning to care for Matt.

Evan could not shake how natural it felt to have Kelly in his home. Matt seemed to have acclimated without a hitch, hugging Evan good-night as if he'd always been a part of their lives. Evan had scored points with the little guy for having him on the show this morning. Steve Fiore loved the way Matt charmed the entire audience—right down to the cameramen—with his Urban Hero antics. The show was a win-win for everyone. Now, if Evan could just hit a home run with Matt's mother, maybe these welcoming evenings would happen more often.

Once they were alone, however, her smile melted with the last bite of dessert. "Do you think this fight will end well?"

He pushed the plate away. "If I have anything to say, it will."

Kelly grew silent, obviously struggling to take another deep breath. He could only imagine how overwhelmed she must feel. He stood, took her hand.

"Come on, bring your coffee. Let's sit more comfortably."

He led her to the oversize couch in the living room. "This is where I relax when I need a little escape. I have some great music." He pointed to headphones on the coffee table. "Feel free to use them if you want to truly get lost in the sound."

"No headphones necessary. Just being here is escape enough."

After adjusting the music to a soft volume, he sat at the other end of the couch, giving her the space he suspected she could use. Did she really just say that she was happy to be here?

"Do you mean that?"

She sighed. "You make me crazy, Evan. You are bossy, overassertive and stubborn, but you are kind and honest. You make me laugh. And neither have you deceived me nor lied to me. I rely heavily on those excellent traits to vindicate you from your other faults."

He laughed. "Faults?"

She smiled. "I told you. Aggressive men intimidate me. I'm sure you understand that by now."

"Kelly. Please do not compare me to men like Buzz Campbell." He tapped his chest. "The insult cuts pretty deep."

She looked contrite. "Then, to whom should I compare you?"

He looked around as if searching for an answer. "Oh, I don't know…maybe *Thor*?"

She almost spat out her coffee when she laughed. Wiping her mouth with her hand, she said, "See? Your ego overrides any good sense you have!"

He sat back, drinking in the laughter in her eyes, the color rising on her cheeks, the way light from the kitchen haloed her gorgeous red hair falling easily around her shoulders. She had changed from her work clothes into a full-length sundress with an Indian print the same coppery color as her hair. He loved the way the soft fabric lay against her curves, hinting that beneath the print lay heaven.

Kelly tucked her bare feet under her skirt and sat facing him in a—dare he believe—welcoming posture. While she might not trust him yet, she certainly was attracted to him. And she smelled so good. Like summer and sea and honeysuckle. Oh, yes, he would like evenings like these to happen more and more often—like every day.

Dare he test the waters?

"Are you comfortable here?"

"When you are sleeping, I am."

"What?"

She chuckled. "I can let my guard down when I know you're not going to say something I have to contradict."

"Come on. You know I'm a marshmallow."

She reached over and tapped the cushion between them. If he had been sitting right in that spot, she would have touched him. "Actually, truth be told, I'm surprised how comfortable I feel here. Your hospitality is most welcoming. Thank you."

They both sipped, watching each other over the rims of the mugs.

Evan cleared his throat. "May I say something?"

"Could I possibly stop you?"

He leaned closer. "Not this time."

"Well, then, if you want to apologize for bullying me earlier, I will accept it."

He leaned even closer. "I apologize a thousand times over, but that is not what I want to say."

She shot him a cautious glance. "What is it?"

He crooked a finger. "Come closer."

She leaned farther back into the corner of the couch. "There you go, telling me what to do."

He smiled, hoping to disarm her. "Come on now, sweet Kelly. Trust me. Come closer."

When she cautiously leaned in, he captured her chin with the pads of his fingers, slowly drawing her even closer to his mouth. He whispered, "I want to kiss you, woman."

She didn't pull away. Instead, desire mingled with concern in her eyes. "Do you think this is a good idea?"

"Oh, Kelly Ann Sullivan, I think it is an excellent idea. You are, by far, the most seductive, impish, intelligent, courageous and beautiful woman I have ever met. And your lips? Most intriguing of all."

She didn't pull back, but eyes widening, watched his mouth as he spoke. When she bit her lower lip as if trying to decide what to do, he leaned in ever so slowly and grazed that lower lip with his. When she closed her eyes at his touch, he kissed her. Pressing gently against her mouth to feel the silk of her lips against his, letting the power of his mouth invite her to press closer, lean into him, let him kiss her more fully.

She did.

He slid a hand along her neck, letting his fingers splay in her hair. His palm cupped the soft column of her throat, her rising pulse echoing against his hand. He kissed her more deeply, letting his tongue enter her parting lips in tentative invitation, tangling delicately with hers then retracting to kiss those luscious lips more. He didn't want to scare her. He just wanted her to feel how much she meant to him with a kiss.

Keeping his cool wasn't easy. Her lips were igniting an inner blast of heat like he'd never felt before. Whether it was the beauty of her innocence pounding his caveman self awake, or the fact that he was finally kissing this woman who had intrigued him for so long, she was proving to be more enticing than he could ever imagine.

He began to pull away to catch a breath. He'd have to take it slow.

But she would have none of it. Without breaking the kiss, she blindly reached and found a landing spot on the coffee table for her mug. With both hands, she captured his face and kissed him in return with the confidence of a woman who'd made a decision.

His mug just made the edge of the table. Not wanting to lose the moment, he pulled her against his chest, cradling her in his lap, returning her kiss with the same hunger with which she drank up his.

Oh, God, she kissed like Venus on fire.

The weight of her body felt so right. His hands took on a life of their own, hungrily exploring her curves beneath the silken fabric—the delectable dimples in the small of her back, up her torso, palms skimming the sides of her breasts, up to her neck, her shoulders, down her back to the sweet turn of her buttocks. A soft moan rose in her throat and vibrated right through him, urging him to make his kisses deeper.

It didn't take long to see where this moment was leading. His body already betrayed that he thought this was a good idea. An excelllent idea. His mind raced with reasons to stop while his soul tore into overdrive devouring her kisses.

"Kelly…"

He leaned forward, the momentum of their weight splaying her on her back against the couch cushions. She hesitated only for a second before welcoming him in her arms. Not wanting to be too aggressive, he stretched out alongside and pulled her close so they wouldn't tumble off the couch.

"You okay?" His voice reflected his hope that she'd say yes.

Her lips curved into a small smile. The passion in her eyes was like a narcotic hitting his bloodstream. Without saying a word, her mouth sought his again. He hungrily claimed her lips, happy to accept her actions instead of her words.

It had been a while since he'd been with a woman, but he'd been with enough to recognize the extraordinary chemistry sparking between them. Kelly's genuine and natural instincts, her heartbeat against his chest, the incense of her perfume, all drove Evan not to think, only to feel, respond, kiss, touch, crave so much more. Her hands exploring his face, shoulders, chest, stomach, the sweet taste of mocha on her tongue, the feel of her body against his own intoxicated him into a spiral of wanting more.

Instinct told him that, knowing Kelly as he did, if they made love she would become bound to him. And he'd be lost to her. This would happen as surely as they breathed. Their intimacy could be good. So very good. He could use their chemistry as proof that they could consider marriage. But did he want her to love him when her emotions were as volatile as they were now? When her world was turbulent and unreliable? When he couldn't even promise that they would defeat Campbell in the end? With the strength of a superhero, he broke the kiss.

"Kelly…"

Her green eyes, darkened with want, slowly focused at the serious timbre of his voice.

She searched his gaze, concerned. "What's wrong?"

He rested a finger on her lips. "Wow."

A crooked grin crossed her mouth. "I'm a little short on practice. I hope you're not disappointed."

She hadn't pulled away. In fact she nestled against him, familiar and content. He liked that. His voice dropped low with intent. "I want to make love with you, Red."

She stilled. "I..."

He entwined his fingers in hers. "I know. That is why I'm stopping. I don't think it is a very good idea right now—for either of us."

Swallowing hard, she nodded. "You are right."

He sat up and pulled her into his lap. Her eyes grew wide when she felt the effect she'd had on his body.

Grinning he said, "Not to worry. I'll be okay in a minute."

She rested a hand against his chest right where his heartbeat pounded. She met his gaze. "I'm embarrassed. I'm not really sure what I'm doing."

He pressed his hand over hers where it lay over his heart. "Oh, I don't know, sweetheart. Feel that? I'd say your instincts are pretty damned good."

KELLY INHALED A needed breath in an effort to still her own beating heart. Her reaction to Evan's kiss had sent her senses reeling to the point of losing herself. Feeling awkward now that he stopped her, she welcomed the warmth of his arm around her shoulder and his closeness. At least he wasn't blowing her off. Oh, Lord, she had practically lost it—all over him. Damn if that kiss didn't awaken the sleeping giant of her tamped-down libido!

"I should probably head to bed."

He chuckled. "My kingdom if you turn that into an invitation."

"And who very well stopped me?"

"I know. I'm regretting it."

He lifted her chin, kissing her mouth one more time. Her insides leaped, wanting the kiss to linger, go deeper, drive her over the brink. She had been denied love for so very long that she felt starved, and Evan handled her with a perfect mixture of strength and tenderness. He seemed safe. Natural. And was rapidly filling her emptiness.

While desire pooled in her core, panic slowly trickled down her spine. Evan said he wanted to make love. She'd seen enough movies to know that making love could be erotic, pleasurable, momentous. Those glimpses were her only defense against the one experience that haunted her. Evan's easy, sensual manner made her curious to know more. God knew she loved kissing him, feeling the closeness of his body, but she had to admit one fact about getting close and naked: she was scared.

She broke the kiss. "I am tempted to make love with you to erase the bad memories from my assault."

He pressed his forehead to hers. "Is that the only reason?"

She hesitated, warmed by the hope in his eyes. "Of course not."

"Then tell me. Why are you tempted?"

How could she tell him? It wasn't just her need for physical contact. Evan had taken the time to reach into her world and develop a sense of intimacy between them. She tapped his lips. "You are like two sides of a coin to me."

He grabbed her hand and kissed her finger tips. "I already know about the bossy side."

A purr rose in her throat. "This particular side has captured my affection. You just gave me my first true kisses. They felt wonderful. You feel wonderful. I think I could trust you if we made love."

He swallowed hard. "Oh, I know you could, Red. Believe me when I say that I didn't make my offer of marriage to you lightly."

And that's when the coin flipped.

Her breath caught in her chest. Here he was, pushing again. She and Evan needed time. Time to get past this awful mess with Campbell. Time to spend in each other's company. Time was the great prover of all matters of the heart, and Evan was looking for shortcuts.

"Marriage, Evan? You've not even been home six months. Up until then, I hadn't seen you for seven years—with no contact in between. I'll hear no more talk of marriage, thank you very much."

"Kelly, on paper it doesn't make sense." He tapped his chest. "But, here? I can't explain it. Everything about you seems right to me. Everything. Right down to Matt. I'd even like to make a few kids of our own someday."

Having Evan's kids? Oh, Lord. He was serious. As much as she would welcome marriage and a child or two with the man she loved in the future, she couldn't handle talk like this. Not now. More directly, as much as she had fantasized about erotic trysts with the enticing Evan, marrying him was not on her agenda. Her little boy deserved her undivided attention.

Besides, Evan said nothing about love. Chemistry? Sure, neither of them could deny that fact, but chemistry wasn't enough. He had yet to ask how she felt about him. His entire assumption that they should marry was based on how *he* felt. That made the thought of marriage to him impossible. Evan was too aggressive. She and Evan would require a lot of time together before she could even consider marrying him. His words were like a bucket of ice water.

"Oh, Evan, you paint a pretty picture, but I'm not prepared to consider marriage to you or anyone. Please don't take offense."

She felt his body tense. "Now, how should I not take offense?"

She climbed from his lap. "Because my decision has nothing to do with you or this lovely moment." She smoothed out her dress and pushed back her hair in a lame attempt to correct her disheveled state. "So, you were right. This wasn't a very good idea for either of us."

He ran a hand over his face in complete confusion. "How did we just go from kissing passionately to arguing?"

She shrugged. "You're Irish. Figure it out."

"Kelly."

She held out a hand. "No, Evan. I'll bid you good-night. I should be up early, so I'll start the coffee."

CHAPTER ELEVEN

NEXT MORNING, EVAN was headed for makeup when Steve fell into step beside him.

"We need to talk, Evan."

"Good morning to you, too, Steve."

Evan wasn't in the mood to deal with Steve's frenetic energy right now. He had worked hard this morning to tamp down his frustrations over the botched evening with Kelly last night. She had been pleasant this morning, handing him a nice hot cup of coffee in the predawn hours and thanking him again for asking his mother to watch Matt while she did the morning shift, but Kelly had clearly returned to arm's-length status.

He could understand why an offer of marriage would make her step back. She could have teased him or suggested they move a little more slowly. But the utter rejection? She clearly was attracted to him—at least he thought she was. Given their chemistry and her dire situation, he thought her pragmatic Irish logic would consider the wisdom in a marriage proposal. Maybe she simply wanted his offer of refuge and nothing more than to remain friends?

No. No way. Not when she kissed him the way she did last night.

In an hour, he'd have to pretend Kelly's rejection didn't affect his attitude during this first interview. Wouldn't you know, Steve had insisted on featuring a Mormon man and his five wives hoping to raise some heated debates on the station's website. Evan would be questioning a man with five wives while he couldn't get one sultry redhead to say yes.

Now, Evan knew what Steve wanted to discuss and didn't need him breathing down his neck first thing. The set of his boss's jaw spoke volumes. They'd been friends for too long for Evan not to know when Steve was about to drop a bomb.

"Can we talk after the show? I'm not in the greatest mood right now."

"Does it have anything to do with Kelly staying at your place?"

Evan punched the elevator key, its red light like a beacon to stop the conversation now. "What would Kelly have to do with my mood?"

A look of disbelief flooded Steve's face. "You have the ticket to the hottest story in the country staying in your home and you're reporting nothing. I don't know about you, but if I was the top-ranking morning anchor in the state with no story, that woman would be messing with my mood."

The elevator doors slid open. Evan ignored them, but Steve gestured for them to board the empty car. "Get in. It's more private in here."

When the doors closed, Evan rounded on Steve. "Look, I spoke with her. I have a strategy in place."

"What does that mean? I need a story. Now."

"She won't talk now. She wants to protect Matt." He met his boss's hard gaze. "I don't blame her."

"Sounds to me like you are a little too close to the subject to be objective about your job."

"I have a story in the works."

The doors opened. Steve didn't miss a beat. "You and I both know that if this involved any other person, you would have already aired two features—one from Campbell's side, the other from Kelly's. But no. You are stalling, and I have a show to run."

Damn it all. Steve was right. Evan was stalling. The last thing he wanted was to admit that very fact. He sat in his chair at makeup. Tanya put a towel over his shoulders to protect his shirt and began their morning routine.

Steve leaned against the counter in front of him, arms crossed. "What do you know?"

"Campbell served Kelly with a court order for DNA testing. He's going to take her down if he can. I'd like to set up a strategy to protect her."

Steve released a long breath. "Evan, you don't have the luxury to protect her. Get her to do an interview."

"She refuses."

"Then present your take on the situation. Challenge the senator to answer you live, on the air."

"I thought of that."

"Then what are you waiting for?"

"I want to put the bastard in jail. I don't want to jump the gun and give him the chance to slip through loopholes."

Steve's antenna definitely perked up. "Why do you want to put Campbell in jail?"

Evan closed his eyes. He'd said too much. "The story runs deeper than you think, Steve. This is one time you will have to trust me. If you want a blockbuster story in which NCTV reveals the real story and saves the day, you'll have to let me do this my way. Kelly has a lot at stake here."

"Evan, listen to me. You're not the cavalry. You are a morning show host with a conscience. Play on that, but you'd better say something leading and important this morning, or we're going to have a problem."

"Are you threatening me?"

Steve slapped a hand on his shoulder. "No, but I'll tell you what. Dean is sawing at your ladder. He's been getting some dirt on this situation and if you don't report on... oh, even what you and Kelly had for dinner last night, I'm going to let Dean run with what he's accumulating."

"You wouldn't!"

"Give me news, McKenna. I want a story. You have a direct line to Campbell. And so does Dean. Call Campbell. Find out his side of the story. Meanwhile, I want you to report your view of how this is affecting Kelly and Matt. First thing on the show. Before the Mormon interview."

WHILE EVAN'S DOORMAN effectively kept reporters from the front of his building, Kelly didn't have the same protection at Neverland. The limo driver pulled up to the curb only to have a clot of rabid religious picketers—mostly women wearing Campbell for President buttons—outside of Neverland chanting intolerance for what they believed was Kelly's immoral behavior in seducing a good family man. One of the placards declared that she was unfit to raise a child.

Her blood chilled in her veins. The driver escorted her to the door to ensure no one would accost her. Angry right down to her toes that her personal life was being invaded and judged by strangers, once she entered Neverland Kelly sent Evan a heated text telling him what was happening. She could ignore these people, but she didn't want her son to witness a moment of it. When she returned to Evan's this afternoon, she would bring Julia McKenna flowers for keeping Matt safe.

Bunny met her at the door. "I already called the police. As long as they stay on the sidewalk and don't do any physical harm, we can't disperse them."

Kelly tapped a finger to her lips. "Why don't you prepare a few trays of doughnuts and coffee? Have them brought out to the picketers. Tell them we appreciate how much their presence is bringing in customers. Let's see how long they stay."

Bunny laughed. "I'll get on that right away!"

A quick survey of the diner showed that business was still moving at a brisk pace. All the regulars were there. New faces watched her with open curiosity. She made a point to greet these folks. When anyone raised a question about the senator, she just waved away the inquiry saying that her attorney wouldn't let her discuss the situation and recommended they try the pastries. When she finally had the chance to talk with Evan's attorney, for sure he would instruct her to say the same.

While plastering a smile on her face, inside she fumed. The seven long years she spent breaking the victim shackles that Campbell's assault placed on her emotions were not going to be trashed again by the man's egotistical and deviant personality. Because Buzz Campbell once took liberties with her body, he had changed the direction of her dreams. Last time, he'd left her scrambling to keep the fabric of her life from tearing to shreds. This time, she'd employ damage control from the get-go. This man had no right to invade her life, and if he thought he did have a right simply to cover his own tail, he had another think coming. She'd learned so much since he last messed with her. He would not get the chance to abuse her again. She wasn't sure how, but she would fight.

Patrons by the window were clearly amused by the picketers circling outside Neverland. Some gestured and interacted with them through the windows, others cast concerned glances in Kelly's direction. A sigh escaped her throat. This situation was too big for her to handle alone. She might have to trust Evan's advice to air her story. But how could she defend herself and not accuse Campbell of rape? No way could she reveal that horror and not hurt Matt in the long run. She'd talk with Evan more about it tonight.

Darn it all. Did that make him right, once again?

Thinking about him sent a flutter through her stomach. The curve of a smile traced her lips. As much as she detested his pushy insistence that they consider marriage to protect Matt, the memory of their few minutes on the couch had simmered below the surface of her thoughts since awakening this morning.

Handing him a cup of coffee in the silence of the kitchen before the city began bustling conjured an intimacy between them that she hadn't expected. The familiarity in those quiet moments seemed so very natural. Evan still looked sleepy despite the perfect navy suit with a yellow tie draped around his neck, his hair still a bit tousled from sleep. He smelled good, like fresh air and promise. Concern about her rejection from last night was clear in his eyes. He hadn't said anything further, but the issue lay between them like a dangerous bog neither of them wanted to tread.

That peaceful exchange with Evan while Matt slept down the hall offered a sense of permanence she had never experienced. The attraction to the possibility of being with Evan on a regular basis had tilted her equilibrium—in a good way.

She mentally shook herself. Taking an armful of empty plates to the busing station she mumbled, "Get a grip, Red."

Truth be told, she was taking her first intimate moment with a man a little too seriously. Here she was, twenty-seven years old and mooning over her first kiss—or more correctly, her first make-out session. No wonder she was so preoccupied about last night. With the way Evan kissed, all she wanted to do was make up for lost time, and hurry. Holy Saint Raphael, could that man make a woman forget where she was!

"Hey, Kelly. Check out the TV."

Bunny pointed to the screen, then gestured out the window. NCTV cameras were trained on the picketers. One of the customers at the counter reached for the ever-present television remote and made the sound louder. Sure enough, Evan was on air with the exact scene occurring outside Neverland featured behind him on an oversize monitor. Evan was addressing the camera.

"Kelly Sullivan is my friend. Moments before we went on air she sent me a text saying that protestors were picketing outside the Neverland diner with malicious accusations. The slander being tossed around since the irresponsible reporting against presidential hopeful Buzz Campbell pulled Miss Sullivan into the spotlight. It is causing irreparable damage."

He took a moment to pause and looked thoughtfully into the camera. "I'm here to tell you folks, the truth of the story is far different from what has been reported. This reporter is taking those accusations against Kelly Sullivan to heart. If Buzz Campbell or Jay Doyle wants to take issue with Kelly Sullivan, they are going to have to come through me." He pointed at the camera as if pulling a trigger. "We'll be back after this station break."

The scene faded to a commercial.

Kelly's supporters in the diner broke into cheers, standing and clapping on her behalf.

"Go get him, Kelly!"

"Evan McKenna for president!"

"Nail the bastard!" one raucous truck driver yelled.

"Oh, God." Kelly's heart practically stopped in her

chest. He'd done it. Evan had exposed her on the air. In
that moment the possibility of trusting Evan shattered.

Damn his ambitious self. She was nothing but a story
to him. He had probably planned on kissing her last night
to soften her up for an interview. She beelined for the
kitchen. She needed to scream and no one would hear her
from the walk-in freezer.

EVAN WASN'T BACK in his office for two seconds before
Sarah charged through the door. She indicated the blinking light on his desk phone.

"The senator is holding."

He blew out a breath. He had been expecting this moment. "Thanks, Sarah. Close my door, please?" He loosened his tie before pressing the speakerphone.

"Good morning, Senator."

"It was an excellent morning until I heard your show.
What the hell are you doing, son?"

"Listen, Buzz. Let's not mince words here. You and I
both know the truth. Kelly Sullivan doesn't deserve to be
dragged through the mud to cover your ass."

The senator was silent for a moment. Evan was more
than willing to let him ponder his words.

"That woman was trouble from the first day she walked
through my door."

"Sir?"

"Irish redheads. Always trouble."

"I'm not so sure I know what you mean, Senator."

"Let's just say there is something you should know."

"Shoot."

"Your buddy Dean has been very helpful. He's secured
the DNA sample I needed. Matthew Sullivan is my son."

Evan closed his eyes at his own idiocy. The juice box
in the trash can. Dean was a dead man. But the traitor-

ous slimeball could wait. Right now, Evan needed to protect Matt from this pompous ass. He schooled his voice to sound confident, even after Campbell had dropped this bomb to throw Evan off balance. "I had no doubt of that fact, sir. Tell me something I don't know."

Campbell chuckled. "Oh, I'm sure there's not much you don't know."

Evan released a breath. "Look, Senator. Right now, my objective is to ensure that a woman whom you once hurt very badly doesn't get swept up in your net of filth a second time. I don't care what you do, but take your focus off Kelly Sullivan."

"Sorry, son. Not going to happen."

"Excuse me?"

"As this country's next leader, I am not going to let some simpering hussy who seduced me in my sleep keep me from recovering my son. It will be my word against hers. Do you really want to try me?"

Evan's skin crawled at how easily the man let a lie roll from his mouth. "And to think you almost had my vote."

"Oh, I'll get your vote, as well. You'll see."

How could Campbell be so damned sure of himself? Did he really believe there would be no punishment for his criminal behavior? "Senator, I cannot imagine that you would take a boy from his mother when you are nothing but a stranger to him."

Buzz sighed as if he was making a difficult decision. "Actually, he is my son. It is taking every ounce of my self-control not to go after him right now. Whether I do or not depends on how much Kelly cooperates. I know the law, Evan. Should I decide to be nice enough to claim joint custody at best, that pretty redhead will be in my sights on a regular basis. I could make her life real interesting."

Evan's gut twisted. "What does your wife say about this situation, Buzz?"

"Right now, she doesn't believe a word of the story. She doesn't know about the DNA results. But if this gets sloppy, Madeline will support me. She believes in me and everything I tell her. She is a good wife."

Evan's inner caveman began pounding his rib cage. Buzz Campbell had no idea how dangerous an enemy he just made in Evan, but he'd find out in due time. Evan lowered his voice, if only to maintain his temper. "Buzz, right now, I don't feel like there's much of a difference between dealing with you or the devil."

"Then it looks like I'm making my point."

Evan steeled himself. "Okay, Senator. So let's suggest a new scenario. Let's say there is no DNA test results. Let's say the real father surfaces to make Doyle's accusations about you and Kelly turn into slander for a campaign smear. Will you back off Kelly?"

Campbell laughed. "Well, well. Sounds to me like my former nanny has caught you by the short ones, McKenna. Would you do all that for her?"

Evan's blood ran hot. "You have no idea."

Again, silence.

Evan pressed on. "So? If I make this happen will you cooperate?"

"I'm a family man, Evan. My wife and daughters mean the world to me. But, I've always wanted a son. Kelly Sullivan is a problem. Make the story go away, or the boy is mine. Do you understand?"

EVAN FOUND DEAN in Steve's office. Using every ounce of control not to take a swing at the fool, Evan dragged him out of the chair by his shirtfront. "What kind of reporter betrays his team, Dean?"

Dean struggled but couldn't break Evan's grip. "Hands off, McKenna. If you weren't acting like such a wimp over Neverland's newest celebrity I wouldn't have to go behind your back."

Evan released his grip, sending Dean tumbling back into his chair. Evan turned to Steve. "I want this SOB fired."

Adjusting his tie, Dean said, "Why, because I'm investigating a story that you won't cover?"

"This is not about the story, Dean. You invaded my office like a slimy little mole to do dirty work for the highest bidder."

Steve held out his hands. "Okay, gentleman. Let's slow down here."

Evan turned on Steve. "Dean supplied Matt's DNA to Campbell after taking the sample from my trash can."

"I know."

Evan stopped. "What?"

"Dean told me what he was doing. He had my permission."

"After I told you I was working on a strategy?"

Dean jumped from his seat and had the balls to poke Evan in the chest. "Kelly's been denying Campbell his kid for all these years."

Evan had to restrain himself from getting physical with this jerk. "You have no idea what you've done, Dean. So, shut up before you make a real idiot of yourself."

Steve stood. "Take it easy, Evan. Nothing has been leaked. The only people who know the results of the test are the three of us and Campbell."

"I don't believe Dean has the integrity to keep the information confidential. A year from now he'd sell the facts for cash."

Steve gave Evan a hard look. "You underestimate Dean's dedication to the truth."

Evan pointed in the direction of his office. "I just got off the phone with the good senator. He is not adverse to ruining the Sullivans' lives to protect his run for the White House. So don't give me that holier-than-thou attitude, gentlemen. You may very well have trashed two innocent lives for headlines."

Steve crossed his arms over his chest. "We're doing our job, Evan. Can you say the same?"

Steve knew Evan's unshakable focus when committed to reporting a story. No one would better recognize that Evan was stalling for time, but Evan didn't like that Steve lacked trust in him to hold the story.

"I'm doing my job, Steve. It appears that for the first time since working together that I'm not moving fast enough to please you. I don't like your tactics on this one at all. You heard what I said on TV this morning."

"Only because I threatened you."

"No, because I know a hell of a lot more than you do." He swiped a hand across his mouth, unwilling to accept this turn of events. "I can't believe you threw me and a woman you've known for years under the bus when her entire life will be adversely affected. This runs deeper than you know and instead of trusting me, you've pushed me into a position of damage control instead of good reporting."

"You're too wrapped up with Kelly to do your job."

"Maybe I am involved with Kelly, but I'm still doing my job. In this particular instance the personal welfare of these two individuals is more important than reporting a half-baked story. Given the direction we're going, this will turn into a witch hunt destroying that small family while

Campbell comes up smelling like a rose. Nothing is further from the truth."

"What is the truth? Why aren't you reporting it?"

What could he say to that? Evan had promised Kelly he would not reveal the rape. He needed Steve to blindly back him on this one. He raised a hand. "Remember when I had a lead on the human trafficking ring in Russia? I needed time to get the locals to give me their stories. We earned an Emmy on that one. What's so different now? If you give me a few more days I will have a story that will not only put this station on the map for investigative reporting but distinguish us as a force that sways the direction of justice."

Thank goodness Steve remained silent long enough to consider Evan's words.

Evan pointed at Dean. "He's not helping the situation as a loose cannon."

Dean puffed his chest in defense. "Hey, I didn't do anything you wouldn't do if the tables were turned."

Steve shook his head. "Evan, the difference between Russia and Campbell is timing. This story is too hot to keep quiet, not to mention that this station doesn't support Campbell's political party. I'm being pressured. We don't have the luxury of a few days. I'm scheduling an interview with Dean and Campbell for tomorrow's news."

His friend could have gut-punched him and not made as much impact as speaking those words. For almost a decade, Evan had worked side by side with Steve to achieve the positions they now held. Each understood what the other personally sacrificed to reach their goals. Now, his boss and the man he thought of as a friend was tossing him over for a story. When did Steve derail from what was important?

"You would cut me out like that?"

Steve had the good grace to look contrite. "Evan, this is business. I know you understand."

"Oh, I understand, Steve. I also understand that this is my story and your interview with Campbell is not going to happen."

"Oh? Why not?"

Steve had a strange look of satisfaction in his eyes that made Evan angry. Was his friend manipulating him to get results? Something inside twisted at the thought that their long-forged trust was suddenly becoming an issue between them.

"Because I just made a deal with Campbell that he can't afford to ignore. I can guarantee you that Campbell will hold off on his interview with you until he hears from me."

Evan backed out of the office and headed back to his own, struggling to grasp his next moves through the blaze of anger searing his mind. Had the investigative reporting world gone crazy? He didn't even want to consider how Kelly would feel when she learned how she'd been betrayed. He already knew she'd be furious about this morning's show. Now with this DNA evidence hanging over their heads, her back would be against the wall. She'd have to make some pretty hard decisions—and fast. Evan had no illusions. He would end up being ground zero when the bomb dropped.

He punched a number on his cell phone. When Michael Sullivan answered, Evan felt the pressure in his chest release enough to form his next thought.

"Top of the morning to you, Father. We have ourselves a situation. Are you free for lunch?"

CHAPTER TWELVE

KELLY FELT NUMB as she flagged down a taxi during evening rush hour. When a cab finally stopped she jumped in, grateful to escape the few reporters who flanked her with questions she waved away like annoying, buzzing flies. Now she focused on her destination. Michael had asked her to meet him at Tavern on the Green before she headed to Evan's to collect Matt. When she'd explained her distress, he listened with the familiar calmness she knew so well, but something was clearly on his mind. The simple fact that he was in Manhattan had her on alert. If he had good news he would have told her over the phone. She didn't think she could handle too much more bad news after the chaos from Evan's morning show.

The hostess led her to the table where Michael sat looking out over Central Park. Dressed in his black priest vestments, he portrayed an excellent example of a distinguished, savvy man of the cloth and she didn't think this way just because Michael was her brother. If he were a stranger she would have taken a second glance at him. Michael's quiet confidence and handsome, intelligent face could well inspire a person to attend one of his services just to listen to his particular view on humanity's collective soul. She would depend on her confidence in Michael's honest point of view when he delivered whatever information had him concentrating so hard as he looked out the window.

"You look like you're deep in meditation."

He stood, a smile immediately crossing his lips. "Kelly."

His hug felt so very good. She breathed in his familiar woodsy scent and felt an immediate tie to home, turf and family. "I am glad you are on this side of the ocean, Michael. Hugging you makes the world seem wonderful."

"Aye. Please, sit. I'm hoping you'll feel the same after we chat."

Now, that comment didn't sound promising. She declined the menu the waitress offered. "I'll just have coffee."

Michael ordered the same and a slice of cheesecake.

Kelly studied her brother. "What's wrong?"

He shook his head. "We have work to do on damage control of huge proportions."

Thinking they were both on the same page, she said, "So, you saw Evan's broadcast this morning, as well. I am so angry with him. Thank you for saying Matt and I can stay with you."

Michael shrugged. "You may not need to stay with me after all."

"Why not?"

"I had lunch with Evan."

An unbidden heat flushed her cheeks. "So that's why you're in town?"

He nodded. "I'm not going behind your back. He asked me to meet him."

"Why?"

"Evan spoke with Senator Campbell after his show. News is not good."

No doubt, Buzz Campbell had reacted to Evan's challenge. Her defenses rose like a cone over a nuclear silo. "I am not surprised. What did he say?"

Michael expelled a long breath. "It seems that Campbell has obtained the DNA results he wanted. He has proof that Matthew is his son."

Her throat tightened. "How?"

"One of Evan's coworkers took a discarded juice box Matt had used."

She slapped the table. "I knew he shouldn't have gone in that day!"

"It may have been for the better. Legally, Campbell would have had you surrender Matt for testing anyway. In the long run this saved your son discomfort."

A wave of despair filled her; Kelly's worst nightmare was coming to pass. "So, now what?"

"You may be angry at Evan for his public statement but it had the desired effect."

"What do you mean?"

Despite the concern in his eyes, Michael smiled. "Campbell wants to play hardball. Evan seems to have just the bat to slam the old boy out of the field."

"That seems impossible."

"Well, the plan is tricky, but it can work if you cooperate."

"What do I have to do?"

Michael's gaze homed in on hers. "Marry Evan."

"What?" She fell back in her chair. "Surely you jest, Michael."

They both fell silent as the waitress arrived with their coffees. Kelly took a moment to catch the breath lodged in her throat. Watching the woman place the beverages, oblivious to her distress, made the entire situation seem fake. How could Michael waltz into her life after eight years and expect her to share coffee with him in a civil manner and accept an arranged marriage while her world crumbled around her? When the waitress departed, Kelly dived right in.

"Don't you go adopting Evan McKenna's insanity, Michael. I need your levelheaded thinking here. A good attorney can handle what needs to be done."

"Not this time, Kelly. Listen to me."

"I won't, Michael. I don't trust Evan's motives. I can't believe you agree with him!"

"Kelly, this is not about you or Evan. Do you or do you not want to keep your son?"

She stopped cold. "How can you ask such a question?"

"Because you are losing focus on what is important here."

"I won't accept a lie."

Michael shrugged. "To save your son you just may have to rethink your position. Campbell said that if Evan can erase any link between you, Matt and the senator, he'll make the DNA test disappear. Otherwise he'll use the test and his muscle to take Matt from you—permanently."

The earth shifted beneath her. "So, it is finally happening. Buzz is coming after me."

Michael shook his head. "Only if forced. Seems the White House is more important than you or Matt, thank God. With these accusations hanging over his head, he'll demand custody of Matt to correct his mistake in the public eye. He won't be nice about it if you give him no other alternative. Bottom line—he'll take Matt and keep you out of the picture."

She knew the bastard would slam her hard. "How can marrying Evan fix this?"

"It's as he promised the other day. As your husband he can protect you and Matt. You both can claim that Matt is Evan's. Right now, no one knows about the DNA test. If Campbell retracts his request, no one else can legally demand it. Campbell will sue Doyle for defamation of character and will throw money where it's needed to silence this story. You and Matt can slide out of the spotlight and continue with your lives."

Kelly shook her head. "Campbell always wanted a son. I do not believe he will go away quietly and leave Matt untouched."

"Well, Evan has a plan to ensure he will go away."

"What is that?"

"Meet with Evan so he can tell you. I'll take Matt out for a movie. You two need to talk."

EVAN WAS ALREADY at the penthouse. He and Matt called hello to her while running through the apartment playing some war game with guns that shot light, and vests that sounded when hit with it. Still there, Julie McKenna greeted Michael with a handshake and Kelly with a hug.

"Matt is a delight, my dear. We had a lovely day together."

Although grateful beyond words for her help, Kelly forced a smile she didn't feel. "Thank you, Julie. Knowing Matt was safe made it easier for me to work."

Julie grabbed her purse. "I'm meeting Evan's father for dinner. Please keep me posted on events."

"Certainly." She walked with Julie to the door, glad for the short distance and that the woman had nothing further to say. Closing the door behind Julie, Kelly glanced at her brother. "Looks like Matt is no worse for wear."

He smiled. "Evan has a way with the boy. I like him."

She didn't have a response that made her feel comfortable. "I'd like to get this over with."

She headed down the hallway into Matt's room, where Evan and Matt were wrestling over Evan's gun. Matt's lay on the floor, out of power. "Hey, Matt. Break it up. Uncle Michael wants to take you to a movie."

The two looked up from tangling. The camaraderie they

shared reflected in the laughter in their faces. Evan looked completely in his element with her son, who was not going to let his competitor win. When Evan smiled at Kelly, Matt grabbed Evan's gun and scrambled off the bed with a hoot.

"I won!"

Evan sat up, running a hand through his tousled hair. "Sure did, Matt-man. Great game." The two shared their secret handshake.

Kelly's breath caught in her throat. If she ever dreamed of how a father would behave with her son, nothing came closer than this moment. Damn Evan for being the perfect and the worst man for her. There was no way around this one. She'd just have to cut her losses and keep moving. "When you get back with Uncle Michael we'll leave, Matt. I'll gather up your things while you're gone."

Matt looked deflated. "Why, Mom?"

Evan stood up. "Yeah. Why?"

He stood close to Kelly. The heat of his body, the intensity of his gaze almost had her forgetting why she wanted to run from this man. Closing her eyes to regain her equilibrium, she exhaled a breath. "You're kidding, right? You have to ask that question?"

Recognition crossed his features. "This morning's show."

She nodded once. "Exactly. Michael tells me you two met for lunch. I'm staying long enough to hear your strategy." She gave Matt a nudge. "Come on, honey. Uncle Michael is waiting."

When Matt and Michael departed, the walls seemed to close in on her, despite the open rooms of the penthouse. Evan pulled a menu from a drawer in the kitchen. His easy manner compounded her unease, as if he was confident he would sway her to his decision when she never felt more certain that she did not belong here.

Evan held up the menu. "This place serves excellent sushi. Have you eaten?"

She waved away the offer. "No, thank you. I had coffee with Michael. Feel free to order if you want something."

He reached into the refrigerator for two waters, twisted off the caps and placed one on the counter for her. "Well, then have a seat and wet your whistle. We have to talk."

Her chin lifted. "Why are you so comfortable giving orders?"

He almost choked on the water he was guzzling. "You're right, Red. Please, would you like a seat while we chat?"

Kelly felt an odd mix of anger and amusement. His willingness to correct his bad behavior had an irresistible charm.

Watching her with those commanding blue eyes triggered the memory of his kisses. The fact that her brother was pushing her to marry Evan made the moment feel surreal. She felt like a pawn at the hands of others plotting her future. Nothing raised her ire more than not having a say in her own life plans. Offense would be her best defense with this headstrong man.

"I see you've convinced my brother to support your ridiculous idea."

He winced. "I can't tell you how much it hurts that you consider marrying me ridiculous."

"You're asking me to make a lifetime commitment at a huge risk to the personal happiness of both of us, not to mention running the awful possibility of confusing my son."

Evan's voice softened. "I would love for Matt to be my son, too."

The bare truth in his eyes hit like a thunderbolt. Dare she believe that Evan really wanted this? No. This morning's broadcast proved he knew how to manipulate an au-

dience, whether a crowded room or a party of one. "So
you are suggesting I marry you so that you can have a
ready-made family?"

He closed his eyes as if fending off her glib suggestion.
When he looked at her again intention filled his eyes. He
took her hand in his, his grasp sure, his fingers warm as
they intertwined hers with as much intimacy as if he'd
touched her naked heart.

"No, you hardheaded woman. I am suggesting you
marry me because we have chemistry. We have an un-
canny comfort between us. We banter to the point that
others enjoy our fun. Ask anyone in Neverland. I heard
there's a secret pool running at the diner on whether we
become an item by Thanksgiving."

She pulled her hand away. The tingling running up her
arm caused way too much of a distraction. "You're kidding."

He rested his hands on his knees, leaning forward. "Let
me finish."

She leaned back in her chair, half intrigued. "Go on…"

"Whether you will admit it or not, I see your face light
up when I come into Neverland. I know my pulse beats
faster when you smile at me—heck, when you smile at anyone else. I enjoy my seat at the counter with the star on the
floor. I adore the way you handle your camera. I appreciate
how courageous you are. How compassionate." He stopped
a moment, inhaling a deep breath as if to fortify himself.
"When you made me coffee this morning, I thought nothing would be sweeter than waking up with you beside me
every day. And the way we kissed last night convinced me
that we need to kiss more—a lot more. I'm actually having
trouble keeping from kissing you right now."

The thought of such intimacy between them made a
flush heat her face. "Evan, stop…"

He held up a hand. "No, Kelly. I'm saying that right now, circumstances, over which we have little control, are forcing us to make a decision that perhaps—given the luxury of time—you and I might end up choosing anyway. I am suggesting that to keep Matt safe and in *your* custody, we take the leap."

His words left her breathless. In any other situation, she could easily believe him. But given this morning's show and Michael's insistence she accept Evan's plans, how could she be sure he wasn't on some hero's quest to save the day for her and Matt? Evan had a noble streak in him. She'd seen enough of his broadcasts when he'd gone over the top to help folks caught in unreasonable situations.

His over-the-top approach to his career had shot him to the top ranks as a celebrity very quickly. America loved him. Although he never told her, Kelly knew he had friends like Brad Pitt and Bono. He was mentored in his early years by the great Walter Cronkite. Could she handle life with a man who could wield serious power should he choose?

Then again, ambition could turn a man away from integrity. What if Evan delivered these smooth-talking lines to get her to capitulate so he could have exclusive coverage of her story? Her situation raised some pretty serious social and political issues. She knew Evan well enough to know his ambitious nature would thrive on creating havoc for Campbell while sinking his teeth into changing current laws to protect women. This type of story was perfect for Evan. With her cleaved to him, Evan could muscle out every other TV station from gaining access to her. When all was said and done, they could divorce. Right? So many celebrities changed their minds like they changed their couture.

Bottom line: Sure Evan liked her and threw a net of

pretty convincing arguments, but was he offering marriage because he loved her? He hadn't said so. Not enough collateral for this levelheaded Irish woman who had sacrificed way too much to create her current situation.

"Evan, at the risk of hurting you I must say that under any other circumstance I would be flattered beyond belief by your offer."

"But?"

She hardened her gaze. "But I'm not convinced of your motives."

Her words caused him to sit back in his chair. He frowned. When he spoke, his lowered voice carried hurt. "Kelly, don't you feel the connection between us?"

She inhaled a long, slow breath. "Yes, Evan, I feel an attraction. But marriage? I can't answer you. And if you insist, I'll have to say no."

He released the breath he'd been holding. "Okay. I understand. I'm being bullheaded and you don't like to be managed."

Despite her distress, she grinned. "Yes, there is that."

"Your back is against the wall, Kelly. You don't know how seriously you should take my proposal."

A lump rose in her throat. There was that casual threat again—the same one Michael had delivered.

"Does my lack of choices have anything to do with the damage control over the DNA issue Michael mentioned?"

His mouth pressed into a hard line. "Afraid so."

She swallowed hard.

"Look," he said, "let's go out. We can sit at a table like civilized adults and continue this conversation."

"I'd prefer we talk about it here. Now."

He watched her for a long moment as if assessing the

situation. He grabbed his phone. "Okay, we stay here. I have to make a call. Does seafood work for you?"

As THEY SAT at the kitchen counter eating chilled whole lobsters, Evan silently fumed about the damned issue with Buzz Campbell hanging between them like a hangman's noose.

How was he going to work around her suspicions? He already knew that she distrusted his motives. Honestly, he couldn't blame her, but somehow he had to convince her that when it came to feelings for her, his were the real deal. Even his mother had noticed his attraction to her. When she kissed him goodbye this evening she whispered that she couldn't believe she was going to have a grandchild so soon. He had to love Mom. She never missed a thing. Now, if her words would fly from her lips to God's ears.

"What are you thinking?"

Kelly watched him with concern. He wanted to slide his hand beneath that sheaf of hair and feel the soft skin of her neck once more like he did last night. He cleared his throat.

"I was thinking about my mother. She likes you."

Kelly arched an eyebrow in reply. "Really? I suspected she thought I may be another project for you."

He chuckled. "You have yet to understand Julie. She's testing your mettle. She likes what she sees."

He didn't take his eyes from hers as they sipped their wine. "I hate that this incident with Buzz Campbell has put a wedge between us."

She shrugged a shoulder, drawing his attention to the smooth whiteness of her skin over the toned muscles of her upper arm. He itched to brush his fingers along the dusting of freckles at her shoulder.

Kelly must have seen the emotion on his face because she blushed. "Look at the bright side."

"What's that?"

"If it wasn't for the senator, I wouldn't be sitting here, and we wouldn't be having such a meaningful conversation."

He chuckled. "Then I should vote for the bastard."

Her smile faded. "What is going to happen, Evan?"

He reached for her hand and was surprised at the tremor in her fingers. "Damage control. We can pull this off, honey."

She momentarily tightened her grip in his before releasing his hand to toy with the stem of her glass. "I'm prepared to fight, but I don't understand how marriage fits into the equation."

"This is where it gets tricky, Kelly. Again, I must ask you to keep an open mind." A thought occurred to him. "When did you get your citizenship?"

"Two years ago."

Evan nodded. "Good. That's one track Campbell can't take."

"Having me deported?"

"If you only had a green card, he certainly could rattle your cage with that one."

"So what is it that we haven't touched on, Evan?"

"My phone conversation with Buzz this morning after the show." He winced. "For which I'm sure you'd like a piece of my hide?"

Her back stiffened. "They are separate issues and the answer is yes to both."

"Which would you prefer wrestling first?"

"Why did you do it?"

"The show? Steve is pressuring me. He insists I'm too close to you to conduct the proper investigative reporting. He's letting Dean run all over with leads and he's been talking with Campbell."

"Can't you stop them?"

A look of disappointment crossed his face. "That's what I did this morning on the air, but you misunderstood me."

"How?"

"Kelly, if I didn't say something to challenge Buzz into talking with me, Dean was going to interview him on the air. If I made it hot enough for Buzz to call me, which he did, I knew my conversation with him would derail Dean's inroad."

"What did you tell him?"

"Nothing specific, but enough to let him know I knew the truth.

"That son of a bitch is threatening to take custody of Matt and smear your reputation from here to California. The only way we can stop him is by concocting a lie that takes all focus off him as Matt's father. If we do that, he'll make the DNA test disappear and leave you alone."

The firm set of his jaw betrayed his anger about the predicament. "I won't let him muscle your son away from you."

"He made the threat real?"

He nodded once. "Yes."

Her heart pounded. God damn Robert-the-Buzz-Campbell for being the heartless soul he was. "You would be comfortable lying to the world about Matt's paternity."

He inhaled a deep breath. "Against a monster like him? Yes. For now."

"What do you mean?"

"Once we get you and Matt in the clear, I'm taking him down. If we put Buzz in jail he can never touch Matt. The law will find him unfit."

She looked away. Could they go up against such a formidable man with deep pockets to cover his tracks? Evan might have connections but Campbell had puppet strings. They'd lose. But Campbell was breathing down her neck.

No doubt he would enjoy toying with her again—bringing her to ruin.

This time, she reached for Evan's hand. "I want you to understand something. Seven years ago, Buzz was all too clear in what he would do if I ever told anyone what happened between us. While he used guilt and threats to silence me, he also assured me that being his lover had become part of my job description. He considered his rape a means to subdue me. He planned on coming back for more."

Color started to rise in Evan's face. "You're kidding."

She looked away. The avenging fire burning in Evan's eyes was too much to see.

He pulled her closer, wrapping an arm around her shoulder. "Come on, honey. Tell me."

She exhaled a breath. "Buzz thought I'd kowtow enough to obey him. He is very cunning. He reversed the blame of his actions on me—making it my fault. I believed him so well that it was my shame that drove me from his house the next day. Counseling at the women's shelter taught me how insidious the mind of a repeat rapist is, especially if he is familiar with the victim. Control is half the thrill for them. All it took was one scathing phone call from him after I fled to know the man is not only dangerous but devious. When I found out I was pregnant I knew he could never learn about my baby. Now you understand why."

"So, since someone cornered him, he's coming through with his threats."

She inhaled the warm scent that was Evan's. Why did his arm around her shoulder feel so comforting and his concern without accusation burrow deep in her heart?

"I think he's manipulating you, Evan. Discovering he had a son has most probably tapped two emotions in him—one, excitement over a male heir and two, another chance to control me once more. He's sick enough to make this travesty a sporting event between us."

Evan frowned. "He did sound competitive during our phone call."

She searched Evan's gaze. Right now she needed to draw strength from him. She spent all these years keeping a low profile but had failed to plan a strategy should he come after her again. Part of her was still intimidated by him, plus she'd been so busy with the simple task of day-to-day living she never had the luxury of time to invest in the probability of *what if*.

Evan's confidence offered strength to bolster her, but it wasn't enough. Evan didn't quite understand the magnitude of Campbell's determination. She rested a hand against his chest. "My sweet noble Irishman, answer me this. When has a politician ever been held accountable for a sex scandal? Buzz might lose his bid for the presidency, but he'll still be around to make life hell for us. You know he will. And you'll become a target for him, as well. I have no doubt he could single-handedly ruin your career. We can't permit that."

Evan's smile was devilish. "You underestimate the McKenna magic."

She laughed. "I wish I had your surety."

He kissed her forehead. "What do you want to do, Red?"

There he went and did it again. Endeared himself to her by asking her what she wanted instead of insisting he had the answer. Could this man actually be different from the other aggressive men she knew? Would he consider her an equal? She rested against the circle of his arm to think. What *did* she want?

She'd already decided against coming forward and accusing Campbell of rape. That meant the only alternative was to marry Evan, tell the lie and pray Campbell's focus on the White House was enough to keep him away—for now. She didn't think Matt would have a problem accepting Evan for a father. He already had a bad case of hero worship. If she took one step at a time to eliminate the most dangerous possibility first, perhaps they could buy some time to formulate a long-term plan. Of the two evils, Evan's proposal seemed the least foul.

God forgive her.

Since they sat in such close proximity and doing so felt so damned right, she cupped his cheek with one hand. "I'll marry you, Evan. The sooner the better, don't you think?"

IF EVAN HAD FINALLY achieved her consent and the soft touch of her hand made him want to do all sorts of things to that mouth of hers, why did Kelly's answer leave him wanting? He should be grabbing her and kissing her right now, but all he could do was stare. She'd said yes and he felt like an idiot because while his heart crashed around his chest at the possibility of a life with this woman, she was buying into his proposal as a business arrangement. She had calculated the lesser of two evils between him and Buzz Campbell and chosen him.

Should he admit this when they toasted their wedding?

He released her and sat back in his seat hoping to read some emotion in her face but she simply watched him, peaceful as a nun. Wasn't the heat of their make-out session the other night burning a hole in her mind like it was his? "You'll be okay living with me?"

She frowned. "Well, the marriage will just be on paper, no? We won't have to consummate the vows or anything, will we?"

That sinking feeling anchored right in the middle of his chest. He wanted to say *hell, yes, we'll consummate,* but then again he hadn't asked her to marry him on bended knee offering undying love. He was getting what he offered: an arrangement to solve a crisis.

Swallowing his rising disappointment, he grinned. "My answer would be yes, but I'll let you call the shots."

She gave a small smile. "That is most proper of you."

He reached for her hand. She let him take it. "We'll have to get a license in person. Let's go immediately after my show in the morning."

"Don't say anything on the air."

"We'll have to announce it at some point."

"I know, but I need a little time to adjust to the idea."

He wanted to say that he didn't need time to adjust. He liked the idea just fine. "Can I at least kiss you to seal the deal?"

She hesitated but heat filled her eyes. A small triumph pounded his caveman chest. *Yes! Their kisses had affected her.*

Stubborn woman as she was, she bit her lower lip and shook her head. "I don't think it's a good idea."

Should he just lean in and steal one anyway? With any other woman, he would. Kelly was a different story. She'd drawn a line in the sand over their agreement and she'd hold firm. He felt like John Wayne chasing after that fiery redhead Maureen O'Hara in the classic movie, *The Quiet Man.* He could just hear the heroine now… *We'll not have a marriage until I have my things about me.* Evan would have to make Kelly's world right to earn her affection. And damn it all, he was up for the challenge.

Matt came to mind. "So how do you want to deliver this information to Matt?"

A hum rose in her throat. "With as little facts as possible. He's still young enough to take things at face value."

"Will you tell him I'm his father?"

"Do you want me to?"

"Of course, but how will we couch it?"

She shrugged, guilt ripe on her face. "I'll tell him first. I'll say I was giving you both time to get to know each other. That way I'm not quite lying."

Evan tapped a finger to his lips. "That could work."

"He won't question further. He'll be glad."

Evan grinned. "Me, too."

"What's good is that we can send him back to school. He is such a straightforward kid that if anyone says anything to him about Buzz, he'll just say he already has a dad and they don't know what they're talking about."

"I'd keep him close a few days longer till the media dies down some more."

Kelly winced. "I thought performing this charade— um, marriage—was going to keep Buzz away from us."

Evan ignored the slight. "So he's promised. I will ask my attorney to draw up guardianship papers. I'd rather have everything nice and tidy before getting back into our normal routines."

"Okay. Matt will catch up easily. We'll keep him home a few more days."

He squeezed her arm. "Hey, if it's the tuition you're concerned about, don't be. You're marrying a rich guy, remember?"

She laughed. "Oh, my. Neiman Marcus, here I come!"

"If you don't have a charge card I'll be sure you get one. They have great shoes."

She stared at him in disbelief. "Really?"

"You didn't know that?"

"Yes, I know about the shoes. I'm surprised that *you* do."

They sat in amiable silence for a moment. They really did have so much to learn about each other.

He didn't want to break the sweet moment, but one more topic needed to be tackled. "Red…"

"Yes?"

"Michael won't like being left out. When we spoke at lunch he sounded pretty excited about officiating at the wedding."

"He'll understand."

With raised eyebrows, he let his gaze drift out the window.

At his silence, Kelly added, "We'll have a civil ceremony. I know my brother won't want to be party to sham nuptials."

"Hey, don't call us a sham. Our marriage could grow into something."

He didn't like the way her lips pressed together.

"No church."

"Okay. Maybe someday we can do this right. Then we'll have Michael marry us."

She laughed. "Evan, as much as I appreciate what you are doing for us, you may soon find that you regret marrying *me*. Let's not make this more than it is and just get ourselves through today."

IT WAS STILL DARK outside when Steve Fiore stuck his head into Evan's office with a cup of coffee in his hand.

Evan looked up from his computer. "You cut your hair."

Steve ran a hand along his silvered temple. "All of them, actually."

Evan smiled. Both men were used to starting their days before the sun rose. Evan liked the familiarity between them. When Evan was overseas they'd consulted with each other by phone before Steve started the morning segments. They'd been doing this same routine for years. Now it was more enjoyable because they had a few minutes of each other's company in person.

Steve got right to the point. "I didn't get your notes on today's show."

Evan frowned. "Didn't Sarah send you the write-up on the wounded warriors piece? I'm interviewing an ex-air force officer who lost two years of memory from a bomb blast. She's a fascinating and funny woman. Said she can't promise she'll remember to show up—and if she does show I shouldn't be surprised if she can't remember my name. I'm looking forward to the interview."

Steve shook his head. "I got that one and the other two. I'm talking about Campbell. I see no notes on him."

Evan motioned to the door. "Why don't you close that and come in. I have to say something."

As he shut the door, Steve said, "Don't tell me you have nothing."

"I have plenty. Please, sit." Evan motioned to the chair and waited until Steve sat because the man wasn't going to like what he was about to hear.

"I cut a deal with Campbell."

Steve's coffee mug stopped in midair to his mouth. "What do you mean?"

"The senator wants this story to go away. He wants all eyes looking at someone else rather than him as Matt's father."

Steve chuckled. "Well of course he does. The guy was caught with his pants down."

Evan held his friend's gaze, swallowing the urge to get angry because this inference pointed to Kelly, as well. He gestured to his screen, where he had filled out the preliminary information for the marriage license. "I've asked Kelly to marry me. She agreed. We're going to announce that Matt is mine."

"What? Are you crazy?"

Evan grinned. "Maybe."

"How could her son be yours?"

"Matt? Come on, Steve. You know his name."

"Answer me."

"When I first met Kelly before heading overseas she was pregnant by the senator and didn't know it. We're going to say that I'm the guy from the one-night stand she always referred to when people asked about Matt's father."

Steve's jaw dropped open. "That's a lie."

Evan shrugged. "How do you know?"

"We have the DNA results."

"What DNA results?"

Eyes narrowing, Steve caught on. "Campbell said he will make the test disappear if you take the heat?"

"Yes. Me or anybody. I'm happy to take the spotlight. Hell, I like the kid and the mother's not half-bad."

Steve stood. "Not gonna fly, Evan. Not with me."

"Why not?"

"Because we know the truth. Dean knows the truth. This is too big an issue about a man who wants to run our country to let it simply disappear. For goodness' sake, which head are you thinking with, McKenna?"

Evan wasn't going to answer such a stupid question. He picked up his favorite pen and clicked it a couple of times to control himself. "If you air anything about Kelly being tied to Buzz, he won't back you. He'll make you look ridiculous."

Steve's jaw hardened. "Buzz doesn't have the only copy of the DNA test."

Evan stood to meet his friend's gaze. He had suspected that test was going to cause more trouble than Steve let on. "Look, Steve. That man will destroy Kelly if he can, then take her son. What happened to your moral code in protecting the innocent?"

"Then she shouldn't have had an affair with him. We have an obligation to the American people."

Biting back his response made the muscles in his neck ache. Steve didn't know about the rape because Kelly had sworn Evan to silence. Keeping this information from Steve was the hardest secret he'd ever kept. Kelly was wrong, and Evan was trying to work with her to finally get her to reveal the truth. If Steve knew this information he'd support Evan. All he'd have to do is imagine some jerk assaulting his wife and he'd be on board.

"I really need you to trust me, man. You've always had my back before. This story runs deep and there's more at stake here than meets the eye."

Steve sucked in a harsh breath. "I'm getting pressure from upstairs, Evan. This is one time that *you* have to work with *me*. I need a story."

Evan's internal alarm sounded. Steve was skirting the truth. They'd both taken chances on stories before at the risk of catching hell from upstairs. It added excitement to their jobs and the resulting stories usually earned them bonuses. The television station owners liked their maverick attitudes even though they bellyached about reining them in. Either politics or Steve's push for ratings was derailing him from the altruistic motives that used to drive them both. When did Steve change? The thought made Evan furious.

"Bullshit, Steve. I'm thinking you want a sleazy story to dress up into some vigilante piece because Campbell doesn't belong to the political party that this station—or you for that matter—supports. Am I reading this right or are you flexing your political muscle to chase ratings?"

Steve looked like he took a punch. "Evan you've known me too long to…"

Evan interrupted. "Yes, and I've never known you to turn your back on an underdog. Aiding the oppressed is what made us such a great team. Improving lives is what elevated our reporting. What is our motto? Changing the world, one life at a time. Have you forgotten?"

Steve's voice rose. "You're in love with the woman and not thinking straight."

"Maybe I am in love, but I am most certainly thinking straight. I know what really happened, Steve. I need your support. I'm working on Kelly. If I can get her to go on the air we'll have a helluva story for the American people. But first, I want to take the heat off her. That bastard is capable of *taking away her son!* Do you understand that?"

Steve stared at Evan, digesting the information as if it was too early in the morning to be doing battle with his friend. "So what is your strategy?"

Evan released a sigh. "Marry Kelly. Claim Matt as mine and clear the air. Then do some digging to get evidence that doesn't include my future wife to prove Campbell is unfit as a presidential candidate. You can give whatever information I find to Dean and let him run with it. I don't care."

"Do you hear yourself, Evan? Marrying a woman to protect her from scandal?"

"It's been done before, Steve. Besides, I care for her. Seeing this nightmare unfold on her simply hammered home my feelings. You've seen enough to know it's true."

"I don't like it. It compromises your position. If you get caught lying it could ruin your career."

Evan held open both palms. "Well the only ones who could make me a liar are you and Dean. Would you do that?"

Steve didn't answer.

This was the first time in ten years that Steve was taking a hard-line stance with him. The cold reasoning in his eyes said it all.

Evan let his pen drop onto his desk in resignation. "Wow. That's too bad. I'm doing this, Steve. Kelly and I will be married in twenty-four hours. I'm planning on making quite a show of our marriage and my son on Monday's show."

Steve shook his head. "You with your black hair. Her kid is blond. Who will believe you?"

Evan grinned. "There is a deep Irish gene pool on both sides. I'll make it work."

Steve sipped his coffee and winced—it must have gone cold. "I have to talk to the chairman about this. I'll get back to you."

"Make it happen, Steve. Trust me. We will sink Campbell in the end and we'll both be able to sleep at night."

WHEN EVAN ENTERED his penthouse, Kelly had the television on, already deep into the second news show at NCTV, which meant she had seen his interviews. Kelly stood at the counter in the kitchen, a cup of coffee in her hand. Matt sat at the counter concentrating on a coloring book.

"Did you like the show?"

Kelly punched the air. "One for the team. Loved the interview with the air force gal."

Evan laughed. "She was a hit."

Matt jumped to his feet. "I'm going with you today. Mom told me!"

Evan pulled Matt into his arms, his grin matching the boy's. Evan hugged him, glad that the kid had accepted him. He whispered only for Matt to hear. "You okay with having me as your new dad?"

Matt leaned in. "Are you my dad?"

Oh, God. Here's where the lies began. This kid could be shattered if the truth ever changed. He sought out Kelly across the top of his head, her eyes riveted on them. At her nod, he looked back at Matt. "Yeah, Matt. This is great news to me."

"What took you so long?"

Evan laughed. "Well, I suppose your mom wanted to make sure you liked me."

Matt gave him their secret handshake. "Can we live in the penthouse?"

"Sure! We'll play basketball every night after your homework."

Matt frowned. "I have homework?"

"Well not yet, but you will someday."

The thought of watching this kid grow up hit with the enormity of the decision he and Kelly had made. Now, if he could just get her to trust him—heck, finally love him. One day at a time. First he had to get them in the clear with the senator.

Evan put Matt back on his feet. "You finish coloring. I have to talk with your mom before we go."

She approached him, coffeepot in hand. "Will you be having your usual breakfast, Evan?"

"Don't know if I can eat. I'm nervous about our next appointment."

CHAPTER THIRTEEN

THEY ASCENDED THE few steps to the Manhattan Marriage Bureau on Worth Street. Kelly had taken Matt with them because Julie was busy. Bunny had too many distractions at Neverland to keep an eye on him, and Michael had a packed day at his parish. She did manage to set up a playdate with Jared, but Donna couldn't pick Matt up until after two. Trying to balance her efforts to keep calm with the license application while keeping Matt in tow didn't give her much time to tap her own reactions to what was happening.

Perhaps that was a good thing.

Evan had taken her hand while they walked at an easy pace down the street, as if they had all the time in the world to absorb their surroundings. She in turn, held Matt's hand and had to tug once in a while when he gawked at memorabilia sold at vendor stands.

Kelly's mouth dropped open at the number of people applying for licenses at computer kiosks in the newly refurbished historical building. Kelly had checked online. The city had provided everything to make a wedding complete, from flowers to photographers, costume jewelry to a beautiful wedding chapel. New York City's mayor wanted to give Las Vegas a run for its money and make Manhattan the number one hot spot for marriages in the U.S.A. Looking around, Kelly believed he was doing it.

"I completed the initial application information online earlier this morning."

Kelly frowned. "You did?"

"Yeah, but I didn't have all of your info. Come on."

Evan led them to an open window where a young man waved them forward. When they approached, recognition clicked in his eyes. Clearly a celebrity follower, the grin that creased his face had Kelly slowing her steps. Evan squeezed her hand in reassurance and cast her a smile. Below his breath he said, "Piece of cake, darlin'. This happens all the time."

The guy adjusted his black-rimmed rectangular glasses. "Evan McKenna, NCTV, right?"

Evan glanced at the nameplate in the window. "Yes, Thomas, and this is Miss Kelly Sullivan and we're applying for a marriage license."

Thomas's glance rested on Matt, who stood on tiptoes to see the man.

Thomas leaned closer to have eye contact with Matt. "Hello, little man. Are you here as witness?"

Matt's eyes lit up with pride. "My mom is marrying Evan. He's my dad."

Thomas had the good grace to say nothing. From the raised eyebrows and the grin tugging at his mouth, he clearly recognized Matt and Kelly from Jay Doyle's scandalous report. Kelly had no doubt his friends would be hearing about this encounter all too soon. Knowing how fast their actions could be broadcast should this young man choose to pick up a phone, Kelly became convinced that the sooner they got married the better. She wanted Campbell's concerns about being targeted as Matt's father appeased and to get him off their backs as quickly as possible.

Evan said, "We're already in the computer, if you'll just search my name."

Thomas typed Evan's name into his keyboard. "Here it is." He held out a hand and smiled. "I'll need identification from both of you to begin…"

On the ride back uptown, Kelly felt numb. She sat in the back of the limo with Matt between her and Evan watching the city pass by, yet seeing nothing. The entire scene in the marriage bureau occupied her mind. Those few minutes had seemed surreal. Watching Thomas efficiently process their license, print it out and hand it to them for signatures left her breathless. At exactly eleven-fifteen, her hand trembled when she took the pen Evan offered her to sign first. She was relieved when her name flowed with little trepidation, leaving a feminine, Catholic school-honed signature that presented confidence.

Evan signed his space with a flourish in clear, beautiful penmanship. She found an odd satisfaction in liking his signature. If his handwriting was any reflection, she could feel sure that she'd just bound herself to an honest and happy man.

Yet still, she didn't feel the excitement a woman should feel about marrying a man she could never live without. Perhaps she was never meant to know true love. She glanced at Evan. He was on the phone with his attorney confirming their appointment to perform the ceremony in his office at two tomorrow. Her stomach knotted. She exhaled a cleansing breath. She could do this.

Matt broke the silence, disappointment clear on his face. "That was boring. I thought we were going to a party."

Kelly laughed. "The party will be another day, honey. This was just the business end of getting married."

She and Evan hadn't discussed a celebration. Honestly, she'd just prefer to get married and carry on their days as if nothing had changed. She tried to inhale, only to discover she could not.

Evan caught Kelly's gaze over Matt's head. "You okay?"

Was she okay? Yes. And, no. Yes, because she was doing what needed to be done to keep her son safe. She would be eternally grateful that Evan had chosen to help protect them. His sacrifice alone endeared him to her. Then, no, she wasn't okay, because deep inside she wanted to be in love with Evan. As much as they had formed a beautiful friendship, and heaven knew his looks could set any red-blooded woman to making designs on him, she wanted to feel head over heels, full of love and trust for him. Those feelings did not exist and she felt guilty.

She pressed a hand to her chest. "I'm a bit overwhelmed, that's all."

His understanding smile warmed her.

"This will all turn out okay, Kelly. I promise you, I wouldn't be offering you marriage if I didn't feel in my heart that it is the right thing to do."

Again, that nudge. He didn't say because he loved her. So, did he mean that marrying her was the right thing to do politically? Was he protecting her, the underdog, once more as he was nationally known to do? Was he taking Kelly and Matt on as a personal crusade to elevate his career, and then would he divorce her when the dust settled and the scandal lay behind them?

Well, if he did, she should be grateful. Damn her suspicious heart, but she just could not bring herself to trust that Evan was taking these actions for love. To do that would mean she would become vulnerable. She didn't think she could ever trust anyone enough to give herself over like that.

She managed a smile and made sure her eyes reflected her appreciation. "Never underestimate how grateful I am, Evan. What you are doing for us is beautiful."

He kissed her fingers. "I want to do this, Kelly. I think we have the beginning of something good between us."

She smiled. It was the best she could offer.

Kelly's phone rang. She looked at the ID. "Hello, Donna." She listened, letting her gaze move from Evan's to Matt's. "Yes, we're on our way back."

EVAN SLID AN arm around Matt as he watched Kelly speak to Jared's mom, aware that Kelly was the most interesting woman in all of Manhattan for both him and Matt. This little boy loved his momma—she was his world. Evan wanted to make both of them the center of his world. Evan's chest tightened with hope that one day the bond of love that encircled Matt and Kelly would widen to include him.

He watched Kelly smile as she spoke, soft lines creasing the corner of her mouth. Evan wanted to kiss that mouth so badly he could taste it. Wisps of her ginger-colored hair had fallen loose from her braid, framing her face with a glow. Her perfume had intoxicated his senses as she leaned into him to sign the marriage license in the small window space at the bureau. He had inhaled a slow steady breath of the warm fragrance, just as he did now, knowing that her perfume would be in his life for a very long time— if he had his way. He was discovering that each moment with Kelly was magic. Yet, from the way she'd taken his pen from him to sign the license, he had no illusions and knew she was terrified at the prospect of marrying him.

He'd do everything he could to allay her fears between now and tomorrow's ceremony, and every day after that until she understood that he meant to be a pivotal force in her life. One she could depend on and trust until the day she died.

Kelly ended the call. "Donna will meet us at the penthouse to pick up Matt."

"I'm going to Jared's?"

"Yes you are, honey. You've been so good these past few days and Jared has missed you."

Matt punched the air. "Yes!"

Evan smiled at the two of them, not believing his dumb luck. He was about to have an afternoon with Kelly all to himself, if he could just keep her from running off to Neverland.

BY THE TIME Donna and Jared arrived, Matt was bouncing around the penthouse with excitement. He was so thrilled to see his buddy he actually hugged him. The mothers laughed. Evan wondered if these two boys would remember this moment ten, twenty, thirty years from now. Did childhood friends last a lifetime as they used to when the world moved at a slower pace?

Donna hefted Matt's backpack. "Since tomorrow is Friday, why don't we throw some pajamas in? If the kids are having fun, we'll make it a sleepover. I can keep Jared home from school for a day."

"Can I, Mom?" Matt jumped up and down, tugging at Kelly's arm.

She glanced at Evan, who grinned. "I remember being excited like Matt, only it was to convince my mom to let me and my buddy sleep in a tent in the backyard."

A look filled her eyes as if she were imagining Evan as a ten-year-old boy full of exuberance and unable to contain himself. She smiled at Matt. "Sure, honey. Get your pajamas and toothbrush, but you have to promise to brush your teeth before bed."

The boys barreled into Matt's room. Just as Evan was wondering if Kelly would say anything, she hugged Donna. "I appreciate you taking Matt. He's been wonderful, but chafing at the short tether he's been on since this debacle with Campbell."

Donna's concerned glance took them both in. "It's been a bit of a roller coaster, I'm sure. Jack and I are happy to help. We'll keep Matt safe. You all can use a break."

"Evan and I are to be married at two tomorrow. Given the circumstances, it would be best if Matt was otherwise occupied. Thank you, and please thank Jack for us."

Evan's breath caught in his throat when she used the word *us* so naturally.

Donna laughed. "So soon! How exciting. And you told me nothing was brewing between you two." She kissed Evan on the cheek and hugged her friend again. "When you called this morning to say you were getting your marriage license, I nearly fell off my chair. Now this."

Evan draped an arm around Kelly's shoulder. She looked like she could use a little support. "Kelly is such a private person that no one knows that we dated before I went overseas. I am more than happy now to claim my family once and for all."

Donna looked dumbfounded. She turned on Kelly. "A man like Evan? You kept him in the dark?" She palmed her own forehead. "What were you thinking, girl?"

Kelly laughed. "Oh, you know how I feel about bossy men, Donna. I needed to get a bead on Evan's flexibility issues before I could count him in."

Much to Evan's surprise, she reached up and kissed him sweetly on the lips. Briefly, but long enough to leave an impression on him—and Donna. If she was putting on a show of affection, she was doing a damned fine job. He wondered what was going through her head to present this change of heart so fast.

The boys skidded to a halt at the door. Donna already had the backpack open to receive the added items.

"Bye, Mom. Bye, Dad!" Matt hugged Evan around the legs and kissed his mom on the cheek when she bent over. Evan didn't miss the odd look on Kelly's face, as if she'd just taken a gut punch.

Then, the door closed, leaving Evan and Kelly staring at each other in the silence. Evan wasn't going to question the conflict of emotions rising in her eyes. Instead, he took the one step between them, pulled Kelly into his arms and kissed her mouth with tender and insistent pressure. She didn't resist. He inhaled the heat and taste that was unmistakably Kelly urging him to kiss her welcoming mouth until she lost her balance and they tumbled against the door. A murmur of protest rose in Kelly's throat but faded as she returned his kiss with ardor.

Spurred on by her willingness, Evan kissed her more deeply, pressing her against the door with the full length of his body. She molded to him in all the right places, wrapping her arms around his torso and if possible, pulling him closer. He cupped her face with both hands, capturing her lips over and over, exploring her mouth, their tongues tangling as if they'd kissed every day of their lives. He was on fire with the taste of her, the warmth and softness of her mouth, the body heat rising through her clothes. And oh God, the press of her breasts into his chest with the rhythm of her breathing just about undid his sanity.

He broke the kiss. "Kelly…"

"He called you Dad."

"Matt?"

She gave him a pleading look, her green eyes hungry, her voice husky with desire. "You stopped me last time, Evan. If you do it again now, you may not get another chance."

He grinned. "Then as you wish, Red. I'm all yours."

He swept her up and headed across the penthouse in

slow easy steps, kissing her along the way while relishing the easy weight of her in his arms. This woman was soft, sexy, comfortable. Her perfume mingled with her kisses, invading his senses like an addiction. He wanted to make this first time with Kelly an encounter she'd never forget— and would want to experience over and over again.

She laughed. "You should put me down."

"No chance. Consider this our first dance." Humming a nameless tune, he slowly spun them around, kissing her neck and nibbling at her ear.

She let her head fall back. "Where are you taking me?"

"To my cave. I'm making you mine. But, more importantly, I'm thinking we're going to need a condom...or several."

He almost died as pleasure lit those enticing green eyes. "Oh, Lord. I hadn't even thought..."

He kissed her again. His mouth against hers, he said, "I like that about you, Red. It means you don't sleep around."

She chuckled against his lips. "You could say that."

They took their sweet time getting up the stairs. He put her feet on the first rise and leaning forward kissed her until her lovely behind found purchase against the higher steps. With arms planted on each side of her, he brushed his chest against hers as he claimed her mouth and she arched backward. Kelly pulled him onto herself, then rolled onto Evan, pushing him against the stairs. He liked that. He used his arms to ascend the steps, letting his butt settle on each riser as Kelly climbed between his legs, her reach for him pushing her breasts into his chest while kissing him with enough pressure to keep the momentum up the stairs. Then, he'd stop climbing. The feel of her was so overwhelming he just had to wrap his arms around her, capturing her between his legs to drink deeply of her kisses. They'd stop for breath, smiling at each other until they started kissing and climbing toward their destination again.

When they reached the top, Evan landed on his back. Kelly snaked her arms around his neck and settled on top of him, making him harder than he already had grown. A soft purr vibrated her throat. She hungrily sought his lips while his hands restlessly explored her back and the curve of her luscious behind.

He had to get this woman into his bed. It had been too long since he'd made love. He had spent way too many hours imagining this moment with Kelly and here she was, blowing his mind. Exceeding expectation.

He stopped thinking. His caveman pounded his chest and his senses took over.

KELLY COULDN'T THINK as her inhibitions swirled into nonexistence. If she ever worried whether or not she could give herself to a man, she need wonder no longer. Touching Evan was sheer electricity, as if once connected she could not let go. Kissing him felt perfect. Delicious. HOT. His mouth sent surges straight down to her womb where her need to have him rose like a Phoenix from ashes.

Logic be damned. She wanted this man now. She wanted Evan to know it. When Matt had called him *Dad* with such surety, that one word blasted the wall that she'd put between her and Evan. Once the door closed, his voracious look in those come-hither blue eyes triggered a need in her that she'd ignored for too long. Evan was doing everything in his power to make the world safe for her and Matt. But most importantly, he had given her son the gift of a father.

Right now, she couldn't care less as to why. All she wanted to do was thank him, body and soul. Only, she couldn't tell who was getting the better end of the grati-

tude. The mere sound of Evan's voice whispering her name
between kisses sent her reeling.

What was it about this man that she could not resist?

Oh, God. It had to be his touch. Those hands were
wreaking havoc on her body. His kisses, driving her wild.
When he stood and offered her his hand, she almost cried
for the distance between his body and to hers.

"Come on, Red. Let's get comfortable. We have some
work to do."

She slipped her hand into his. Sure as the sky was blue,
she had waited way too long to give herself to a man.
She could feel her attachment to Evan pulling like a magnet from sheer need alone. Even the strength of his hand
turned her on.

The night curtains in Evan's room were drawn back, but
gauzy sheers covered the windows hinting to the impres-
sive city skyline. She noted the spacious room painted in
muted tones but her gaze riveted to the bed. Evan's bed.
Modern, platformed. Charcoal-silver silk covering. Large
down pillows. Evan turned her to him, taking her with another knee-melting kiss.

He pressed his forehead to hers, exhaling a satisfied
sigh. "I dreamed of having you in my bed, woman."

She nipped his lower lip with her teeth. "And if I'd only
known you kissed like this I wouldn't have taken so long."

He answered with a harsh laugh. "Well now, we'll just
have to make up for lost time."

They tumbled on the bed together. He bundled her
against him, kissing her softly, slowly, holding her close.
When he slid his hand along the length of her leg, mur-
muring how smooth her skin was, tingles shot up and
into that place deep inside her growing hotter by the second. She pressed against his hand with abandon until his

hand slipped under her dress on a slow but urgent mission upward.

Sprawled next to her, his body seemed much larger than hers, but she liked the power of him. That fleeting thought surprised her but she lost concentration when his hand burrowed past the lace of her panties to her soft mound beneath. He captured her mouth to silence her gasp, kissing her long and deep, his fingers teasing her hot spot. Then, with both hands he explored upward, tracing the smooth plane of her stomach with one hand while the other slid underneath to caress her behind. He kept kissing her with slow, deep, languid kisses trailing from her mouth down the pulse of her neck until she was drunk with want. Pressing himself against her with the weight of his erection heavy against her thigh, she didn't think she could tolerate another moment of his teasing. She wanted him inside her. She wanted him now.

They could take their time later.

She tugged at his shirt, but he wasn't stopping long enough for that. He kept kissing her, exploring her body, pulling her panties down. She bent one knee to slip the garment from her leg, giving Evan access to her. A moan of pleasure rose in his throat. His gaze drank in the length of her leg as his hand retraced its path up her thigh. He bent his head, kissing the inside of her knee, his mouth and tongue following his hand up to her most sensitive area gently exploring and nuzzling the silken amber curls at her core.

She thought she'd scream with want. He must have sensed her body tense. His hand and mouth abandoned their sweet torture to push her sundress up. His kisses traveled upward, tasting the soft skin of her belly. He raised himself, his eyes seeking hers with the heat and torment of a man who couldn't wait much longer. She sighed at the sheer emotion coloring his face.

The power of his body over hers didn't frighten her as she had feared. No, it had the opposite effect. This was one possession to which she'd surrender. The heavy weight of him made her feel safe, wanted and most of all, understood. Evan was responding to her body like a symphony in motion. Everything felt right. Holy Blessed Mother she wanted more!

She reached for his belt. When he realized she was trying to undress him, his heated gaze turned questioning. She met the fierce want in those blue eyes and whispered, "I can't wait."

His mouth softened into a roguish smile. "Ah, Kelly."

He pulled off his shirt while she struggled with his belt buckle. She stopped for a moment to lay a hand on the nicely honed plane of his abs. He smiled, then helped her undo his pants and dark briefs until he kicked them free. He took the moment to pull a condom from the drawer next to his bed before she reached for him once more, tangling his tanned, muscled legs with hers. The brush of the hair on his legs teased her thighs, sending frissons of delight up her spine.

She pushed against him while he made quick work of the condom, but he pushed back, easing between her legs. The raw sensation of his skin against hers sent pinpricks of pleasure through her. Evan slipped the sundress farther up, the flat of his palms skimming up her torso, over her breasts and along her arms only to tangle in her hair as the dress piled above her head on the bed. Rising over her once more, he nipped at her breasts brimming over the top of her lace bra while his hand slipped beneath her back to unclasp the hook. She arched to accommodate him and felt his hardness pressing against her. The sound of his heated breathing drove her further into mindless desire.

He stopped to behold her naked body, a murmur of appreciation escaping his lips.

She'd have none of it.

With both hands she grabbed his face, raising her mouth to his. The action brought him down on her, planting his erection closer to her essence. He covered her breasts with his chest, searing his skin to hers. He kissed her hard and entered her at the same time, entwining his fingers in hers and stretching her arms over her head to capture her completely. She rose her hips to meet him, her body tightening. A moan escaped her lips as he buried himself deep inside her.

He broke the kiss, panting, his eyes dark with passion. "Are you all right, Kelly?"

Trying to catch her breath, she nodded. "Oh, yes. I want this." She drank in his gaze. She'd never seen him look like this. Erotic. Sensual. His focus intently on her, his face flushed, a lock of black hair falling into his eyes. "I want *you*, Evan."

With a groan of surrender he captured her mouth once more, kissing her with a passion Kelly never imagined existed. As their bodies moved to the timeless and urgent rhythm of love, she finally understood what it meant to connect with a man by desire—as lovers. Holding her gaze with a look of exquisite torture, Evan drove her to orgasm with an explosion that rocked her body, mind and soul until the world fell away and nothing existed except this man in her arms, crying out in climax as her body claimed him and he, in turn, responded to her ultimate need.

DINNER HOUR HAD come and gone when they finally came up for air. They'd made a trail of lovemaking from Evan's loft, to his shower to back downstairs in Kelly's bed. Now showered again, sated, their hair still wet and both naked beneath light robes, they sat next to each other on the couch, feeding each other sushi that had just been delivered.

Evan refilled her flute with his favorite Winston Churchill Pol Roger champagne that he'd opened to celebrate the moment—and their meal.

He toasted her with his glass one more time. "Woman, you are an amazing lover."

She sipped her champagne, a playful light in her eyes. "'Tis all your fault, to be sure."

"Mine? How?"

"Aye. You are so dastardly handsome and those mitts of yours know exactly how to touch me."

He smiled. "That's because you are every man's dream come true."

"So, I didn't disappoint you?"

"You're kidding, right?"

Small color rose on her cheeks. "Technically, you are not my first, but you are the first and only man I've known by choice."

She'd been such a natural lover that this fact had immediately slipped away with their first kiss. He chuckled. "Did you know your brogue becomes more pronounced when you've been sexually satisfied?"

Her grin reached her eyes which seemed softer and less tense than they had earlier today. "Does it now? And how would you be knowing that I've been satisfied?"

He buried a hand in her loose-flowing hair and pulled her close for a slow, deep kiss. He whispered, "Does, *Oh, God, I'm coming!* count as proof—over and over again?"

She laughed out loud. "I said that?"

He fed her another piece of sushi, watching as her mouth slid the morsel from the chop sticks. "I rest my case."

He popped a piece into his mouth. They chewed in amicable silence.

"So tell me, Red."

"Yes?"

"Why the change?"

She swallowed. "Meaning?"

"Well, when we got the license you insisted our marriage would be in name only." He motioned to their nakedness. "Now, here we are."

She pressed her lips together as if trying to choose her words. "The answer is simple. Matt. He called you Dad and something inside me shifted. I…"

A hook of hope caught his gut. "Yes?"

"I wanted to thank you. Let you know how grateful I am."

He felt deflated. "Not that I'm complaining, but this was all one big thank-you?"

She bit her lower lip. "It started that way but lasted for about ten seconds. Then my body took over and nothing you could have said or done would have stopped me. I wanted you."

He looked cautious. "So, should I read into what you're saying?"

"Please do not, Evan. At least, not yet."

"Does it make our impending nuptials tomorrow seem easier?"

The smile of gratitude that filled her face practically stopped his heart. "Aye, Evan. I'll not be shunning you anytime soon."

Evan's phone began ringing from the kitchen counter. Evan frowned at the ring tone. "That's Sarah. Why would she be calling now?"

EVAN ANSWERED HIS phone. "Hey, Sarah. Everything okay?"

"Hate to bother you, Evan, but you have to turn on the ten o'clock news. I just got wind of an interview Dean did with Senator Campbell this afternoon."

"What?" Evan looked at Kelly, knowing his tentative bond with her just fell through the floor. Steve hadn't even given him the benefit of twenty-four hours to implement his plan. Damnation. He had been so close. "Why that son of a…"

"What, Evan?" Frowning, Kelly put down her chop sticks.

He held up a hand. "Okay. Thank you, Sarah. I'll talk with you in the morning."

He reached for the remote. "I want you to brace yourself. I didn't tell you, but Dean was the one who sneaked the DNA test on Matt. He interviewed Campbell this afternoon. It's on the news."

Kelly jumped to her feet. "Please tell me you're kidding."

Evan glanced at the wall clock by the bookshelf. Five minutes until showtime. He sat on the couch, pulling her down next to him. He wrapped an arm around her shoulder but already her body had stiffened. Tension creased the corners of her eyes. "Don't lose your cool, Kelly. I talked to Steve the morning. When I left, he wasn't airing anything on Campbell until he heard from me."

Then he remembered. Steve said he had to run Evan's request by the chairman and would get back to him. He never called. And truthfully, Evan had become so wrapped up with Kelly that he forgot. The big-screen TV erupted to life on the NCTV channel. A beer commercial played. Evan closed his eyes as the truth hit. He had just been screwed by his friend and boss.

Kelly was watching him. "Why are you upset, Evan?"

He could tell Kelly already suspected foul play. He shook his head. "I had an argument with Steve this morning."

She gestured to the screen. "Over this."

"Yes." *How much should I tell her?*

"What did he say?"

He released a breath. "He accused me of being too close to you. That under any other circumstances I would be using your story to pin Campbell against the wall. He wanted to know why I was keeping you from the spotlight."

The late night news began rolling on the television.

"Did you tell him?" Though her voice was soft, her eyes held suspicion.

"Absolutely not."

"Okay. So, how did you answer him?"

He was having trouble tamping down his own anger. Not five minutes ago they were as close as lovers could possibly be without the *L* word being spoken. Now, he would have to defend himself. Knowing Kelly as he did, chances were slim they'd ever survive the broadcast, especially if Dean did what he suspected Steve set up him up to do.

The anchorwoman outlined the evening's features. Campbell and Dean were front and center in order of delivery as she read the teaser for the story, *"Will the discovery of a hidden love child hurt Senator Buzz Campbell's bid for the White House?"*

"Oh, God!"

Kelly had turned dangerously pale. She fell back into her seat, defeated.

"I will kill that bastard!" He looked at Kelly. "I have to see what they reported. Can you watch this?"

"Shut it off. Please!" She choked on her own words.

He snapped the TV off. He'd get on the computer and

snag the file. But first, he had to do damage control—one more time, damn Steve's bones. Kelly sat with her arms hugging her knees to her chest.

"Kelly, I did not condone this. You have to believe me."

"I don't know what to believe right now, Evan."

He snapped the TV back on. "Then we're going to watch this. Unless we have the facts we'll jump to conclusions and someone will get hurt."

Evan and Kelly listened as the woman explained that Dean had spent the afternoon at the Campbell home on Long Island. A photo of Buzz walking his back lawn with wife and dog filled the screen behind her as she explained that the interview took a turn for the worst when Dean asked the Senator to address the sexual harassment allegations by his former administrative aid. The reporting switched to the interview tape.

Dean and the senator sat in wingback chairs with a coffee table between them in what looked like the Campbell's living room. Dressed in dark slacks and a crisp blue button-down opened at the neck, Campbell sat with his one leg crossed at the knee, master of his castle. Dean wore a dark suit, a closed leather file in his lap.

Kelly groaned. "Oh, Lord. I remember that room."

Evan wanted to pull her into his arms. The turmoil in her eyes harpooned his heart. They watched while Buzz listened with a momentary frown as Dean asked about Helen Thompson and her interview with Jay Doyle. Shaking his head, Buzz glossed over those allegations like a pro, making Helen and her accusations sound like an ungrateful employee with a grudge because she had flirted with him and he didn't respond to her advances. Buzz had moved on in his career and left her behind with an excellent reference for employment elsewhere for which she completely deserved.

Dean didn't even blink. He accepted Campbell's conde-
scending yet well-played answer as if there was no other.

Evan knew before he spoke that Dean was going in for
the kill. He had seen the same ruthless look settling on
Dean's face in office meetings when he'd worked around
another reporter's back to get a story. Dean must have considered this interview one hell of an opportunity to further
his career because this broadcast would destroy his ties
with Buzz, and Evan. When this interview was over, Buzz
would have nothing to do with Dean ever again. He'd probably work on destroying Dean, but Dean was too green
to be aware of that danger. Not when Steve and the boys
upstairs probably promised to protect him.

As for Evan? He'd let Campbell do his dirty work regarding Dean. Evan had more important issues to clean up.

Dean opened the file and extracted a sheet of paper.
The camera panned on both men. Evan didn't miss the
momentarily raised eyebrows when Campbell recognized
what Dean held.

"Then, Senator, can you explain this DNA test showing that the six-year-old boy of the woman reported as this
family's former nanny is your son?"

Buzz did what all good speakers do when caught with
their back against the wall he gave an indirect answer.

"Well, I'd have to be able to believe a report like that,
son. Trust the source and all."

"But, Senator, I obtained this report from a DNA sample
I obtained from the boy, along with a DNA sample of your
hair in a comb in the NCTV makeup room. This is, indeed,
fact. I supplied you with a copy and asked you to explain it
for the American people, but you remained silent."

Buzz Campbell looked like he wanted to explode. He
placed both feet on the floor and leaned forward, not caring about the camera angle as much as, Evan suspected,

caring very much to make an impression on the viewing audience.

Kelly started trembling. Evan tried to bundle her in his arms, but she pulled away. She rose to her feet, terror filling her face as she stared at the screen as if the devil himself stood before her.

When Campbell spoke, she flinched.

"One of the most unfortunate aspects of wanting to be a servant for the American people is having my personal life aired in public. I did not respond to you, Mr. Porter, because this information came as an utter shock to me. A shock of such magnitude that I had to speak with my wife and my pastor before I could come forward.

"Let me tell you. This news does not make me happy, but for reasons other than you might suspect. This nanny of whom you speak was a trusted member of our household. We all loved her. I would like to spare the poor woman from airing the details. Let it suffice to say that she developed a crush on me of which I had no idea. One night I feel asleep on the couch after working late and she seduced me in my sleep.

"She is a beautiful woman and it was a weak and less than lucid moment before I realized what was happening and it was too late. I fired her immediately. She left the next morning. Madeline has forgiven me, which is all the absolution I require. Now, she joins me in wanting to know for sure if this boy is really mine. If he is, we intend to file for custodial rights. This was an issue I had hoped to settle privately because clearly Ms. Sullivan never approached me with paternity for a son. Clearly, her shame for what she'd done caused her to protect her privacy, as well."

He pressed his lips together as if making a hard decision. "I would like to believe the American people understand I am a man who can make dire mistakes just like any other man. But, I am also willing to claim responsibility for my actions and make amends. I plan to do that, Mr. Porter. Now, this interview is over."

The senator did not rise. He simply sat back in his chair and stared at Dean as if the man was invisible. Then the camera cut.

Kelly stared blindly at the screen, struggling for breath. She didn't know what to do to stop the pressure building inside her like a volcano ready to explode. "He's going to take Matt!"

Evan stood, grabbed her by the arms and made her focus on him. "We can fight him, Kelly."

She pulled from his grip. Pointing a damning finger at the television, her voice rose in panic. "How, Evan? If I didn't know the truth, I'd be pitying the poor fool for being seduced by a wanton woman who ran off with his baby! I can't fight him. The man will say and do whatever it takes to clear his name."

Evan folded his hands as if praying to punctuate his words while achingly aware that Kelly was naked under her robe and that her most sublime affection for him had just been crushed. He had to reach her. Make her believe he could help. "Kelly. Please. You must listen to me. We can raise public support for your position and win, but you have to do as I say."

IN THE BLINK of an eye, it all fell together in Kelly's mind. The understanding poured through her like an arctic blast to the face. She looked at Evan as if seeing the man for the first time. She shook her head, mistrust making her want to scream while suddenly all too aware of her nakedness at this excruciating moment. The fact that seducing her this afternoon played a role in his grand scheme made her think murder wasn't good enough for how deeply Evan had betrayed her.

Her voice fell dangerously low. "You planned all of this. Didn't you?"

Disbelief filled Evan's eyes. "Porter's interview? No! Absolutely not!"

She took a step back. "Oh, no? Let me guess. Now, you're going to tell me that you will interview me on television where I will tell the world that Buzz Campbell raped me and I've been hiding all these years to keep that monster from taking my son."

He closed his eyes, his arms dropping to his side. "Yes, Kelly. That is exactly what I was going to advise. I've told you this before."

The despair that crossed Evan's face almost had her believing she was wrong. But no. She knew the truth. Evan had been wooing her, making her feel safe. He lured her into accepting the lie of a false marriage and lying about Matt being his son so that Steve could blast the truth on camera and force her to make a stand to save her son and her own pathetic pride. Evan had manipulated her—from the first day Jay Doyle aired his story straight up to this point.

She palmed her own forehead. "How could I have been so stupid?"

"Kelly, you are completely mistaken. I am telling you the truth. I cut a deal with Campbell to become Matt's father and marry you in order to shut him up."

"Yes, but that was just a small piece to your elaborate plan with Steve to achieve your ultimate goal which is to throw Campbell out of the candidacy and use my baby to do it. This was all about the goddamn story, Evan. And, don't you dare lie to me."

He stepped into her path as she tried to leave. Her eyes

were alive with a fury he'd never seen. He'd lost her, he knew it. This broadcast was what she had feared most. Someone pushing her against the wall with nowhere to go. How could he make her believe him?

"Please listen to me! I fought with Steve this morning because he threatened to conduct this interview. I thought I convinced him to wait, but believe me Kelly Sullivan, by all that is sacred and holy, after learning the truth from you about Buzz, I didn't give a damn about the story. I wanted to do what is right to protect you. It's why Steve has been on my back all week."

She'd have no more of his lies. She tried to move around him, but he stepped in front of her until she met his gaze once more.

"As for Campbell? Hell, woman! I was going to support the man for president until I learned what he'd done to you. Believe me. I can do my homework and take Campbell down in ways that won't involve you." He invaded her space, inhaling her sweet scent because he knew she was on her way out. "I cut that deal with Campbell because *I love you*, Kelly Sullivan. I love Matt. I was glad and willing to tell the world a boldface lie to make you mine. And *that* is the God's honest truth!"

It had taken her some time to pack up her belongings and then bundle Matt's clothes and toys scattered around his room. *His* room. No longer. The possibility of a life with Evan had been too good to be true. Why had she been so naive?

Evan had the good grace to help her pack. Sullen and silent, unhappiness on his face as if etched in stone. He'd said that he loved her. If he'd said those words just an hour before, she may have believed him. But now? Her response was to turn on her heels and walk away.

She didn't believe his words. Couldn't. Not with the pall of deception between them. He let her go, but his parting words still echoed in her mind. *Believe it or not Kelly, I love you. Promise to call me if you need me. I want to talk this through.*

She had answered, "You shouldn't have done it."

He shook his head, pain filling his eyes. "I didn't, Kelly."

But the elevator arrived and she stepped in, her world reduced to two suitcases and a satchel filled with toys. She wouldn't let Evan call a taxi for her, let alone help her with her things. She didn't trust herself to be in his company another minute. After the way they had made earth-shattering love, she was too damned raw to look at him.

Luckily she'd arrived at Donna and Jack's late enough that Matt was asleep. She had no idea how she would break the awful news to her son that the man he called Dad for the first time in his life had just vanished from the picture. Every one of her worst nightmares were coming true.

Donna and Jack had already been in bed when she arrived and hadn't seen the news. They assured her that her arrival was welcome and offered her the couch to sleep on. When she told them what happened they sat stunned.

Jack looked at her as if she was suspect. "So did you seduce the senator?"

She momentarily closed her eyes, her head aching at the realization that those would be the first thoughts that jumped into everyone's mind. Amazing how seeds of doubt and mistrust could be so easily planted by a convincing argument.

She huffed in annoyance. "Well, surely you know me better than that, Jack?"

He opened his palms unabashedly. "I do, but I'd still like

you to answer me because you'll be hit with the same question from all directions until you feel battered and bruised."

"I already feel bruised. Betrayed. Dishonored."

Donna had grabbed her hand from where they sat together on the couch. "I believe you, Kelly. This whole ordeal must be awful."

Jack insisted. "So, what happened, Kelly? Is Matt Buzz Campbell's kid?"

"Shush, Jack! Matt might hear you," Donna said.

He waved a hand. "He's been asleep for a few hours now."

"I don't care. Voice down."

Kelly waved a hand. "It's okay. Matt sleeps like the dead." She looked at this couple whom she'd only known since Matt started day care two years ago. But what did it matter? If she intended to fight Buzz Campbell, which she did, she'd have to get comfortable telling her closely guarded secret out loud—over and over again.

"Okay, I will tell you what Evan knows. But understand one point. I require your discretion with this information. It could wound Matt terribly and I will do nothing to hurt my boy."

Jack nodded. "Fair enough."

She took a moment to collect her nerve. She'd spent seven long years making the assault become a memory of little importance. The joy and love she received from her precious son had made the task easy. Never speaking of it had somehow deadened it in her mind. Made it seem as if it had happened to someone else—another Kelly from long ago.

Building a life for Matt, renovating Neverland, developing her network of friends had all worked as a catharsis for what truly mattered in life. Retelling the story made her feel dirty again. The shame of the attack was gone.

Through counseling she'd learned to understand that she had been a victim of someone else's actions, actions of which she'd done nothing to attract.

But recounting the event brought the moment alive in her mind. She'd often wondered if her rooms had been set on the other side of the Campbell house more for Buzz's convenience rather than her own privacy. When she'd awakened to see Buzz standing over her bed, she knew the family would not hear them in those late hours.

He had torn her favorite nightgown down the front, using his body to hold her down. The sound of the tearing fabric still echoed in her ears because the cold air suddenly accosting her skin contradicted the heat of his probing hands. When he'd raised himself to release himself from his pants, she used the moment to scramble for the door, but he'd locked it when he'd entered and snagged her around the waist, pulling her back. Her actions did nothing but excite him more. He wasted no time.

What embedded in her mind so deeply during this ordeal was her helplessness against his strength. The salt taste of Buzz's hand as he held it over her mouth, the scotch on his breath invading her nostrils, the wild almost insane excitement in his eyes reflected in the dim light as he pumped inside her, stealing her virginity and uncaring that he hurt her. Then psychologically, he humiliated her with ugly words of how she had seduced him to give her what she wanted while her body and mind decried his violation. And worse. When she had an orgasm even as she struggled, her body's betrayal had brought Campbell to climax. Sated and arrogant, with his full weight on top of her, he had wiped her tears and caressed her face as if they had been the most intimate of lovers.

The experience was awful. Blinded by tears when he'd gone, she had kicked the ruined nightgown into her closet because she couldn't bring herself to touch the garment. She'd curled up on the floor in her shower and wept under the steaming water, wanting to die.

These were the memories that resurrected when she recounted the story. These she had to tamp down to keep her words sounding neutral.

She met their gazes and as bluntly and calmly as possible said, "Buzz Campbell raped me."

IF KELLY THOUGHT the cameras and reporters had been bad the first time, she was sadly mistaken. Camped out five-to-six deep in front of Neverland, passersby had to step into the street to get around the sidewalk. Gratefully, she had left Matt at Donna's while she tried to put their world in some semblance of order. Now, any thought she had about stopping at Neverland to touch base with Bunny in person was shot to hell. No way would she exit the taxi.

She slouched down in the seat. "Don't stop, driver. Keep going."

After gawking at the crowd in front of Neverland, he glanced at her in the rear-view mirror. "Hey, aren't you the gal who owns that joint? The one they're jawing about on television?"

She considered denying it, but then decided she'd start her campaign at the grass roots. "Yes. But, I'm here to tell you. The senator is lying."

"Really? That's not his kid?"

Oh, God. Dare she say it? "What I'm saying is that I didn't seduce him. The senator lied."

The guy whistled softly. "What are you gonna do, lady?"

Her laugh caught in her throat. "There's the million-dollar question." She didn't even know where she should go to avoid the press.

Yes she did. Michael. When all else failed, she now had family right here in the good old U.S.A. They might find where she was hiding, but Michael would make sure they didn't get to her.

She speed dialed Michael's number. As it rang she said to the driver, "Would you mind returning me to the place you picked me up?"

EVAN BURST INTO Steve's office angry enough to punch the man. He had called Steve several times after Kelly left last night, but got voice mail. Now, Steve had a ton of explaining to do. His reasons had better be a matter of life or death—and that might not be enough.

At the look on Evan's face Steve stood. "If you hit me, I'll press charges."

Evan could not remember ever being so angry. He wasn't a violent man but he sure felt like he could put a dent in something. "What the hell have you done, Steve? I specifically asked you not to disclose the DNA information on the air."

"You force my hand, Evan. I had no choice."

"Me? How?"

Steve's steely blue gaze grew hot with conviction. He pointed out the immense office window reflecting the orange traces of dawn creeping into the sky behind the nightlights of the city. "You were going to lie to the world on camera. If the truth got out your career would be finished. I'm not about to let that happen, even if you are."

"So you had Dean expose Campbell yesterday before I could announce my wedding and my son this morning. How convenient. Why don't you tell me the truth, Steve? You just wanted NCTV to be the first to blow this story wide-open. You don't give a shit about Kelly, Matt or *my* well-being, for that matter."

"Don't be ridiculous, Evan. If Kelly has a gripe, she needs to nail that bastard's ass. Now, she has the ammunition to do it."

Evan stepped back. "Are you kidding me? Who made you God? These are people's lives you're talking about here. You used to understand that, Steve. You and I. Remember? We were going to make reporting what it was meant to be. Somewhere along the line you've become a bottom-feeder just like the rest of them."

Steve's nostrils flared. "I am delivering responsible news, Evan." He poked the air with his finger. "You are not. You got your goddamn heart wrapped up in that redhead and are holding back facts. If I didn't shoot that newscast it wouldn't be long before other stations got wind of the story."

"You are wrong, Steve. No one knew about the DNA except us. And no one knows the truth behind the story, except me. You've always trusted my judgment. You've always given me whatever time and resources I needed to bring a story to light. What is it? Political pressure from your boss? Ratings? That fat bonus to pay off your beach house? *You* caved here, Steve. Not me."

The two men were practically nose-to-nose. Their voices no doubt were carrying down the corridor as folks starting coming from their offices to view their argument from the fishbowl that was Steve's sprawling office.

Steve glanced at the onlookers then turned back to Evan. He released a held breath. "You know something, Ev? I think this is one time you've put too much emotion into your story. I'll have Bethany sit in for you this morning and we'll run the interviews you've already taped. Why don't you take a long weekend and think this one through. We'll talk again on Monday."

Just like that, Steve was tossing a left-handed threat.

He was sending him home for what? To rethink how important his job was? Recount the ten years he and Steve have built between them? His commitment to moral journalism? Did Steve want him to take time off to remember how hard he'd worked and how far he'd come in achieving his heart's dream? Was he supposed to reevaluate whether his own stance on Kelly was right for the good of the station and his job?

Like a finger snap, it hit. Nothing meant more to him than Kelly. Even when he was in Europe she had invaded his thoughts and curled up in his mind like a soft caress. Now over these past months, her strong will, drop-dead gorgeous Irish grin and those smiling eyes had burrowed into his heart. He was hooked on her sexy brogue and alluring body. She'd snagged his heart for good last night when they made love and she looked at him with passion and awe in her eyes like she'd never known such magic, never felt such happiness. And Matt's face when he had hugged his legs and called him Dad. He almost groaned knowing he'd lost these two precious people in his life because his boss and friend ignored his request in favor of making headlines.

No, Evan didn't need to take a few days off to ponder his future. He knew exactly what to do.

Meeting Steve's gaze, he sighed. "Forget it, Steve. I don't need a long weekend. You can give my job to your new rising lackey. I quit."

Steve scoffed. "You can't quit. We have a contract. You're mine for the next three years."

Evan headed for the door. "So sue me."

"WHAT DO YOU mean, you quit your job?" Julie McKenna and Evan's dad, Sean, were having their morning coffee in their suite at the Ritz. They had come in for the wedding. Of course, Julie became distressed that he wasn't on the television when they had turned on the show to watch their son. "Who'll do your show?"

"Bethany Dodge. She'll do fine."

Sean refilled his cup from the steaming coffeepot. Evan shared the same aqua-blue eyes as Julie, but he had inherited his dad's tall, lean build. Strands of silver hair streaked Sean's jet-black hair as it would eventually streak Evan's. Sean's light brown eyes reflected the intelligence and humor that Evan so admired in his dad. Those eyes never missed a trick. Sean McKenna was a master at assessing situations and human behavior in their true light. As a man in his sixties, Sean proved an excellent role model of vitality and success in both his private and professional life. Evan felt nothing but pride and love for his father.

Sean added sugar to his refreshed cup. "Is it safe to assume a drastic measure like quitting your job involves this woman who's been ensconced in your home?"

Dad was using his subtle way of omitting Kelly's name and their expected nuptials to infer that he'd yet to meet the woman Evan intended to marry. "Kelly, Dad. Yes and no."

Julie sipped her coffee. "Uh-oh. Sounds like a news report in itself."

Evan expelled a breath, more fatigued by this turn of events than he wanted to admit. "For the first time in ten years, Steve refused to trust me on Kelly's involvement with Buzz Campbell. He wanted a story first, while damning our duty to protect the source. He did a ton of damage releasing the interview. I won't work that way."

"Couldn't you have simply argued over the points beforehand and come to a conclusion?"

Evan took the coffee cup his mother handed him. "I thought we had done that. It wasn't until Sarah called to warn me about the interview airing that I'd even known. I thought the piece had been tabled."

Sean nodded. "I watched the interview. That bastard senator is lying through his teeth."

Evan put down his coffee cup in frustration. "Like a Persian carpet on a sultan's throne, Dad. He has so knotted up that story."

Sean ran a hand over his unshaven chin. "So, from your ferocity about this story, I'm taking it that what your mother told me is true?"

Evan met his father's gaze. If he could trust anyone in this life to back him, it was his parents. "Kelly's experience with Campbell consists of one encounter which was not condoned by her."

Julie frowned. "This turn of events is serious."

"You have no idea, Mom."

"But if you quit, how can you help her?"

Evan shook his head. "Don't know. Haven't figured that out."

Sean tilted his head as a thought occurred to him. "Are you still getting married today?"

Evan answered with a laugh. "Oh, I doubt that very much, Dad. I'm not expecting to see Kelly any time soon after last night's broadcast."

If Sean was relieved Evan wasn't fulfilling his marriage plans, nothing showed on his face except concern over the fact that his son was upset.

Julie laid a hand on his arm. "Don't tell me she's blaming you for the story."

Evan nodded. "She thinks I've drawn her into some elaborate scheme to use her and Matt as a means to bring Campbell down in his candidacy. She's left the penthouse and refuses to talk with me."

"Oh, dear."

He looked at his parents, ready to bear his soul. "When I came home and found her running Neverland and still single, I have to tell you, I just about howled with my dumb luck. Now, I'm afraid I've lost her."

Julie's smile worked all the way up to her eyes. "Well, I'll be damned, Sean, my dear. I believe our boy is in love."

Sean grinned. "He is all moo-eyed like I was the first day you stepped into my line of vision, my love. Looks like we've got to help this poor bastard."

Under any other circumstances, Evan would have laughed, but he was too miserable to appreciate the humor. He didn't miss the shared look between his parents that only time-honored love could bring. He'd come close to starting a relationship with a woman capable of developing that same affection. His gut twisted at the loss.

Julie sipped her coffee, delight all over her face. "I do like Kelly and her son is a good boy."

"Yes, dear, but let's get to the point here." Sean looked at Evan. "If you wanted Steve to table the interview, what did you have in mind?"

For the first time since the news report last night, Evan felt a glimmer of hope returning. He leaned toward his parents, elbow on his knees. "File for legal guardianship of Matt then start knocking on doors. If Campbell can be brought up on assault charges and we put him in jail, Buzz will be considered unfit to be around Matt and will lose all custody rights. The boy will be safe."

Julie sat up. "You mentioned this at the penthouse."

"That's right, Mom. Her brother agrees with me. I may never be able to adopt Matt, but I surely can gain legal guardianship of him if I marry Kelly and we get Campbell arrested and convicted."

"So, where is Kelly now?"

Evan shook his head. "Either at her friend's house or in Brooklyn."

Sean reached for his cell phone. "Actually, son, that girl needs to marry you today. Exactly as planned. What's her number? I want to have a little chat with her."

CHAPTER FOURTEEN

THE GARDEN ROOM in the back of Michael's rectory reminded Kelly of their family parlor at home. The oak floors gleamed with a good polish, a comfortable leather couch flanked by upholstered armchairs nestled around a circular glass coffee table over a beautiful silk rug of deep greens pulling in the colors from outside. The view into the garden through the bay windows framed the lushness of the small enclave.

A Steinway parlor grand piano occupied a corner behind the couch, where Matt currently plunked out discordant tunes with one finger. Kelly sat on the couch facing Michael with her bare feet tucked beneath her. They'd been speaking quietly and indirectly so as to not allude to anything that Matt might overhear and become distressed over.

Clearly, Michael was getting frustrated with his inability to speak directly. He stood. "Let's take a walk in the garden, shall we?"

Once outside he didn't hesitate for a moment.

"I saw the broadcast last night, Kelly. I think you are making a huge mistake. If Evan said he had nothing to do with that interview, I believe him."

"Well, I don't. You don't know Evan as I do."

Michael shook his head. "No, dear sister, I don't think you know him at all. The man I interrogated over lunch for the first time the other day is nothing but honest, sincere and, dare I say, madly in love with you."

She looked up, stunned. "Really?" Then she waved away the notion. "It doesn't matter. I can't trust him."

"And why not?"

"He's manipulative."

"You mean he's focused and achieves his goals."

"Well, then he's pushy."

Michael shrugged. "So you push back. You do have a backbone, girl. Look at all you've done for yourself up to now."

They walked side by side, pacing the length of the lawn. "Kelly, please understand, I'm not one to insist a woman marry a man she does not love, but Senator Campbell will take your son from you unless you take steps to make his reach more difficult."

She stopped in her tracks. "You want me to marry Evan?"

His lips pressed into a determined line as he formed his answer. "Do you have feelings for the man, lass?"

"Campbell?"

"No, Evan. Don't be daft."

That damned lump rose in her throat, surprising her with the threat of tears. "Michael, we made love last night. He was my first. We had just finished discussing how taking vows today would not be so difficult, given the...um... compatibility we discovered with each other."

He laughed. "You're blushing!"

"Michael, he terrifies me."

Michael shook his head. "No, he doesn't. You're mixing him up with the only experience you've ever had. The only man who hurt you—oh, wait. *Da* is a bit of a chauvinist, as well."

She sighed. "You see my point. I *love* my freedom."

Concern filled his eyes. "If New York law is as skewered as it seems on this issue, I don't think you can afford that luxury any longer. You need to be marrying Evan. Today."

"What if I am right? What if he really is doing all this for headline news?"

"What if Evan is telling the truth and he can muscle Campbell into a corner?"

For the first time in days, she felt a fire rise in her heart. Buzz Campbell—out of her life forever? She was so busy believing he could not be beaten that she hadn't considered the *what if* of Evan's professional prowess.

Wonder filled her voice. "Do you really believe we can get him convicted?"

A chuckle rose in his throat. "The Evan McKenna I had lunch with can certainly rattle that cretin's cage." Michael grabbed both her hands. "If you think Evan has been manipulating you, then turn the tables. Use him to save your son from an evil man."

She sighed. "Evan says he loves me."

Michael punctuated his point with a finger in the air. "Good, then give him the chance to prove it." He put an arm around her shoulder. "Besides, after all is said and done, if you're unhappy I will personally annul your marriage. Do you think you can find the courage to save your son the only way that will work given the present time constraints?"

Matt burst out the back door, Kelly's cell phone in hand. "Mom, phone!"

Kelly glanced at the caller ID. Connecticut. She didn't know anyone from there who would have her number.

"This is Kelly."

"Kelly, my dear, this is Sean McKenna. Evan's father."

If he hadn't announced himself she would have thought she was speaking with Evan, only his voice was stronger and carried the brogue of her home turf. She looked at

Michael with bewilderment when he gestured to ask who was calling.

"Mr. McKenna. How do you do?"

Michael mouthed, "Evan?"

Placing her hand over the phone she whispered, "His father!"

When Sean began speaking she returned her attention to the call.

"I'm here in Manhattan with my lovely wife. We arrived last night to attend your wedding. It's already close to noon. Will we be seeing you shortly?"

She was so flustered, her mouth opened and closed a few times. "Well, sir, there has been a complication."

There was only a short pause. "Well, Evan is right here with us. He's explained your situation as delicately as possible. I have yet to meet you or your son, but Julie is smitten with you both. I trust her judgment completely. That said, with all due respect, I concur with Evan that it is in your very best interest to make this wedding happen today."

Just like Evan, the man was nothing if not direct. Kelly closed her eyes, inhaling a deeply needed breath. She was a woman who always believed she'd get nudges toward the direction she should go when indecision confounded her. This man whom she'd never met before must certainly be a nudge. She felt herself capitulating. Michael watched her with unveiled concern.

A small chuckle escaped her throat. "Well, sir, I can see clearly from whom your son gets his straightforward personality."

Sean McKenna's laughter on the other end actually made her smile. She would like this man. "I think you mean pushy, eh? Ah, we Irish. A stubborn lot."

"Aye, sir, but you must know I'm not happy with this current turn in events."

KATHLEEN PICKERING   225

He lowered his voice. "I understand. Believe me. I do. But I want you to know that we McKennas want to support you one hundred percent. We'll put all our guns behind you. Evan is willing to put on a suit if you'll meet him at two as arranged."

"Why would you do this for me?"

The man sighed. "Our son is in love, lass. We've lost loved ones before due to political strife. We'll not see it happen again in his life."

Evan had either told them the truth or was working his story on his parents in order to get Kelly where he wanted her. Kelly's eyes shot from Michael to Matt then skyward, her gaze landing on the church steeple next door. Dare she believe that perhaps she truly was wrong about Evan?

"Will you be there?" Sean McKenna's voice held concern.

She released her held breath. "Aye, sir. I'll show. Only, please understand if I'm a few minutes late. I'm not dressed for the occasion."

EVAN ALTERNATED BETWEEN sitting in a chair to jumping out of his seat and staring out the twenty-first-floor window of his attorney's office. Quince Jacobs, a bespectacled middle-age and well-manicured man with sandy-blond, receding hair was not only the family's long-trusted attorney, but Sean's neighbor and close friend. Evan had already discussed the possibilities of adopting Matt with him, only to confirm that it would be practically impossible while Campbell lived and claimed a tie to the boy. Quince concurred Evan's best bet was legal guardianship with a handful of possible caveats. For now, that would be enough.

Quince had expressed reservations about Evan's plan to marry Kelly due to the urgency in Evan's request. He knew the McKenna family long enough to understand how passionate they became about social injustice. He didn't want the son of his best friend with a considerable financial standing to become legally bound to a woman for the wrong reasons—especially without a prenuptial agreement. Evan assured him that his motives went deeper than a rescue mission. Once he was married, he'd explain the situation in detail. Otherwise, he had politely informed Quince that there was no changing his mind.

The clock on the desk said five minutes until two o'clock. Sean and Julie were making use of Quince's time chatting business in the sitting area of his office. Champagne chilled in an ice bucket on the bar with six delicate champagne flutes on a tray beside the bubbly. He'd stopped at Van Cleef's on the way over and bought two simple gold wedding rings. He'd guessed Kelly's ring size, using Julie's hand as a guide.

Now and again he caught his mother glancing in his direction. No doubt she wondered—as did he—if Kelly would show. She'd been all the way out in Brooklyn already determined not to marry him. To make an about-face like that was not easy for her to do. She could change her mind again and leave him stranded.

That thought, even though this marriage was one of convenience for her, made his mouth go dry. Not only did he want to do everything in his power to protect her and Matt from Campbell, but he wanted Kelly for himself. In his mind they were a perfect match. He could only hope that once they'd tackled the bull that was Buzz Campbell, they'd have a clear road on which to start their adventure together.

Or, she'd want out.

Or not show at all.

Both options twisted him up inside. He wanted a fighting chance before she walked away for good.

A quiet knock on the door and the secretary stepped in. "Miss Sullivan, sir."

Evan's heart punched against his ribs as Kelly stepped into the room. She looked stunning. A formfitting sheath of sheer peach draped her body like a hug and stopped just above her knees. Her hair was pulled up at the sides and caught with a sprig of baby's breath at the crown of her head. Delicate pearl earrings dangled from her lobes. The matching high-heeled sandals did beautiful things to her legs as she walked in, her head high, her eyes shining and her softly glossed lips slightly parted. Her cheeks looked pale, probably from nerves, but it gave her an ethereal fragile look, making Evan want to pull her into his arms and assure her she was safe with him.

Michael escorted her wearing his black priest vestments. On his heels came Matt in a pair of navy pants, a white shirt and polished black shoes. Matt ran up to Evan, who hunched down on one knee to greet the boy.

"Matt-man!"

"Hey, Dad! Mom said I could come if I dressed up."

Evan didn't miss the expressions on his parents' or Michael's face at Matt's easy use of the term, *Dad*. Evan loved it. This little boy's trust in him helped cement that he was doing the right thing. Evan stood to greet his bride.

"Kelly, you look amazing."

She gave a guarded but grateful smile. "I didn't have much time."

He bent to kiss her cheek and used the opportunity to whisper, "What made you change your mind?"

A look of determination filled her face. "I need you, Evan. I can't get around it."

Not willing to misinterpret anything, he searched her gaze. Then he smiled. "I'm glad."

Julie bustled forward. "Kelly, you had us thinking you'd be late shopping for something to wear. Here you are right on time and looking like an angel." She pulled Kelly into a hug. "Under the best of circumstances a wedding can be nerve-racking. You must be feeling overwhelmed."

Kelly laughed. "I wish the circumstances were different, Julie. Your support means the world to me."

Sean McKenna offered her a fatherly hug and a kiss on the cheek. "With one look I can see why Evan fell so hard. You are a beauty. And redheaded." He chuckled. "Evan is a braver man than I thought!"

The heat of a blush rose on her face. "Thank you…I think?"

Michael held out his hand. "How do you do, Mr. McKenna. I'm Michael Sullivan." He glanced from Sean to Evan. "There is no mistaking you for Evan's father."

Sean clasped his hand. "Happy to meet you, Father Michael. Will you co-officiate the ceremony?"

"I'm here to give the bride away. Though Kelly, Evan and Matthew have my blessing." Michael clapped Evan on the back as they shook hands. "Your son is a fine man."

Evan laughed. "I'm glad to be on your good side, Father."

Quince greeted them, then gestured to the group. "Now that we are all here. Shall we begin?"

The small party assembled before the desk. Evan and Kelly took their places before Quince. The wink he shot Evan said that from what he'd just witnessed he understood Evan's choice in a bride. He acknowledged Quince's concession with a satisfied nod.

Michael and Matt stood next to Kelly. Sean and Julie

next to Evan. Kelly handed her small bouquet of roses to Julie.

Evan was surprised at how calm he suddenly felt despite his racing pulse because Kelly's delicate perfume invaded his senses and all he could think about was how that scent on her neck intoxicated him while her arms and legs were wrapped around him last night. A wave of tenderness tightened his chest.

He met her gaze. "Are you ready?"

THE MOMENT FELT SURREAL. Kelly nodded first then forced the word from her lips. "Yes."

The smile crossing Evan's mouth tugged at her heart. He seemed so calm. So sure that they were doing the right thing. She wished she could have his confidence. Instead fear nipped at her insides. Until she remembered Michael's admonishing words. *Evan is the perfect weapon...*

Weapon, indeed. He looked so unbelievably handsome right now in his dark suit, his black hair brushing his collar, those lips—oh, Lord, she could still feel them trailing down her neck. She thought she'd melt if he kept watching her as if she was the only person on earth. The attorney cleared his throat as if waiting for them to stop staring at each other.

When she looked away, Evan turned his attention to Quince, as well.

He began.

"Evan Thomas McKenna, do you take Kelly Ann Sullivan to be your wife?"

Evan's smile was devilish. "I do."

"Do you promise to love, honor, cherish and protect her, forsaking all others and holding only unto her?"

He nodded once as if the seriousness of the moment settled in his mind. "I do."

The minister turned to Kelly. "Kelly Ann Sullivan, do you take Evan Thomas McKenna to be your husband?"

Kelly released a breath. With the way Evan was watching her, if nothing else in the world mattered, she would not hesitate to reply. "I do."

"Do you promise to love, honor, cherish and protect him, forsaking all others and holding only unto him?"

Oh, Lord, was she lying? "I do."

Quince addressed Evan. "Do you have the rings?"

He pulled them from his pocket. He gave Kelly an apologetic look. "I had no time to engrave them. I was thinking we could get to that task when we are clear on what we'd like to say."

Behind her, Michael cleared his throat.

She gazed at the circlets of gold in his palm. He'd gotten rings. She hadn't even thought of them. Now he was concerned because they hadn't been engraved. She wanted to reach up and press away the crease forming between his eyebrows. This simple gesture, holding rings in his open palm, weakened her knees. He cupped her hand when he handed her the one he'd chosen for himself as if depositing a precious talisman in her care. Was the man a hopeless romantic?

"They are beautiful, Evan. Just as they are."

His smile reflected relief.

She wanted to kiss him.

Quince continued. "Evan, repeat after me. 'I, Evan Thomas McKenna...'"

Evan didn't wait for Quince to lead him. He took Kelly's hand in his. Placing the ring at the top of her finger, he began, "I, Evan Thomas McKenna, take you Kelly Ann Sullivan, to be my wife. To have and to hold, in sickness and in health, for richer or poorer. I promise my love to you all the days of my life. With this ring, I thee wed."

He slid the ring onto her finger with the utmost care. When it fit, he breathed a sigh of relief. He lifted her fingers and kissed the ring.

The slip of gold along her skin made Kelly light-headed. She watched his bent head as he kissed the ring and decided Evan was either a consummate actor or he meant every word he said. While the delicate band felt light as a feather and cool on her finger, she felt like she'd just accepted the weight of the world.

Quince was watching her. He sensed her trepidation because gentleness filled his gaze. "Repeat after me, Kelly…"

She gave him a grateful glance. "Wait, let me see if I can do this. You correct me if I make a mistake."

He nodded. "Okay."

Her heart thudding in her chest, she reached for Evan's left hand. The heat of his palm in hers had the same effect it did last night. Electricity. She inhaled a deep breath and placed the ring on his finger, just above the first knuckle.

Staring at the gleaming gold band, she said, "I, Kelly Ann Sullivan, take you, Evan Thomas McKenna to be my husband." That damned lump started rising in her throat. She swallowed hard. If she was going to get through this she needed Evan's help. She raised her gaze, letting the intensity in his sky-blue eyes pull her in like a magnet. "To have and to hold, to cherish above all others, in sickness and health, through good times and bad, whether richer or poorer. I promise my love to you all the days of my life. With this ring, I thee wed."

She slid the ring on his hand, not believing her own actions because she'd just spoken words she could not honestly claim. Yet somewhere inside, the moment seemed true. Matt had stepped around Michael to get a full view of their exchange. She glanced down at his beaming face and tears sprang into her eyes.

Her baby was happy.

They now had a fighting chance.

Evan was watching her as if concerned she'd disappear in a puff of smoke. She managed a trembling smile. She owed it to Evan to be as true to her word as possible.

Quince said, "We're almost finished." He lifted a passage from the desk behind him and read,

"Evan and Kelly, just as two very different threads woven in opposite directions can form a beautiful tapestry, so can your two lives merge together to form a very beautiful marriage.

"To make your marriage work will take love. But it also will take trust—to know in your hearts you want the best for each other. It will take dedication—to stay open to one another—to learn and to grow even when this is not easy to do. It will take faith to go forward even when never really knowing what tomorrow will bring. In addition, it will take commitment to hold true to the journey you both commit to share.

"Evan and Kelly, you have agreed to live together in matrimony and have promised your love for each other. I now declare you husband and wife." He smiled at Evan. "Congratulations. You may kiss the bride."

Kelly wanted to run. Panic bubbled inside her as Evan leaned in for the kiss. She shouldn't have done this. It was unfair to Evan. Unfair to her. She'd lied about promising her love. She felt something, but was it *love?* His arm snaked around her waist, pulling her against him. His eyes, intent only on her, said he would not kiss her unless she permitted it. It was that look—that restraint that made her understand that this marriage was not a power play. When her lips parted, ever so slightly, the corners of his mouth turned up. Before she could close her eyes he captured her lips with his, pressing the full weight of his intention against her mouth. She kissed him back, knowing she couldn't stop herself if she tried.

THREE HOURS LATER, after an early dinner at Aquavit, Kelly, Evan and Matt found themselves back at the penthouse, the doorman behind them with the suitcases Kelly had lugged out last night. She felt like the silver ball in that pinball machine in the game room.

It was still early, so there was no chance of putting Matt, or herself, to bed. She'd had several glasses of champagne to still her nerves, so felt a tad tipsy. The champagne, however, did nothing to relieve her conscience. Marrying Evan had been a consummate lie.

She would burn in hell, for sure.

She felt equally guilty because dinner had been delightful. The party, including Quince, was small enough that conversation flowed easily. Michael, Sean and Quince discovered they shared the same passion for golf, which had Evan rolling his eyes because it was the one sport his father could never get him to try. Sean and Michael exchanged stories about life in Ireland, making Kelly laugh at how much of a mischief-maker Sean had been as a boy in Dublin. Matt had been laughing right along with the men just like a little man, himself. His eyes grew wide when Sean insisted with a grin that Matt not try any of his nonsense.

When Quince asked her about Neverland, she shared how ownership of the diner came into her hands, again grateful for Herby George's generosity. She swallowed hard when she voiced how she hoped he'd be proud of the changes she made. The pride in Evan's eyes as she spoke took her by surprise. She wasn't sure why. She supposed that, despite his compliments in the past, her success never really mattered to him.

Seated next to her, his body was so close she could feel

his heat, smell his cologne, his size imposing enough that she had to look around him to answer Quince's question at the end of the table. At his side, she felt an odd mixture of vulnerability and security. Evan asked Matt, who sat on her other side, what he thought of his mom running Neverland. When her son answered that she was the best, he and Evan reached across her to slap a high five that had the table smiling, and had him leaning into her enough that she briefly rested her head on his shoulder as she laughed.

What really shook Kelly was that the pride she saw in Evan's eyes when she told her story about Neverland was the same pride she'd noted in Julie's eyes for her husband when he'd been recanting his teenage escapades. Kelly wasn't sure what to do with the warmth Evan's look stirred in her. Julie's pride reflected the deep affection that had grown for her husband through the years. Her charm and sense of humor simply seemed like another link binding these two charismatic people together. Hearing stories from their life together, including the tragedy of losing her brother, showed that the strength of character, trust and devotion they found in each other had carried them to this wonderful life they shared today. Watching Julie so comfortable in her own skin and willing to share her joy with everyone around her reflected her contentment with the choices she made in her life, including her husband.

To find a love like that would take Kelly's breath away. Evan's glance made her see how far away that chance was for her. He might be showing her affection, but she'd taken vows under a lie. It didn't matter that she had the chance to meet and like her new in-laws—oh, it felt so strange to say those words—which could make this union so much easier. Her marriage to Evan was doomed. It was founded on an unworthy foundation that she had created. She was the cornerstone to the impending calamity. She had to set the record straight.

Evan tipped the doorman and closed the door. Sheer horror must have crossed her face because he laughed.

"You look like a deer in headlights, woman. Relax. It's me. Evan."

"I know who you are." She looked down at the ring on her finger. Her hands were shaking.

"Hey…"

Evan came over and slowly wrapped her into his arms. She let him hold her because right now, the enormity of the situation threatened to knock her off her feet.

"No pressure, Kelly. Let's just take it easy. Before being husband and wife, we are friends. And as your friend, I really want you to calm down."

"Hey, Dad! Let's play pinball!"

The fact that this momentous occasion had very little effect on her son's world helped put her shock into perspective. The only difference was that her son was now calling her husband, Dad, and liking it. Her *husband!*

Evan called over Kelly's head. "You start, Matt-man. I'll be right there."

Kelly stepped from his arms. "I'm sorry, Evan. I feel like I've done us both the biggest disservice."

He frowned. "Getting married? Really?"

Her gaze settled on Matt as he fed a quarter into the pinball machine. She lowered her voice. This was not easy to say. "You know I'm using you to save Matt."

He lifted her chin to draw her attention to him. "I know, Red. I asked you to accept this exact plan a while ago. Remember?"

She nodded. "Yes."

"So now, we enjoy the rest of our lovely wedding day

as a family. Tomorrow, we begin our work as a team to remove Buzz Campbell from your life. Forever, if possible."

"That is why you married me?"

He shook his head slowly. "Why I married you can keep
for another time. Suffice it to say that I have no illusions
as to why you married me. When this mess is cleaned up,
if you want out, I will give you a divorce without question. Is that fair?"

Her throat tightened. "You would do that?"

He chuckled. "Willingly, but not happily."

The smile creasing her lips made her heart feel lighter.
"I just didn't want a lie between us about why I took those
vows."

He reached down and kissed her lightly on the lips. "No
lies here, Red. I understand."

"Thank you." She couldn't understand why suddenly
she felt so shy.

Evan held up a finger. "However, I have a caveat."

"What is that?"

"You must go on the occasional date with me. I almost
had you on a theater evening before this whirlwind struck."

Inwardly she sighed in relief. That was easy. She thought
it would involve sleeping in the same bed or something.
She hadn't quite come to terms with how they'd tackle
that subject yet.

She grinned. "I think I can surrender to those terms."

Heat lit his eyes. "Careful now, Red. I am vulnerable
to words such as *surrender.*"

She laughed out loud. "Well, then I *agree* to those
terms."

The pinball machine hit the jackpot because the bells
and whistles went off.

"Dad! Look at this!"

"I'm going to play pinball with my son. Would you like to cheer us on?"

She swallowed her answer. The conviction behind Evan calling Matt his son floored her. He was taking his role seriously. It occurred to her that Evan's drive to keep Matt from Campbell wasn't just about helping her.

Oh, God. So much to consider. She needed to be alone for a while. She glanced down at her dress. "I'd like to take some time to change my clothes and get more comfortable."

Appreciation filled his smile. "You look spectacular, Mrs. McKenna. If the situation was different, I'd be helping you peel out of that dress, very, very slowly."

Her heart skipped a beat. "Please, Evan."

He bit his lower lip. "I understand." He spread his arm in a flourish in the direction of her room. "Please make yourself comfortable. Right now, that's the best I can hope for."

TONIGHT WAS TECHNICALLY the first night of their honeymoon. Matt had been in bed for about an hour. Kelly's first impulse was to retreat to her room for the evening, but her inner coward refused to take root. Now that she had taken this enormous leap into the unknown with Evan, she decided it best if they delineated some ground rules.

She'd changed from her dress to a pale yellow sandwashed gypsy skirt with a white tank top and white ballerina slippers. She'd twisted her hair into a braid that fell on one shoulder and caught the end with a leather tie. She'd removed all jewelry except for her wedding ring, which she fingered nervously now as she sat on the balcony. The city lights framed the undeveloped dark space that was Central Park. She took small comfort knowing that a chunk of Manhattan had been preserved with woods.

Evan emerged through the door, tray in hand and a lap blanket over one arm.

"What do you have there?"

"A little something to sweeten the end of a beautiful day."

He placed the tray on the table. An opened bottle of Pol Roger champagne chilled in an ice bucket. Two flutes. A dish of strawberries and a plate of dark chocolates. With a flourish he opened a crisp white napkin and laid it in her lap. The lap blanket he draped behind her chair. "In case a breeze rises."

His attention tugged on her heart while raising an alarm. "Is this a plan for seduction?"

He grinned. "It could be if you allow it. Otherwise, no. Consider this a tribute to your courage for marrying me."

"Oh, Evan, you are smooth."

He shook his head. "No, Red. I speak the gospel truth. I also have an announcement to make which may require celebration—depending on your point of view."

He filled the glasses, handed one to her, took one for himself and pulled his chair close to hers before sitting.

They touched rims and sipped. He offered her a strawberry. She took it. As he watched her bite into the red flesh and smile as the ripeness exploded on her tongue, she had the feeling that he had wanted to feed it to her himself.

"Hmm. Delicious. Thank you."

He helped himself to one.

Kelly settled back into her chair. "So what are we celebrating?"

He lifted his flute from the table. "In all the excitement of our nuptials today I never had the chance to tell you that I quit my job."

Kelly bolted forward. "What?"

Amusement lit his eyes. "I thought you'd react that way."

"Evan, why?"

He reached for a chocolate and popped it into his mouth. Chewing he said, "Steve didn't offer a good enough reason for why he aired the Campbell interview. I had expressly asked him to support me in exposing Campbell without using you and he ignored me."

She sat back in her chair, dumbfounded. "Evan. You didn't."

He nodded, entirely sober. "I did. I told you I had nothing to do with that interview."

"So you didn't host your show this morning?"

"Nope. Bethany Dodge did a fine job."

"Don't you care?"

She didn't miss the tightness setting his jaw as he thought over his answer. After a moment he nodded. "Yes, I care very much. I love my job. It's my chance to make viewers aware of our moral obligation to each other. But Steve overstepped the line of this code we held between us. He said he'd done it for my own good. I don't believe that was entirely true."

He sipped the clear liquid from his flute. A soft smile curled his lips. "This champagne was Winston Churchill's favorite. We drink in good company. Bully for us."

Frowning, she toasted him once more. Those refreshing, delightful bubbles were wreaking havoc with her emotions to begin with. Hearing that Evan quit his job because of *her* made her want to gulp the remains and refill the glass. He'd waited all day to tell her, as if the information was an afterthought.

"What are you going to do?"

He shrugged. "Honestly? Right now it frees me up to research my original plan to protect you against Buzz. I wasn't kidding when I said I believe we can get him convicted."

"How?"

"Ideally? Plan A is to ask you to speak publicly about what truly happened between you and Buzz. Then get Quince to explain how you had no choice but to hide Matt to protect you both from further damaging interactions with Buzz. That would clarify why you went underground with your child. I can guarantee you that the majority of the population has no idea how damaging the current laws are against women who keep children born from rape."

Kelly practically choked. "No, Evan. I can't do that!"

He held up a hand. "I know, Red. Hear me out."

This time she took a mouthful of champagne and swallowed it in a lump down her throat.

Evan noticed. "Easy, girl. Small sips. This is worth enjoying."

"The way you're jumping from my personal life to your love of this champagne is nerve-racking."

He settled back in his chair. "May I explain myself?"

She was suddenly feeling edgy. His insistence that she do his bidding—exactly what she didn't want to do—had her guard rising. She waved a hand. "Certainly."

"All I'm trying to do is calm you down. Do you really think I don't understand how traumatized you were by this experience with Buzz? Do you think I don't understand how disappointed you must have been when your life turned upside down and steered you away from your original plans? Do you think I don't understand the absolute conviction, courage and strength it took to work those exhausting hours for the past seven years as a single mom to keep your son safe while still finding joy in your child and your life? Do you think that I don't admire your independent spirit? Or that while I might turn you on as a lover—and oh, by the way, a lover like you I have never known—you are such a classy and morally sound woman that you still refused to jump at the chance to marry me, even to lighten your burden?

"I can guarantee that you never even once considered me as a cash source because you are so fiercely proud. Did you know that I don't even think that *I* could sacrifice my happiness to marry a person I did not love in a complete last effort to protect my son? You amaze me, Kelly Sullivan. You absolutely have rocked my world. So finally, I ask you. Do you think for one second that I would ask you to do anything that would hurt you or Matt?"

Her mouth fell open. Evan Thomas McKenna was completely clear on what she had gone through to reach this point in her life. Knew the heartache and danger she faced right now, lost his job over it and married her anyway.

Unbelievable.

He leaned close and intertwined his left hand with hers so their rings reflected the soft candlelight. "I believe it is in your best interest to accuse Buzz Campbell of rape and have the bastard tried, convicted and thrown in jail."

When she went to protest he held up a stopping hand.

"But, I will honor your need to protect Matt, even though I think he would come to understand how much you love him despite his origins. So, mark my words. I will put Buzz Campbell in jail with or without your help. I just want you to be clear on what I'm going to do."

"The devastation runs so much deeper than Matt and me, Evan. I'm thinking of Madeline Campbell and Emily and Mary Kate. I loved that family. If I call Buzz a liar and declare rape, my accusations would damage those three in the exact same manner Dean's interview damaged me and Matthew. I simply will not hurt anyone else over that man's crime. If you have a Plan B, I'd love to hear it."

He shrugged. "Plan B removes you entirely and entails hooking up with Doyle for his contacts with accusations against Buzz. Then I'd conduct interviews of my own and some in-depth probing into Campbell's college days and what not. A man just doesn't wake up one morning and decide to be a rapist. This is a pattern that had to develop over time. I plan to put the trail together and create a profile to convince a judge and jury of his guilt."

She shook her head in amazement. "Remind me never to make you angry."

Grinning, he stood and held out his hand. "What I'd like to do is whoop your tail at a game of pinball."

"Um. I was thinking we should set some ground rules for this marriage of convenience between us."

He thought a moment. "It is convenient, isn't it? I get you to live in my home all the time now." A heart-stopping look crossed his face. "Now if you could only find it convenient to make your home in my bed, that would truly be a marriage."

She wagged a finger at him. "Ground rules, Evan?"

"Okay. But, first a game of pinball. We have all weekend to hammer out the details. It's a perfect way to celebrate our honeymoon."

She laughed at the absurdity.

He put his flute in her hand. "You take the glasses. I'll take the tray."

"I've never played pinball."

He grinned. "I know. I'm thinking we should play blindfolded."

HER PERFUME WAS driving him wild. It would have been one thing if they hadn't made love yet, but he'd already had her. He knew what she felt like, smelled like, sounded like lost in lovemaking, how she moved when he was deep inside her. He didn't know how long he could remain charming and understanding. All he wanted was more. Wanted her closer so he could breathe her air, feel the warmth of her skin close to his body, feel the tickle of her hair on his face. But no.

He'd settled for pinball. It was the only way he'd get close and not scare her off.

At least Kelly was smiling again. He'd done all but declare his love for her on the balcony, but at least he reached her. He was that much closer in getting her to believe that she could trust him. Now, he'd whoop her ass at pinball and get that Irish temper going so she'd compete with him and return them to some common ground. There was no place they needed to be tomorrow. The night was young and Evan wasn't tired. Not when Kelly smelled so good and looked so damned sexy.

Her tank top had ridden up, exposing her flat belly and the soft skin at her hips. The gauzy skirt swayed with her steps, attracting his eye like a bull to a red cape. Last night's tangle with her was all too fresh in his mind. Just coming down the stairs this morning after experiencing her on each rung gave a whole new perspective of how he was viewing his home since Kelly arrived. He wanted to taste her again. Make her his, one more time.

He'd have to be a patient man.

He grabbed a fistful of quarters from the bowl. He lined the coins along the side of the glass top of the machine. Kelly refilled their flutes from the tray he placed on the ottoman. She took a bite of strawberry then pressed the remainder to Evan's lips. He bit. Next she broke off a piece of chocolate and popped it into his mouth. The smaller piece she fed to herself. They both chewed, watching each other. Evan hummed his delight.

"What a great idea to mix the flavors. That's what I like about you, Red."

Taking his glass in one hand, Kelly's hand in his other, he maneuvered her to the front of the pinball machine. He hesitated. "Think we'll wake Matt?"

"No. He sleeps pretty soundly. Besides, he ate so much food and dessert, I think he stored enough to hibernate for winter. We should be fine."

He grinned. "Excellent."

He dropped a quarter into the slot. The machine sounded its dastardly laugh as the lights flashed around the face board characters of Flash Gordon, his love interest Dale Arden and the evil Ming the Merciless.

Kelly laughed. "So I press these levers on the side? And I pull back this pin and shoot the ball?"

He gave her what he hoped was a smug glance. "Sure, but it takes coordination and an excellent sense of timing to keep the silver ball moving. Here, let me show you."

He stepped up behind her, careful not to get too close. He loved how she fit tidily within his arms, the crown of her head just below his chin.

She tensed. "Tell me you're not going to use pinball to seduce me."

He chuckled. "No, we're playing pinball because I'm determined not to seduce you."

She was silent a moment. "Oh."

Did he hear disappointment in that one little syllable? "Okay, so you have to relax, Red." He placed her hands on the sides of the machine. "Press the flippers a few times before launching the ball so you can get a feel for their flexibility."

Flexibility. He'd have to use different words.

She tapped the buttons on the side and watched the flippers move. "Okay, I think I have the feel."

The feel. "Yeah, you sure do."

She laughed. "Stop it now."

He had to resist nuzzling his face in her hair. With extreme discipline he stepped to the side. "Okay, when you're ready, launch the ball. Let's see how you do."

Twenty minutes later, Kelly was jumping in the air, cheering herself on. She'd soundly trounced his butt and won the match.

He couldn't help but grin. "Beginner's luck. I declare a rematch."

"Not tonight, buster. I'm not taking the chance of handing my victory over so quickly."

Heat lit his eyes, he knew it. "You are beautiful when you are victorious, Red, but I especially like it when you jump up and down like that."

She swatted at his arm. "Funny man."

Color was high on her cheeks. An excellent mixture of champagne and fun. She was standing with her back to the pinball machine, her hands propped on the glass behind her doing wonderful things to her cleavage.

"What should we do now?"

He knew exactly what he wanted to do next. He didn't dare move from his place by the table where he'd gone for the last piece of chocolate. He gestured for her to have it. She declined.

"Do I get to choose?"

A slow grin crossed her mouth. "Hmm."

"That means?"

She pursed her lips. "No."

"Why not?"

"What would you choose to do?"

He blew out a breath. She shouldn't have asked a second time. In two steps he stood before her. "Given the chance, Red, I would do this..."

Using one finger to lift her chin, he descended on her mouth softly, but with a surety she could not miss. He held himself far enough away so that only his finger and his lips touched her. Gently, he probed, moving an inch closer, letting his breath mingle with hers in a heady mix of chocolate, sweet fruit and champagne.

She pressed back and he moved in, sliding his hands along her jaw to cup her face, his fingertips invading her hairline behind her ears.

She kissed him back like she meant it. God bless Pol Rogers.

When his tongue sought hers, she responded. Mindful of her back, he lifted her by the waist and hoisted her on the edge. Not breaking the kiss for a second, she snaked her arms around his neck and let him step between her legs draped by her flowing skirt.

He wanted to make love to her until she forgot she didn't trust him and fell so deeply and profoundly in love with him that she screamed his name out loud.

When his hands started caressing her belly, her torso, her breasts, she broke the kiss.

The look she gave him held angst. "Evan."

He pressed his forehead to hers. "Yes?"

"I own that I married you today. But, I cannot deceive you. I'm a little drunk. This feels really good, but I don't want to give myself to you again until, if and when, I can declare my love."

"What if I can declare mine? Right now."

She touched his lips with the pad of her fingers. "Thank you, Evan. But I must stand on these terms. Part of the ground rules I wanted to discuss."

He closed his eyes. She'd married him. He'd gotten her this far. He could wait. "I understand, Red. But may I say something?"

A small smile broke on her lips. "Of course..."

"Mom?"

They turned to see Matt standing in the middle of the court. Evan helped Kelly down from the pinball machine with a swift motion.

"Matt, what's wrong, son."

He pressed a hand to his stomach. "I don't feel so well."

And he proceeded to throw up his winter storage all over the polished floor.

CHAPTER FIFTEEN

KELLY SERVED THE bustling Monday-morning crowd feeling a step lighter. It felt good to be back in Neverland with the ordered chaos that was as familiar to her as her own hands. Bunny had been great by covering in Kelly's absence. To thank her, Kelly gave her three days off with pay. Of course, Bunny refused to take them right away, saying something about saving for an escape to the Bahamas. She'd been talking about this escape for four years now. Kelly suspected she never planned to go. Bunny was a woman who liked her routine. It was as simple as that. Kelly decided that after the holiday season she would take Bunny to the Bahamas herself.

Kelly never would have survived the huge undertaking that was the Neverland diner without her employees who had become friends. As she walked by, Jake whistled some tune off-key while he worked the grill, every once in a while glancing in her direction, she knew, to be sure no reporters bothered her. The floor staff laughed and chatted with customers as they deftly served the tables. Her crew worked like a well-oiled machine whether she was present or not. The value of their loyalty knew no price. Neverland thrived because she'd created a family from a colorful group of strangers who had been drawn to Neverland and spent a major portion of their waking time here. She had yet to fire anybody.

She, Evan and Matt may have done nothing on their so-called honeymoon weekend that resembled a honeymoon, but they spent the weekend playing in the penthouse away from prying eyes. Between movie marathons with popcorn and ice cream, basketball shoot-outs, pinball, laser tag, cooking homemade pizzas, they ate up the hours. Interacting as a family helped strengthen this budding friendship that Evan and Kelly were now bound by marriage to grow. Chances were good their union would not last, but at least she wouldn't have to pretend that she was enjoying this private time together.

Another perk to this arrangement surprised her: Evan helped share the responsibilities. He dived right in. Since he didn't return to work, Evan took Matt to school and would pick him up, thus ensuring her son could safely return to his daily routine. It was a godsend that the school had excellent security. Now that the principal understood Kelly and Matt's unique situation, she took extra steps to make sure everyone kept an eye on Matt while he remained unaware of their diligence. After school, instead of bringing him to Neverland, Evan and Matt would return to the penthouse, where he could play while Evan worked from his home office.

Kelly and Evan had taken time with Matt last night to explain how as a new family if anyone was to say anything to him about Kelly or himself, he should ignore them. Should any questions arise, both Kelly and Evan would be happy to answer them.

Matt had frowned. "But, you are my dad, Evan. Right?"

Not sure how to answer and not wanting to lie, Evan said, "Do you want me to be?"

Matt had looked from Evan to Kelly as if that was the dumbest question he'd ever heard. "Well, duh. Yeah!"

Evan tousled his hair. "Tomorrow I'll be sure Mr.

Quince draws up documents to make me in charge of you. How is that?"

Matt lifted his hand for a high five. "Okay!"

Kelly had also been glad to clear the air between her and Evan over their vows. She couldn't just marry him and use him as Michael had suggested, even though she suspected her brother didn't mean for her to be so mercenary as much as he was trying to get her to take the vows. No doubt his tradition-steeped heart believed she'd be safer beneath a man's wing.

Given the lies Campbell spewed in his interview with Dean, this time she agreed completely. But, she had to be true to her feelings. She would not lead Evan on romantically unless she truly felt love for him—though she was sorely tempted. Thinking about his touch made a delicious shiver run up her spine. She wondered how their heated moment on the pinball machine would have played out had she let it…or if Matt hadn't doused the moment as only a child could.

Some of the patrons started to boo and hiss when Evan's show came on and he wasn't at his desk giving the usual morning greeting. Instead, Bethany and Dean sat welcoming each other for the next week while Evan was on leave.

On *leave?*

She and Bunny exchanged glances. Kelly would ask Evan about their word choice as soon as she saw him.

Bunny worked the counter today while Kelly and two other waiters manned the main room. Kelly sensed Bunny's stare before she looked up to see a blonde woman talking to Bunny follow her gaze in Kelly's direction. Kelly stopped dead in her tracks.

Helen Thompson. Kelly hadn't seen her in seven years, but she'd know her anywhere. Dressed in business professional casual with a navy sheath, gold rope choker that was probably real and her hair scraped into a perfect French twist, she held Kelly's gaze until Kelly acknowledged that she recognized her. Helen then sat on the stool at the counter to wait.

Kelly finished pouring coffee for the women at the table and excused herself, working her way to the counter. She could guess what Helen wanted.

"Helen."

"Hello, Kelly. I know this must be a surprise."

The women shook hands. "A surprise, yes, but we were in need of speaking, so I am glad to see you. Would you like a cup of coffee?"

Not wanting anyone to overhear their conversation, she led Helen to the family booth by her office. Bunny followed with coffee and a plate of Kelly's favorite almond cookies.

Bunny gave Helen a harsh look before pouring their coffees. "I know who you are. I recognize you from the Doyle interview. I don't like how you dragged my friend into your little fight. Cheap shot." She looked at Kelly. "I wouldn't share your cookies with this one."

Kelly laughed. "That's enough, Bunny. Can you ask Jake and Kristin to spread out and cover my station for a bit?"

She turned her attention to Helen. Lifting the plate, she said, "Cookie?"

Helen glanced in Bunny's direction. "No, thanks."

"Oh, don't be silly. If Bunny was really irritated she wouldn't have brought the cookies at all. Take one. They're excellent with coffee."

Kelly broke a piece of the cookie and munched it, giving herself a chance to pull her wits together about this woman sitting across from her. She was determined to stay cool despite the fact that she'd been angrier than a nest of hornets when she'd first heard Doyle's interview. It took a few days for her to become okay with the fact that Helen had an accusation out on Campbell that needed to be addressed. That was her business. Kelly hoped that Helen hadn't pointed the finger at Kelly as much as Doyle built the scenario on his own. Guess it was time to learn the truth.

"I must say Bunny voiced the exact question I wanted to ask. Why did you drag me into your story?"

Helen put the untouched cookie on the plate holding her coffee mug. "That's why I'm here, Kelly."

She frowned. "Explain."

"On one hand, I'm compelled to apologize, but on the other, I'm not. Once I saw the photos of your son, I understood why you quit working for Madeline." She leaned forward, lowering her voice. "What I want to know is why you haven't pressed charges?"

Kelly sat rock still. She did not want to be pulled into this debacle, let alone admit the truth she'd never spoken aloud before Doyle's interview hit the airwaves. Now her circle of confidence was extremely small. She wanted to keep it that way.

"I have nothing to say, Helen. I left Madeline and the girls for my own reasons."

Helen sipped her coffee, black. "I don't believe you, Kelly. I knew you for three years. Your dedication to those girls showed how much you enjoyed your job."

"How did you know that?"

"Because when Madeline sat down with me to discuss hiring a new nanny, she was perplexed about why you bolted—because you did *bolt*. The night before, all was well. You helped put the girls to bed and retired for the evening. Next day, you were gone before noon. Madeline couldn't understand why you'd given up so much, when you seemed so happy with them."

Kelly's throat tightened. When she'd left the Campbell's she never looked back. Never called. Never sent cards to the girls. Nothing. She simply disappeared.

"I feel awful that I never explained myself to them."

"So, why would you do that if you didn't have the same problem with Buzz that I had?"

Kelly sipped her coffee. She needed something hot to burn the ache running down her throat. "You're charging Buzz with sexual harassment, yet you plastered me all over the screen as Campbell's lover. I'm not so sure I understand the justice you served me, Helen."

Color rose in Helen's cheeks. She was a striking woman. Slender, clear skin. Lovely blue eyes under slightly arched eyebrows. A beautiful smile. She even managed to maintain poise while she admitted cruelty.

"That was Doyle's idea."

"And you let him?"

Anger rose in her eyes. "Okay, Kelly. Truth of the matter is that Buzz Campbell raped me. Not once. Not twice, but four times before I was able to break his hold. After I saw your son I was convinced he'd done the same to you. We couldn't declare rape on television because we had no proof, but a child who is the spitting image of his rapist, except for having your eyes? Well, we might not be able to accuse Campbell of raping you, but we certainly could get your attention suggesting an affair that produced a love child. If we were wrong, you'd step forward to defend yourself."

Kelly sucked in a breath. "That's disgusting."

Helen sighed. "I know. For that, I apologize."

"Why didn't you come to me first?"

Helen frowned. "Jay Doyle did."

"He's a reporter. Why didn't *you* come to me?"

She wouldn't take her eyes from Kelly's. "In a word? *Shame*. I still struggle with my guilt as a rape victim. So, I let Jay contact you. Besides, while I believe I know what happened to you, what if I'm wrong? What if your entanglement with Buzz had been an affair that produced a child? If you had been Buzz's lover, how would I know if you still support him?" She opened her hands in resignation. "Look how blind Madeline is. I'd be standing there alone pointing the finger at a rapist with no proof except my word against a man who threatened to ruin my life if I ever spoke about what he'd done."

A shiver ran up her spine. Kelly understood all too well how convincing Buzz was in making a woman feel like she was to blame for his assault.

"Yet you haven't accused him of rape. Why go halfway?"

"I hate to admit this."

"What?"

"It's a strategy to blacken Campbell's name so he'll be forced to drop from the presidential candidacy."

"I don't understand."

"Think of a snowball running downhill. We're starting with a small stone and a little snow hoping it will grow larger as it rolls. My accusation will go from harassment to assault as we gain momentum."

"With me joining the fray."

"We think Campbell left a trail of women. I'm here to ask you to step forward and tell what really happened. You haven't said a word publicly."

"And it's going to stay that way, Helen. I've carved a good life here. I want to be left alone."

Helen reached a hand across the table as if reaching out for help. "What happened to your moral compass, Kelly?"

Swallowing the reflex to ask the woman the same question, she rephrased her thought. "Let me ask you. Did you seek out Doyle on this issue?"

"No. He contacted me."

"So you signed on for this crusade with the opposing political party to ruin Buzz? Is that an act of moral certitude or revenge on your part?"

Helen sat back in her seat, the wind taken from her sails. "I suppose I deserve that."

Kelly crossed her arms. "Do you care to answer?"

Helen studied her for a moment. "Kelly, I lost my need for revenge years ago. What I do know is that Buzz Campbell is a liar and violent toward women. I don't want a man like him running my country. I welcome the chance to bring Buzz down. I hope we are successful because I've put my personal life on the line. I hope to God Buzz falls and he falls hard."

A rush of guilt swamped Kelly for not taking the morally correct action and speaking out against Campbell's crime, but she'd learned early on. Personal outrage was all well and good when it wouldn't hurt anyone else. Silence was her ally in this instance. She'd convinced herself that dredging up the past would create more ill will and pain for innocent people than do good. Her hands were tied. She strongly suspected that Buzz Campbell knew this as well, which was why he made her the architect of her own demise in Dean's interview.

"Helen, you have my full personal support but I will not go public. My life is my business. I ask that you respect my privacy."

Helen pointed to the wedding band. "I see you are married."

"Yes."

"How long?"

Kelly chafed. She didn't want to answer. "Newly married."

"After fifteen years, my husband left me when I told him about Buzz. He wouldn't believe that I could possibly let a man rape me four times. He even went so far as to confront Buzz." She gave Kelly a hard stare. "Of course, the good senator told Chuck that I threw myself at him. What was a man to do? I was divorced in a month."

"Helen. That's awful."

"Does your husband know about Buzz?"

"My husband is Evan McKenna. He knows."

A strange smile tugged at her lips. "Interesting. I heard he was talking with Jay Doyle this morning. Well, if I can't convince you to step forward. Maybe he can."

"What do you mean by that?"

Helen stood. "It doesn't matter. Thank you for the coffee—and for talking with me."

She slid her business card onto the table and left the diner.

KELLY WAS PISSED! Why was it that just as she started to grasp a fragile hold on the possibility that Evan was genuine in his intentions toward her that someone came along and threw a wrench right in the face of her trust?

He'd already contacted Doyle. Okay. He told her he would. Yet, the look on Helen's face implied that she didn't have to worry any longer because Evan would talk her into pressing charges against Buzz. Kelly's suspicions kicked in. Did Evan truly quit his job or was it an arrangement with Steve? Did he step down from his precious throne to go behind the lines to gain her confidence? Dean and Bethany practically said as much on TV this morning.

What did all of this mean?

Bunny didn't bother to knock after Kelly slammed the

door to her office, but let herself in and closed the door quietly. Kelly knew she was there but continued to stare at the sidewalk outside the window.

Bunny moved next to her and put an arm around her shoulder. "Everything okay?"

Kelly met her friend's dark eyes, which held nothing but concern for her. "Will I ever be able to trust a man, Bun?"

Bunny gave her shoulder a squeeze. "Are you talking about my heartthrob, Evan McKenna?"

Bless Bunny for answering perfectly with a question that truly described her *husband*. She rested her head on Bunny's shoulder. "He is a good man, isn't he? Am I being a fool?"

"Only you will be able to decide that, Kel. It all depends on what you want from your life—and the people you bring into it."

Kelly slid from beneath her arm. "What do you mean?"

She shrugged. "You can either let your past rule you and indulge your suspicions or you can take a man at face value and trust him until he proves himself wrong."

"Other than my brothers, I don't think I've ever been comfortable around a man." *Except Evan.*

Bunny shook her head. "Kelly, don't you understand? When you are always on your guard it makes folks work awfully hard to prove themselves to you."

Kelly frowned. "Do I do that to you?"

"No. We seemed to hit it off right away. But you certainly had Jake dancing a jig his first year here."

Kelly shook her head, a small grin creasing her lips. She'd taken a chance on her burly cook who'd just freshly arrived from New Orleans. "Well, Jake needed to do a little proving. He stank like a bottle of Jameson the morning he interviewed with me."

"Yet you hired him."

"Yes. There was something solid about him. I was willing to take the chance. Besides, he cooked an omelet for me that I still dream about today."

"So, you trusted your instinct."

She understood the look in her friend's gaze. "You're telling me to have faith."

Bunny pinched her chin like a doting mother. "I'm telling you to have no expectations. Let every encounter be fresh with the man whom I suspect you love. Leave a clear space and see what fills it. Time will be the great prover. Evan won't have to work so hard to make you believe him and you get to be free to explore your feelings instead of guarding them."

Kelly sighed. "So many signs point to Evan having ulterior motives for supporting me."

"Like a groundbreaking story?"

"Exactly."

"Okay, let's assume that is true. What do you believe Evan's motive would be for exposing your story? Would he compromise your son or your happiness for his career? For justice? Would he compromise you at all?"

When Kelly opened her mouth to answer, Bunny held up a hand. "Wait. I want you to think about this. Given the Evan you have come to know. Just the man. Not his job. Not the current situation. Simply Evan. What would be his motive for deceiving you?"

She didn't even have to deliberate. The answer came immediately. "He'd have none. The Evan I have come to know would not hurt me."

"Okay, so why are you angry?"

She waved a hand. "Helen Thompson wants me to go public with her in denouncing Campbell. When she learned I married Evan, she seemed to think my compliance was a shoo-in."

"You told her no?"

"Of course."

"Then there is no problem. Evan can't make you do anything you choose not to do."

"You saw Evan's show this morning. They said he's on leave."

Bunny sighed. "I didn't like the sound of that, either."

"Think about it. Now that you know the truth about Matt, you can see that the newsman who uncovers a skeleton like mine in a presidential candidate's closet would end up in history books."

"Not to mention, become a hero for saving the country from a psychopath."

"You and I both know that Evan gave up seven years of his life abroad to build his career to where it is now. He's like a dog with a bone when it comes to morally righteous reporting."

Bunny shook her head. "Well, then, there's only one answer."

"What's that?"

"Ask him."

She clasped her hands together. "But, that is my dilemma. Can I believe what he tells me?"

EVAN HAD JUST settled Matt and Jared with milk shakes in front of the TV to watch the latest Urban Hero video— again, when his cell phone rang. Steve's number lit the screen. He debated whether or not to answer. After the third ring, he punched the button.

"McKenna here."

"You know it's me, Evan."

"Hey, Steve. What's up?"

"I'm calling to remind you that you can't quit. You're under contract with me."

Evan scrubbed his face with his hand. "I know. I told you to take me to court."

"I had the kids announce on your show that you're on leave."

He laughed at the absurdity. "So, getting bad ratings, are you?"

"Did I hear you're married?"

"Are you ignoring my question?"

Steve laughed. "Answer mine first."

"Yes. Kelly and I married on Friday."

"How's that going for you?"

"Shut up, Steve."

"Are you really going to sit on the story of the year—heck, the decade? Buzz Campbell has been blazing a pretty solid campaign trail for at least that long. You can blow the man's entire career up in smoke."

Evan knew this. That's why it was so damned difficult to walk away from this newsbreak when Kelly could get the job done and obtain justice by simply stepping forward. "And your point is?"

"I have my suspicions about the real story behind Kelly's son. If they are true and you get her talking, the sky is the limit for you, Evan. Anything you want at NCTV is yours."

"You used to like Kelly, Steve. Now you sound like a real jerk. See you in court."

The minute Kelly stepped through the door Evan knew something bothered her. She hugged Matt hello and sat with him to hear about his afternoon with Jared before even looking up at Evan. Something happened at Neverland today. That probably explained why she didn't answer his call earlier.

He watched her from the kitchen where he put the final

touches on the salad. Homemade pizzas were already in the oven. The Chianti decanted. "You okay?"

She headed over to the kitchen. Matt climbed up on the stool at the counter. "We're having pizza tonight, Mom."

She tugged on his sleeve. "I can see you helped. You have sauce on your shirt."

Evan grinned. "Matt twirls a mean pizza crust. Wait until you see the heart-shaped pie he made for you."

She kissed her son, who was beaming at her. "For me? I can't wait to eat the whole thing."

Evan gestured to the wine. "Shall I pour?"

"Let me shower and change first. It's been a long day."

"I figured as much. You didn't answer my question."

"Which was?"

"Looks like something is on your mind."

"That's not a question."

He laughed. "No, it's not. I asked if you were okay."

"Right now, I'm not so sure."

"That's what I thought. I'm ready to talk when you are."

She glanced at Matt before speaking. "Helen Thompson paid a visit to Neverland."

That raised his brow. "Let me guess…she's trying to recruit you."

She looked him squarely in the eye. "Yes. And left me with the impression that you'd accomplish the job in getting me to sign on."

"Who's Helen Thompson?" Matt plucked a slice of mozzarella cheese from the cutting board.

She held up a hand. "We can finish this later. I'm going to change. How much time until the pizza is ready?"

THEY'D BOTH TUCKED Matt into bed and Kelly felt like a complete hypocrite. There she was playing house with Evan and her son, but what if that little boy's hopes were dashed when Evan turned out to be a fraud? She closed the door to his room suddenly thinking that there was no place to hide in the huge penthouse from the man who stood there with expectation on his face.

He wanted to finish the conversation she'd started earlier.

"Another glass of wine?"

"No. Thanks."

He pulled a sheepish grin. "I have a feeling this conversation is going to be difficult. Want to talk about it in my bedroom?"

His subtle scent rising on his body heat made her fingers itch to touch him. He looked so sexy barefoot in his jeans and faded gray Led Zeppelin T-shirt stretching across those shoulders she'd tasted naked once. God help her, with his black hair pushed back, those sky-blue eyes were questioning her as if he was remembering the very same moment. Despite herself, she grinned. "Absolutely not."

He held out his hand. "Come on. I'll make some tea. We'll sit on the balcony."

She folded her arms. "Let's just talk."

He made a sweeping gesture. "Okay. Lead the way."

They hadn't even made it across the kitchen when she turned on him.

"Did you or did you not quit your job, Evan?"

He stopped in his tracks. Was that disappointment filling his face?

"I don't lie, Kelly."

"Did you marry me to seduce me into giving you an interview about Campbell?"

Now he frowned. "Are you kidding me? That question isn't funny at all."

She planted her hands on her hips. "That's not an answer."

"What did Helen Thompson say to you?"

She pinched the bridge of her nose debating whether to explain because he'd hadn't given her a straight answer yet, but pressed on. At this point, she'd stepped over the line of caution. What did she have to lose?

"Helen said that Buzz raped her on four different occasions. That she and Doyle made up the story about Matt being a love child to force me to come forward and defend myself. And, she found the fact that we are recently married rather interesting, as if you'd taken vows as a measure to convince me to speak out."

He shook his head. "All that from a woman I never personally laid eyes on let alone had a conversation with. Amazing."

"So that's your reply, Evan?"

He looked at her as if seeing her for the first time. "You know something, Kelly? I was taking a chance marrying you. And I married you because I fell in love. I think I've loved you from the first day I came into Herby's and you overpoured my coffee."

Kelly's breath caught in her throat. "Evan…"

He held up a hand, his aqua eyes flashing with anger. "No, wait. I want to make sure you understand exactly how much you mean to me. Three hours ago, I got a call from Steve. He's not letting me quit because I'm violating my contract. But he offered me carte blanche at NCTV if I can convince you to talk about Campbell on the air."

"This is what I've been talking about."

"You think I don't know that? Do you know what I told him?"

Kelly lifted her chin a notch higher. "What?"

"I'd see him in court."

Kelly stared at him, wanting to push away the distrust

with hope. "How do I know this isn't all just an elaborate ploy between you two to get me to talk?"

"And there lies our problem. You don't trust me. I'm wondering if you managed to survive Campbell's assault in one way, but not in others."

Kelly swallowed hard. Evan was voicing her own worries, and she didn't like the sound of them.

He continued. "Let me be clear, Red. Do I want to interview you and nail Campbell so hard he can't get up? Hell, yes. It's like instinct for me. I see wrong and want to make it right, especially because that bastard hurt *the woman I love*. Will I coerce you to speak out? Absolutely not. I respect you enough to honor your wishes. But nothing I say will convince you otherwise. You're dug in so damned deep behind that wall of yours, that I'll never have a chance to love you the way I want to."

She stepped toward him. "If we'd just been given time like normal folks to build understanding between us."

"It won't work, Kelly. We'll do too much damage to each other before we can get to that place. When this is all behind us and I've put Buzz in jail as I promised, I will file for divorce."

She held out a hand. "Evan…"

He shook his head. "No. I will not live with a woman who cannot trust me. I know what I want from a marriage, Kelly, and Quince said it all too well. Love. Trust. Dedication. I took those damned vows offering you all three, plus one more. Protection. I hoped you'd see through to me and believe me enough to open up. You did. Once. But we got too close and you shut right down with one excuse after another. You'll have my friendship and my protection, Kelly Sullivan, but as for marriage? Looks like I made a mistake. I am truly sorry for us both."

KELLY LAY IN bed staring at the ceiling, where the ambient city lights diffused through the curtains. Inhale as she may, she could not get a full breath into her lungs. Her throat was way too tight, her heart pounding against her ribs.

She lifted her hand to look at the gold band on her finger in the little light there was. The delicate circlet seemed so foreign yet fit perfectly. She turned her hand. Seamless. Perfect. She'd worn this on her hand comfortably for these past days as if it had always been a part of her. Only when she'd reach for something and notice it on her hand did she realize it was there. In those moments her mind would fly back to the fact that she was truly married—and then the guilt would hit. Had she done herself and Evan a disservice simply to meet her own desperate needs? This ring symbolized what was precious between two people. Evan let her know tonight that his intentions had been genuine. Hers had not.

What had she done? It only took four days for him to call it quits. And here she was questioning whether it was because she'd called him on his deception or because she had profoundly wounded the man.

Her gut told her it was the latter. If that was the case, she was a damned fool.

Okay, so she was unschooled in love. God knew the emotional hurdles she overcame to see Matt as a sweet, innocent newborn and not the seed of a monster. She'd done all that good work. Matt's joyful attitude was proof. The price she'd paid was keeping everyone at arm's length, including her friends. A form of self-preservation in order to do what she must had backfired on her in the intimacy department.

Now she knew the difference. Evan had shown her. She needed the love of a good man and he awakened that need like a thunderclap before a deluge. While her heart and soul wanted to stand in that storm with feet firmly planted and arms wide, feeling every drop of wind and rain buffeting her body, her mind had yanked her back into her safe, dry cave. Logic admonished that something as powerful as love from the hands of a man could hurt her and she continued to believe it.

But Evan had shown her otherwise. When he did, she'd responded, albeit with caution. Evan taught her the difference, yet she still hunkered back into her own sanctuary at the slightest provocation. While she and Evan had given Matt a lecture on standing together and not letting other folks tear them down with their ideas, she hadn't applied that philosophy to herself with Evan.

Because she was afraid. Afraid of commitment. Afraid to hand herself over to a man in case he considered her chattel. *Fear*—that four-letter word had just shattered her chance at happiness with the one man she loved.

Loved?

Did she just use that word?

She sat up, looking around as if someone else had spoken. But no. She was alone. Her heart whispered the truth to her. She'd finally listened and let the meaning sink in. And crazy as her world was, she realized the truth when it was too late.

No. She would fix this. She hadn't battled the odds of cruelty and survived just to let fear keep her from love.

How could she prove her love to Evan now that he'd turned away from her? She knew him well enough. When that stubborn Irishman made a decision, moving a continent was easier than changing his mind. She'd have to completely overwhelm him to get his attention.

The answer came like a sucker punch.

She'd have to come forward about Buzz Campbell. Tell the truth on the air and in so doing trust him. She would also be giving him another gift. She'd be putting her *husband* on the map for reporting accurate, timely and responsible news on a story that addressed so many necessary issues. By coming forward, Kelly would make Evan a hero in her eyes for protecting her and *his* son from the man who would tear their world apart for revenge, or worse, for control of their lives.

Oh, God. How could she possibly protect Matt from the fallout? And what about the other innocent people who would be affected by her accusations? There was only one answer. Take each situation, head-on. When she had all the players in place, she would sit down with Matthew and give him his first lesson in growing up.

First thing in the morning, she would call Madeline Campbell. Madeline deserved to know the truth. What she would do with the information was her business, but Kelly had done a huge disservice to the woman, who had been more than an employer, by remaining silent. Just admitting that fact to herself lifted a weight she'd been carrying for all these years. By the grace of God she would find the courage to speak the right words and put her world back on track.

She had a marriage to save. Her *own!*

FROM WHERE SHE KNELT in the end pew, Kelly spotted Madeline Campbell entering the side door of St. Patrick's Cathedral. Madeline dipped a finger into the holy water font and crossed herself. As Kelly had done, she stood for a moment to let her eyes adjust to the softened light. Afternoon mass was about to begin. Tourists and locals began filling pews, making the cathedral look like Grand Central Station.

Kelly had used her stolen moments before Madeline arrived to send some hearty prayers to the Divine. Her task would not be easy. Yet she felt more serene now that she'd decided to tell her story out loud. For real—with the hopes of gaining blessings from the senator's wife. She'd already lighted a candle for Herby George to watch over her for the next hour. All her bases were covered.

She stood. Madeline spotted her. A petite woman, she'd changed little in seven years. Perhaps thinner. Her loose brown hair fell at her shoulders, those large, sea-blue eyes still held youth, her lips were lined perfectly in her favorite soft coral color that complemented her complexion. Kelly always saw Madeline as the perfect match for the charismatic Buzz Campbell she admired before the assault. Madeline was lovely. Intelligent. Genuine. Always quick to smile. Only now, she regarded Kelly warily as she approached.

"Madeline, how good to see you."

A small smile broke on her lips. "Hello, Kelly. My, you've grown into a woman."

She shrugged. "I grew up fast. You haven't changed a bit."

Kelly hadn't explained much to her about why she wanted the meeting. She'd been surprised when Madeline agreed to see her today. Perhaps she had a gripe with Kelly that she'd been wanting to air for all these years.

Kelly reached a hand out. "Can you forgive me for running out on you like that, Madeline?"

To her surprise, Madeline pulled her into her arms and hugged her hard—a bit awkward since Kelly now stood a few inches taller than she. "I've missed you, Kelly. There is so much I have to say."

"Oh, me, too, Madeline. Thank you for coming."

Madeline let go. She pushed a lock of hair behind her ear, a habit she'd always had. "I saw a coffee shop across the street. Let's grab a table while half of New York is packed in here."

Kelly took a last swipe of holy water and crossed herself before leaving. She'd need all the help she could get.

Two coffees between them, the women appraised each other. Kelly stirred her coffee even though it was black then stopped herself. Her stomach burned from nerves. She wanted to start this conversation but search as she may, she couldn't find the right words.

Madeline broke the silence. "Kelly, I came to see you so quickly because there is something I've wanted to say to you for a very long time."

She inhaled a deep breath. She was about to get blasted. "No doubt Dean Porter's interview with the senator gives you reason to see me now."

Madeline frowned. "No. Kelly, please let me finish. This is very difficult for me."

Kelly found herself blinking. "Wait a minute. I'm here to tell you something that is very difficult for me."

Madeline grabbed her hand. "Kelly, I knew Buzz assaulted you *the day you left.*"

Kelly stilled. "What?"

Madeline's gaze began flying around the room as she struggled with what she wanted to say. "I woke up to find you waiting outside for the taxi. You were nervous, fighting tears, talking nonsense. You kept glancing down the drive expecting Buzz to come back from his jog any minute. I knew something was wrong."

The memory of that morning stung hard. Emily and little Mary Kate had stood in the doorway, their hair mussed from sleep, still in their pj's watching Kelly argue with their mom over why she was leaving. She closed her eyes at the memory. "I'm so sorry, Madeline."

The fierceness in the other woman's voice startled her. "No, Kelly. I'm the one who owes you an apology."

"How did you know?"

Madeline swallowed. She sipped her coffee. She pushed that lock of hair behind her ear once more. When she looked at Kelly again, there were tears in her eyes. "I found your torn nightgown in your closet. You'd put your sheets in the wash, but I knew. There was no way that gown ripped itself. My husband attacked you and you left my house to save yourself from having him assault you again."

Kelly fell back into her seat as if she'd been hit by a boulder. "You really knew?"

Tears fell freely down Madeline's face. She swiped at them with the back of her hand, but they kept coming. "Back then I didn't want to believe the truth. I had two small girls. Buzz was my high school sweetheart. We'd broken up during college, but he came home to find me, swept me off my feet and made me believe that everything he was doing in his career was for me—and then the girls. Never did I suspect he had that…that bend…until you."

Kelly's voice choked with emotion. "I could have used your help."

She nodded. "I know. I'm so very sorry. But once I figured it all out, I wanted you gone. I wanted to pretend it wasn't real. I wanted my life the way it was before you came into my house." She gave Kelly a pointed and miserable look. "I wanted to blame you for corrupting my husband. It was how I kept putting one foot in front of the other."

As she listened to Madeline explain herself, the truth of the matter hit home, obliterating any outrage that had risen. The calm that settled over Kelly overwhelmed her. "My God, Madeline. You are as much a victim of that man as I was."

She nodded. "He's sewn me up so tight to his side that I am his lovely little marionette, believing anything he tells me so I won't have to change my comfortable life."

Kelly shook her head. "Maybe so, but I'll bet you another cup of coffee that the real reason you kept your own counsel is because you are afraid of your husband."

"Yes."

"Why are you telling me this now, Madeline?"

"Because until that Doyle report with Helen Thompson, I had no idea that you'd had a baby from the assault."

"But Buzz told Dean Porter…"

She held up a hand. "I was sitting in the room during Porter's interview. I watched Buzz lie right there on camera. He hadn't told me about the DNA test. I hadn't forgiven him, let alone agreed to stand by him in investigating further into who your son was. There I sat listening to Buzz dictating on national news exactly how I was going to respond when anyone questioned me."

Kelly's hand flew to her mouth. "My God."

Fire rose in Madeline's eyes. "I'm finished, Kelly. I can't do this anymore. My soul has worn paper-thin. I don't want my girls growing up thinking that men like my husband are what they should seek for themselves. I know this sounds cowardly, but if my husband goes to jail it would be so much easier for me to file for divorce and start a new life for the girls and me."

Kelly appraised Madeline. She needed one more question answered. "How do you feel knowing my son is Buzz's child?"

Madeline closed her eyes briefly. "Not knowing the child I find him difficult to accept. We both know Buzz wanted a boy. Part of me will have to deal with the fact that you gave him what I couldn't…."

"Stop right there, Madeline! I didn't *give* Buzz anything. By raping me, he took away my choice over whether or not I wanted to have a child. Getting me pregnant was not his goal. He has and never will have any rights to the baby that came from that night."

Now tears filled Kelly's eyes. "My son is such a wonderful child, Madeline. He might have Buzz's coloring—maybe some of his bravado, but that boy has so much Irish in him that it's blinding. I never see Buzz when I look at Matt. I see Matt."

Madeline reached for both of Kelly's hands. "Kelly, if you love that child, I will, too. We'll find a way to explain to our kids how they are related. It'll be strange at first, but we'll make it work. Okay?"

The two women sat in silence. Their coffees cold. Wiping the tears from their faces.

"Kelly?"

"Yes?"

"Why didn't you let me know you were pregnant? Financially supporting the baby must have been unbearable."

Kelly took the time to explain the abysmal New York laws regarding women who became pregnant from rape and chose to keep their babies. "You see? I couldn't let you know. Buzz would have had custodial rights. You would have had to accept my son and me into your world. I couldn't do it to you. To the girls. And mostly, please forgive me for saying this, but I believed if Buzz had access to me, he'd rape me or coerce me to have sex with him again. With my son as hostage, I'd never be free of him."

Madeline pressed her hands to her stomach. "My heavens. I had no idea. I think I want to throw up."

Kelly laughed. "Join the crowd. Every time I think of those cold hard facts I want to puke."

Just by looking at Madeline, Kelly could see the woman was as exhausted by their exchange as she was. Difficult as this discussion had been, both women told the truth—revealed their secrets. Their honesty had rekindled a bond between them that Kelly knew would last for the rest of their lives.

"What will you do now, Madeline?"

She shrugged. "I'm not sure. I'm going to have to speak with my attorney about protecting myself."

A grin broke on Kelly's face. "I have an idea. It's why I called you in the first place."

Madeline must have seen the mischief in Kelly's eyes because she smiled in return. For a fleeting moment, it was as if they were sitting in Madeline's kitchen hatching a plan for the day, just like old times.

"What is your idea?"

A thought occurred to her. "If you can spare a little more time, I'd like to add another person to our discussion."

Kelly reached for her phone and tapped Evan's number.

His voice sent a thrill right down to her backbone even if his tone sounded as cold as an old fish. "Yes, Kelly."

"Evan McKenna, this is your wife. If you are free, I'm wondering if you'd be so kind as to send your car to St. Paddy's Cathedral. I have someone with me I'd like you to meet."

CHAPTER SIXTEEN

THAT EVENING, Kelly reached for two orders from the line, exchanging easy banter with Jake's assistant cook. She turned and almost dropped the plates. Buzz Campbell stood at the counter. The impact of seeing him in person for the first time after his assault felt like cannon shot blowing a hole right through her. Instinct tossed her back seven years to that helpless moment before she instantly got a grip. That was before she'd grown a backbone and knew how to take care of herself. Campbell could no longer cause her physical harm. But he could make a dent in her personal comfort if she let him. That was not going to happen.

If anything, he'd grown more handsome. His confidence made him look larger than life, approachable. But to her he was just damned ugly. She didn't like the way he appraised her as if they had unfinished business that he was more than eager to address.

The grin on his face said it all. "Kelly Sullivan. Had I known you were the fetching redhead that Dean said all the newsmen fussed about over here, I would have come in sooner."

A man in a dark suit stood behind him. She didn't have to glance out the diner window to know the stretch limo double-parked out front was his.

She handed off her plates to Bunny, who materialized at her side. Jake came out of the kitchen and stood next to her, arms folded. The look he gave Buzz made her want to kiss her cook. He'd get a bonus for this one.

Her gaze settled on Buzz. She forced her face to appear calm. What was this? Family reunion day? Had Madeline told him they'd met earlier? After their discussion with Evan, she would think not. However, it wouldn't be unlike the senator to know that his wife had come into the city. Perhaps he was covering his bases.

"What do you want, Senator? I'm very busy."

"I'd like to have a private word with you."

"Not going to happen. Do you have my attorney's number? Or for that matter, my husband's?"

He glanced at the ring on her hand. "I heard. Won't help."

Her stomach twisted. She understood immediately. Campbell was here with every intention of threatening her into doing his bidding. He was gunning for Matt. She could feel his intent radiating off his body. Rage almost blinded her. Panic almost dropped her to her knees. This awful man had the law on his side and all she could do right now was wield a healthy dose of bravado.

"What do you want, Senator?" She stressed the word *senator* as if to say, *asshole.*

His voice was quiet, intended only for her ears. "I'd like to meet my son."

From the corner of her eyes she saw Bunny talking on her cell phone. She hoped to heaven she was calling the police.

Ignoring the quake rising in her knees, she forced herself to match his tone. "I don't have *your* son, Senator. I don't have anything that is yours." She stepped closer as outrage fueled her. Leaning in, palms flat on the counter she said, "I am not afraid of you, Buzz Campbell. I think it remains in your best interest not to believe any documents Dean Porter flashed under your nose. I am married to the father of my child. Your best bet right now, sir, is to get out of my diner before I tell every person here exactly what I know about you."

He flashed the smile that graced millions of television screens throughout the year. Kelly knew that smile. It meant, I can't say or do what I really want to say or do. Clearly he had expected Kelly to crumble against his veiled threat. She had surprised him, but it wouldn't bode well in the long run.

Buzz was here to ensure against exactly what she suggested. He wanted her to remain quiet about his assault, and was prepared to strong-arm her into doing so. If she spoke out, he'd take Matt from her. His message was loud and clear. What he didn't know was that now that Madeline and she had decided to speak out, Buzz Campbell could kiss her derriere.

His face took on a benevolent look. "I am here to let the past die between us. I'm not here to cause trouble. You misunderstand me, Kelly."

"I am Mrs. McKenna to you, and I understand you perfectly."

Her heart banged in her chest, but this bully was not going to get his pound of flesh from her today. She'd never called herself Mrs. McKenna before. Right now, Evan's name on her tongue never sounded more perfect. He had offered her protection and she was using it.

Buzz sat at the counter and leaned closer so their faces were inches apart. The citrus scent of his aftershave invaded her senses setting off the worst of her memories.

"I already have the legal wheels in motion, Kelly. Your son will be mine by Christmas. You should not have run off with him. He deserves so much more than what you've dragged him through."

The breath Kelly inhaled seared all the way down her throat. "You'll have to kill me first, Senator. That child will never lay eyes on you."

Three men sitting along the counter were listening to their conversation. One man, Harry from the construction site a block down, stood. "Hey, Kelly. Do you want us to toss the good senator out for you?"

Jake was already moving around the counter only to be blocked by the senator's aide.

All around them, her customers started to stand. Even an elderly woman. Kelly's heart swelled at the support her patrons were showing for her.

Kelly crossed her arms, feeling like Joan of Arc. "Now get out of Neverland, Buzz Campbell. It looks like no one here is planning on voting for you. Don't ever darken my doorway again. Do you understand…sir?"

Buzz stood and laid a proprietary hand on the counter, spreading his fingers wide, the thick gold band on his left hand gleaming beneath the lights. "You know I'm a family man, Kelly. I take good care of those who are mine and your son is mine. I will see you in court. Madeline and I will be so happy to have Matthew—and you—back in our lives again."

TWENTY MINUTES LATER, Evan pushed through the doors of Neverland. Kelly was seated at a table surrounded by patrons, a cup of coffee between her hands. The place buzzed with everyone's chatter. Meanwhile, her staff was practically jogging to keep up with the food orders. She saw him and reached out a hand.

Her fingers were cold to his touch. She looked pale but fire lit her eyes. He slid into the chair next to her. "Bunny called. I got here as fast as I could."

Harry, the construction dude, slapped Evan on the back.

"You should have seen her, man. She stood up to that SOB like a roaring tiger."

All at once everyone started telling Evan their version of the story. He started laughing. "Hold on now, folks. I think Kelly can fill me in just fine."

Harry motioned to his two coworkers. "Now that you're here, Evan, we'll head home. Just wanted to make sure our girl was okay."

Kelly stood and hugged the man, uncaring if he had dust on his overalls. "I'm fine, Harry. Thanks so much for standing up for me. Free lunch tomorrow."

He waved a hand. "No bother, girl. This was more fun than reality TV!"

Kelly glanced around to the others. "Thank you all for showing your support. I never felt stronger in my life than I did with you all here."

Evan took her hand again. "Let's go to your office."

As soon as the door closed he pulled her into his arms. He was glad she let him. She fit so perfectly. He inhaled her scent of coffee, cinnamon and apple, or was it strawberries? He pressed her head against his chest, kissing the crown of her hair.

"So, you battled Goliath and won?"

She looked up at him, her eyes huge with concern. "This round. And thank you."

He tilted his head. "What for?"

"Your name. Having your wedding band on my finger slowed him down."

"What did he say."

She laid her head back on his chest. "Will you just hold me for a moment, Evan? Right now, I need your strength. He scared the devil out of me."

Tightening his hold, Evan chuckled. "Oh, I think there's

plenty of devil left in there, Red. You're just needing a breather."

She started to giggle. His hands roamed from the small of her back massaging up to her shoulders. He couldn't help it. "I'm proud of you, woman."

She stepped out of the circle of his arms. "We're going to have to speak with Quince."

He sat on the small couch across from her desk and patted to the seat next to him. Once she settled he said, "I did this afternoon. But first, tell me what happened."

Her brow creased. "Buzz said he's already started the process to fight for custody." Her lower lip began to tremble. "He says he'll take Matt by Christmas."

He pressed a finger to her lips. "No he won't, Kelly. Mark my words. He was pushing you around. He wants you to stay quiet about the assault."

"He made me so angry. I can't stay quiet any longer."

"We're going to have a small problem. Proving the fact that Campbell assaulted you may not be enough to keep him away from Matt. That DNA test pretty much cements his paternity. Our focus has to be on proving him unfit as a parent to have access to Matt."

Evan used the word *assault* instead of *rape* because Kelly always seemed to wince when the *R* word was used. The last thing on his agenda was to make his wife uncomfortable.

His wife.

She'd gotten his attention yesterday when she walked into the penthouse with Madeline Campbell by her side. Evan had never met the woman, but he'd seen her enough on television to know who she was. Her small stature surprised him, but it belied the woman's courage.

He'd listened for a full half hour while Madeline explained how her marriage evolved with Buzz, how, even though he was a doting father and a loving husband, their intimate life had started to dwindle. Buzz seemed preoccupied at times with certain women employees. He'd had three women quit from his campaign staff in just as many years. And then she explained her view of what happened to Kelly, and how she'd known Buzz had hurt her. He was floored by her willingness to end it all now. She had decided that after hearing Helen Thompson speak and hearing how Buzz lied on Dean's interview that she would no longer pretend that her husband was a moral and dedicated man.

He had become a megalomaniac.

Kelly's motives were not lost on him when she took Madeline's hand and said, "We are prepared to give you the interview you want to blow Buzz Campbell out of the water."

Kelly was reaching out an olive branch. She wanted to prove to him that she was going to trust him. The guard that rose in his mind was—ultimately, would she?

Hell. He'd give her the chance, but he wasn't going to cave on his decision. That rock-solid wall of hers had bruised him enough. He was not a glutton for punishment—nor was he a quitter. In his heart, he didn't want to give up on her. Only, there was fixable, and those who didn't want to be fixed. Which was this fiery redhead? Unless he stepped on this roller coaster with her he wouldn't find out. This time, however, he'd keep his defenses in place.

He'd taken Kelly by the shoulders. "Are you sure, Red?"

The tears that filled her eyes gave him hope. "I have two reasons for doing this, Evan. The first is to finally do the right thing. Now that Madeline agrees with me to move forward, I feel free to speak. You'll just have to help me explain the situation to Matt."

His heart just about burst he was so proud of her. "And the second reason?"

She became uncomfortable and fidgeted for a bit before planting her feet and looking him squarely in the eye. Those green eyes begged him to believe her. "I want to prove to you that I am ready and willing to trust you. I know you will take excellent care to ensure my—" she looked at Madeline "—*our* story is aired properly. We want to show women who suffer abuse at the hands of immoral men that they can find a safe haven."

She had said words he needed to hear, but she hadn't said that she loved him. It was a start.

After they had bundled Madeline in Evan's car to take her to Penn Station, Evan had to fight every urge to keep from throwing Kelly over his shoulder and dragging her upstairs to show her just how well he could take care of her for the rest of her life. But he resisted.

This was a battle worth retreating to fight another day.

Unable to resist he pulled her into his arms. She let him. He rested his forehead on hers, because, God help him, he wanted her. "You are going to have to do everything I tell you. Do you accept that?"

She had laughed. "Oh, how that irks me." But she settled down, her face sobering and said, "I accept." Stepping on tiptoe, she placed the sweetest kiss on his lips. "I want to deserve you, Evan. You are rare among men."

Now, sitting next to him so full of conviction, he was about to serve her with her first true test. Since he'd finally sat down with Quince and told him about Kelly's accusations against Campbell, his attorney had given him some bad news. Chances were their fight would get uglier before it got better.

He grabbed Kelly's hand. "Buzz came here today to publicly make it look like you two had been lovers and you ran off with his child. He'd rather stick to his story that you seduced him than defend himself against assault charges."

She bit her lip. "I suspected that long ago. I have very little chance of winning. Is that what you're telling me?"

"Yes, but remember that snowball strategy Helen Thompson told you about? If we can get more women to add to your testimony, we can prove he's lying—and dangerous."

"That's a big *if*. The shame of coming forward is impossible for most women."

He held her gaze. "I had to call Madeline and tell her this. She's not going to say anything publicly to support you until we learn more."

"Maybe I shouldn't do this."

There it was. Her fear. Would she rise to meet it head-on? Evan so very much needed his *wife* to trust him.

"No, Kelly. Given the pressure the senator is putting on us about Matt, I think we should go live tomorrow morning."

Her eyes darted in momentary panic. "Why?"

"Because we don't have a choice. With the way today's laws are about rape and keeping the baby, we can't protect Matt from Buzz on just the assault charge. The only way we can keep Buzz at arm's length is to send him to jail or get enough testimony to prove him unfit to be with your son. We can't wait another day."

She exhaled a breath. "Okay. You're right." She thought a minute. Looking totally stricken she said, "What should I wear?"

He laughed out loud.

A knock sounded at the door. Jake barged in carrying a large plate and two napkins rolled with utensils. "Glad to hear you two laughing." He placed the plate on the small table. "Burning all that energy fighting off the bad guys requires a special meal. Crawfish étouffée. I'll bring the beers to wash it down in a minute."

Evan rubbed his hands together. They needed a moment of normalcy to offset today's insanity. God bless Jake for making it happen. "Thank you, Jake. It doesn't get any better than this."

Jake smirked. "Oh, yeah? Come with me to N' Awlins. I'll show you how it's really made."

Knee to knee, Evan and Kelly sat for the first time in agreement on their plans. This battle was going to be tough on Kelly, but he'd use every contact he knew to make her interview the harpoon that put the end to Buzz's threats. Then he'd decide which direction their marriage would take. God knew he didn't want to let her go, but she had to prove her courage here, or she'd lose him forever.

Kelly frowned. "What did you do with Matt?"

Between bites he said, "Michael showed up this afternoon unannounced. He'd had some church council meeting midtown so dropped in. They should be fine until we get home."

"We have to explain to Matt what's going to happen."

He nodded. "I've made an appointment with a child psychologist for some pointers after lunch tomorrow. We should be ready for him by the time he gets home from school."

Time to get the ball rolling. He pulled his phone from his pocket and tapped the keypad on his cell phone. Watching Kelly as the number rang, he noticed that a subtle change in her body language had taken place today. Even though Campbell had wound her up with his threat, she seemed calmer. The tense energy that always seemed to drive her had softened as if releasing the muscles in her body from years of strain. While her eyes still held concern over the enormity of the undertaking that lay ahead, she popped a crawfish from the tip of her fork into her mouth as if eating the tiny morsel was the only thing in the world she had to do right now. Kelly had found peace within herself by making this decision to fight.

He liked that.

Steve answered the phone. "Evan! Good to hear from you."

"Steve. Listen. I'm going to need the talk show set for a breaking news segment after the morning show. Kelly is going live with her story."

The man actually hooted.

Evan shook his head. If it wasn't for the fact that this story involved Kelly, he'd be right on board with his boss's relief. But feeling the razor edge of unbiased reporting cut into his world personally had given him pause. When the dust settled Evan would reevaluate his approach to future reporting. He was still angry and not happy at all with having to go back to Steve because it looked like he was caving to Steve's offer. But the issue at the moment wasn't about him. He had to get the job done for Kelly. He'd do whatever it took.

Steve said, "Excellent, my man! I'll arrange it immediately."

"I appreciate it."

"What's the platform going to be?"

"Assault. Campbell forced himself on my wife when she was his nanny. She became pregnant from the event and hid the boy because there are no laws in New York State protecting her against Buzz taking custody of the child."

"You're joking, right?"

"God's honest truth. It's why I wanted you to let me work through this mess before going live. We are not only going to press charges against Buzz but will challenge New

York State's laws on their stand on protecting women who bear children from rape and keep their babies."

Steve whistled low. "This is bigger than I thought. What made Kelly change her mind?"

"Madeline Campbell. She gave Kelly her blessing to speak out. Seems Madeline suspected the assault back when it happened and pretended it didn't. Now she's willing to back up Kelly's story. Madeline Campbell wants her husband to go to jail."

"This is perfect! We'll be able to work this angle for months."

Steve's impersonal enthusiasm irked Evan. "We're not doing this for you, Steve. So stop salivating."

Kelly put her fork down. From the look on her face, Evan's discussion killed the rest of her appetite. He laid a hand on her leg.

Steve had the good grace to sound contrite. "Evan, I'm sorry. You are correct. Please extend my apologies to Kelly. In the future, you'll just have to kick my butt every time I get out of line. You weren't wrong about everything you said last time when you were in my office."

Evan grew silent. This is what had bound him to his friend for all these years. The man's open mind and willingness to claim wrong were two traits Evan admired.

Steve persisted. "So, do you forgive me for the Dean interview, buddy?"

Evan laughed. "Absolutely not. You and I have a few more topics to hash out. I'm still not sure I'll re-up my contract after it finishes."

"Evan, that interview was not all story motivated. Believe me when I say that as your friend I couldn't let you lie on national television. What would make you any different from Buzz Campbell no matter how noble your cause?"

Evan rubbed his brow. He might just have to accept that

fact as truth. "Like I said. We'll have to talk about it. See you on the set tomorrow."

He ended the call.

Kelly released a deep breath. "You okay?"

Evan shrugged. "Right as rain."

"Then tomorrow we begin."

Evan leaned back on the couch beside her. "We're in for one hell of a ride, Red."

KELLY SAT IN the guest chair on Evan's right-hand side. She'd never been on a television set before. They had just finished the first rehearsal of the interview. While she'd fully expected her nerves to get jumpy she hadn't expected the intense heat of the overhead lights. She wiped the perspiration on her brow with the handkerchief she had knotted in her fist. She was glad for the navy blue color of the wraparound dress she wore because of the dampness collecting beneath her arms.

Her thoughts jumped to Neverland. Bunny and Jake had been doing an amazing job of running the business in her absence. She and Evan had come out of the office last night to see the two of them taking a break. Sitting across from each other at the family booth, they discussed the specials Jake would prepare for the weekend. Before Bunny spotted them, Kelly saw one of Bunny's petite feet resting casually atop her cook's worn cowboy boot.

She suspected something more than dark roast coffee was brewing at the Neverland diner. She liked the idea very much. That thought then jumped after her worries about Julie McKenna successfully keeping Matt away from the television this morning. Her stomach started to flutter with nerves again.

This segment was set to air after the morning news portion, and they were waiting out the commercial break before going live. Evan was in his element, looking handsome, relaxed and focused in a perfectly tailored charcoal-colored suit. To her surprise, Evan reached over and planted a kiss on her mouth long enough to capture her attention. The press of his lips calmed her. He hadn't kissed her since they fought.

His blue eyes held intent. "You're going to do fine, Kelly. Just as we read, I'll ask you questions and you answer them. Pretend it's just you and me sitting on the couch at home."

Her brogue thickened with nerves. "It's not like I've been chattering out loud about this issue for the past seven years, now is it, Evan? Don't be sugarcoating it."

He grinned. "Believe it or not, even nervous you're going to be great. Remember we're fighting for our son."

She swallowed the knot rising in her throat at the way he included himself. "Yes, Evan. I've not forgotten. Let's just get this over with. Shall we?"

The Assistant Director began counting down to black. She felt her face flush just as the cameras went live. She could do nothing about it except watch Evan begin the introduction.

"Good morning, ladies and gentlemen. Before we begin, I want to caution the viewing audience that the topic we are about to discuss will be uncomfortable. We deem it important to present this information to the American public because it answers the questions raised about an illegitimate son in presidential hopeful, Senator Buzz Campbell's interview earlier this week."

Kelly felt the intensity of the cameras from her peripheral vision but as instructed resisted looking at them. She forced herself to take in slow, even breaths wondering if she'd make it through the interview, let alone Evan's introduction, without begin reduced to a nervous wreck.

Evan was leading up to their first question.

"Here with me this morning is Kelly Sullivan, who is the target of Campbell's accusations. Kelly was the Campbell's nanny seven years ago as stated in the news report." He smiled at Kelly before returning his focus to the camera. "I'd like to add that Kelly just recently became my wife. I've taken a personal interest in proving that Senator Campbell has lied to everyone, including his own wife about what happened on the night Kelly's son was conceived."

Evan's aqua-blue eyes turned to Kelly, full of understanding. His gaze helped her to concentrate on his words instead of the nerves making her head buzz.

"I want to make sure everyone understands the enormous amount of courage it has taken for you to speak the truth behind this incident after all this time."

She nodded at his acknowledgment. "Evan, if not for that awful interview, I would still be keeping my counsel about my son. I am not happy to be discussing this publicly." The answer rolled off her tongue of its own volition and surprised her as much as it did Evan. It was not what they had rehearsed earlier.

He shot her an imperceptibly encouraging nod. "And why are you speaking out now?"

It seemed impossible to say these words out loud because her superstitious heart believed words spoken could become real.

She swallowed hard. "Because Senator Campbell is taking legal action for custody of my son. In his own words, the senator said that my son would be his by Christmas. I have to stop him. I do not believe his intentions are honorable."

Evan squeezed her hand. "Let's get right to the point. Senator Campbell insists that you seduced him late one night after he fell asleep on the living room couch. Thus, bringing about your pregnancy. Is that what happened?"

Feeling the heat of an unwanted blush on her cheeks, she shook her head. "No. The night I became pregnant with my son, Senator Campbell entered my bedroom while I slept. He assaulted me." Her throat tightened as she continued. "I had never been with a man before. I tried to escape him, but he'd locked the door, tore my nightgown and forced himself on me."

She inhaled a huge breath, her gaze glued to Evan as if he was an anchor for her ship in a floundering sea.

His gaze softened, encouraging her. She could see by the crease in his brow that emotionally he was right there, tied into her. Her story was upsetting him all over again.

"And then what happened, Kelly?"

"The next morning, I quit. I took a taxi while the senator was on his morning jog because I was terrified of seeing him again."

"Why is that?"

"Because after he…assaulted me, he let me know that this secret between us would also become part of my job description."

Evan continued. "And when you discovered you were pregnant? Why did you keep your son a secret?"

Kelly's voice became quiet. "I learned that if a woman who becomes pregnant from a rape chooses to keep the child, the state considers the accusation of rape as fraudulent and awards the perpetrator joint custody of the child. I believed Senator Campbell was a danger to me—and to my son. If the senator knew about Matthew, he would be granted access to my boy and to me. I could not take that chance."

"So you raised your baby alone."

She nodded once. "Yes, with the help of Herbert George, my employer at the diner."

"What are your intentions now, Kelly?"

They had rehearsed the answer several times. She wanted to say it perfectly. It was the platform from which she would throw the first snowball.

"I am seeking to press charges against Senator Campbell for first degree rape. I would like to see the senator put in jail."

THE PRESS OF news reporters at Neverland Diner once again overflowed into the street. While Kelly thought fending off their questions was a downright nuisance, Bunny and Jake assured her that Neverland was becoming a city hot spot from all the press. Business was booming. A reporter from a national magazine left a business card. The phone had been ringing off the hook from other news stations wanting to interview Kelly. She, in turn, had contacted Helen Thompson to alert her to the morning's interview before it aired so that Helen could add Kelly's actions to the campaign against Buzz Campbell.

In the meantime, Bunny had a niece who was looking for work. Bunny brought her in part-time to help pick up the slack Kelly had left. Kelly applauded Bunny's initiative then had to run out the door again to meet Evan for the meeting with the child psychologist.

Now, Kelly and Evan didn't shield Matt from the few determined reporters who clamored around the car when they drove up to the penthouse garage.

"What do those guys want?" Matt asked.

Evan shook his head. "Your mom made an announcement on TV today and they want to talk to her about it."

Matt's eyes lit up. "You were on TV today, Mom?"

She smiled. "Yes, indeed."

"Did you see Urban Hero?"

"No, honey. That was your special day."

"So who did you talk to?"

She glanced at Evan over the boy's head. "Dad."

It was the first time she'd given Evan that title out loud. The smile he rewarded her with sent her heart skidding in her chest. Saints in Heaven, this man had an effect on her.

Matt had climbed up on his knees to see the reporters who had fallen away as the car eased past the security gate.

"So, why are those guys yelling at you for talking to Dad?"

On the advice of the counselor, Kelly had rehearsed this answer in her mind over and over on the ride to pick him up from school. Given Matt's age, she didn't have to say much. Just enough for him to understand that his mom had a conflict concerning him, but she and Evan would keep Matt safe.

"Matt, do you know who Luke Skywalker from *Star Wars* is?"

"Sure!"

"Well, you know how cool and brave Luke is and how his father was that mean old Darth Vader?"

"Uh-huh."

"Something like that has happened to me. You are my very cool and wonderful son and there is a man who is important in our government. I used to work for him. Turns out, he's a bad man. He is telling everyone that you are his son. I went on TV to make sure that everyone knows that he is not allowed to be your father. I also spoke to Mr. Quince because I'm telling the police on him, too."

Matt let his butt slide back down into his seat. He looked warily from Evan to Kelly. "But Evan is my dad, right?"

Evan held up his fist for their secret handshake. "I am

your dad, Matt-man. I will be your dad for the rest of your life. You are safe with me."

His little face became thoughtful.

Kelly kissed him on the top of the head. "Sometimes we get problems in life. But if we stick together, they all work out."

He looked up at her. The trust in his eyes made her so very proud. "Okay, Mom."

Just like that. Her son's well-being rested in her hands as it always did. With Evan by her side, no one would get in their way.

She wasn't going to give up on either cause.

As they entered the penthouse, Evan's phone rang. He answered when he saw the caller ID.

"Steve. What's going on?"

"Is Kelly with you?"

"Yes."

"Put me on speakerphone."

Evan tapped the icon. "Okay, you're on."

Steve practically cooed his satisfaction. "Kelly, my girl, you were brilliant today!"

Feeling shy, she shot Evan an appreciative glance. "Oh, be still, Steve. I just told the truth."

"Yes, you did. Between your difficult story and that delicious Irish brogue, the phones have been ringing off the tables. Women's rights movements, attorneys, universities, charities. They all want to support or donate or interview you as a sponsor for changing the laws on protecting women on assault issues. I even heard from the governor's office.

"Oh, my."

He laughed. "If you two wanted to start a grassroots movement, you've done a good job. Campbell is scrambling."

Kelly's hand went to her throat. "The power of the media. Wow. I'm a little overwhelmed."

Evan was smiling at her. "We're not done yet, Red. So hold on to your skirts."

Steve spoke again. "Evan, I talked with the board. They want to give you a time slot for your own talk show. Immediately. We have a lot to discuss. When can you both come in?"

Evan laughed. "I'm still mad at you, Steve."

"You won't be when you see the bonus you're getting from today's interview with your wife. You'll have to take her on a vacation. Come on now, buddy. Water under the bridge."

Kelly grabbed Evan's arm. "You might want to consider the offer. After all, the man did save you from lying. Terrible sin, lying."

CHAPTER SEVENTEEN

One month later

KELLY AND EVAN sat on the veranda of their private bunga-low overlooking the Atlantic. Given their new and hectic schedules, they were only able to steal a long weekend. Fall had hit in New York and Evan wanted Kelly as naked as possible all weekend.

Hitting the Florida Keys not only involved less travel time, this isolated, exclusive and lush resort of Little Palm Island offered them every ounce of privacy Evan required.

They'd just returned from snorkeling in the local reefs. Kelly was lightly sunburned and naked beneath the gauzy white sundress that caressed every delicious curve. He was shirtless and had pulled on a pair of baggy white Bahama shorts over his nudity. From the moment they stepped on the mahogany wood ferry taking them to the island yes-terday, they'd done nothing but revel in each other.

Kelly had not only proven herself to him on loyalty and trust, but raised the bar on his own standards. Once com-mitted to him emotionally, it was as if those years she'd stored up her need for love crashed down on Evan like an avalanche. And, God as his witness, he'd never been hap-pier to be knocked off his feet. Her willingness to trust him started the morning of her TV interview, but grew stronger with every signature she placed on Quince's legal documents for pressing charges against Campbell, sworn testimonies and starting the tedious process of requesting Evan's guardianship of Matt.

They soon learned that certain legislators already had requests pending to change the laws governing rape and custody of children born of rape. Her movement to address the state's laws joined these political figures in their cause. Once people learned about the difficulty of this situation, her campaign grew viral throughout the city, the state, the country.

Two women came forward with charges of rape against Campbell, thus reinforcing their position. Quince had assured them that with diligence, they would win the fight to keep Campbell away from Matt until Matt was an adult and could choose for himself. It looked as though, if they could get Campbell convicted, whether he did jail time would be determined by his defense. Either way, Kelly's goal would be achieved. She and Matt would be free of Buzz Campbell.

The last time Kelly and Evan spoke with Madeline, she was already moved out of their house on Long Island. Kelly had helped Madeline find her power, as well. Once her world settled, they would discuss the idea of introducing their children.

Kelly reached to the bench beside her chair. She began snapping her beloved Nikon at Evan in his musings before he realized what she was doing.

"Hey!"

She rose from her chair, still snapping. Moving in for close-ups. Her hair was in a braid over her shoulder. The ties running down the center of the sleeveless dress opened enough to show him the enticing curve of her sun-kissed breasts. With the backdrop of palm trees, crystal-blue skies

and the ocean horizon behind her, the total picture stole
his breath.

He pulled her into his lap. "Enough photos."

She kissed him soundly on the mouth. "I will never
have enough, Evan."

He wrapped an arm around her waist, settling her
against him. She smelled of salt water and suntan lotion.
Her dress had gathered up, exposing those long luscious
legs for his pleasure.

"Are you glad to be back at school?"

She smiled. "Thrilled. Given the women I'm meeting
and the places we've gone. I have a lot of subjects. My
photo album will be the best in the class."

"And Neverland?"

Her gaze drifted out to the horizon. When she looked
back at him, satisfaction lit her eyes. "I think Herby would
be happy with Jake and Bunny as the new proprietors. I
can't think of anyone else worthy of owning it."

"I've never been to a Thanksgiving wedding, especially
in a diner."

"I know. Those two are perfect for each other." She
touched a finger to his mouth. "Like us."

"And speaking of us. Are you happy, Mrs. McKenna?"

Her face grew grave. "You didn't bring me down here
to announce our divorce now, did you?"

Ahh. He loved her humor. Just one more facet of this
precious jewel who was his wife—who would stay bound
to him for the rest of their lives if he had any say in the
matter.

He pursed his lips. "On the contrary. I have something
to show you. Up you go."

Once on their feet, he captured her hand and led her
deeper into the bungalow to their sleeping area where a

four-poster bed nestled in the corner. The balmy breeze lifting the bed curtains carried the scent of the sea. The trail of rose petals littering the bed and floor from last night had been cleaned up in their absence. Now, a bouquet of exotic tropical flowers graced the table next to the bottle of champagne chilling.

He turned Kelly in a sweet pirouette and stopped her to face him. He leaned in for a precious, delicate kiss.

"I have a gift for you."

She smiled. "I love presents."

He slipped the strap of her dress off a shoulder and kissed the soft flesh on the spot where the strap had rested.

"Only, to receive this gift you must be naked," he said, letting his lips trail from her shoulder down along the soft skin above her breast.

A murmur rose in her throat. "That can be arranged with a little negotiating."

He lifted his head. "Oh, yes?"

A grin pursed her lips. "I'm thinking that to accept my gift, you should be similarly attired, as well."

He reached into his shorts pocket. Something hid in his closed palm. "I can accommodate you, Red. Only I'll need your help, after this…"

He pushed the strap off her other shoulder with his free hand. As he hoped, the loose fabric fell down her body, resting momentarily on her hips. He watched hungrily as she shimmied her hips ever so slightly to allow the fabric to fall to her feet.

Loose tendrils of hair escaped her braid, framing her face. High color was rising on her cheeks and those eyes held an anticipation that made his groin tighten. He would not be able to wait another moment. He bent and kissed her wedding band.

"I needed you perfectly naked to know there would be nothing between us when I brought this to your attention."

Question filled her eyes. "What are you up to?"

He grinned. "This."

He opened his hand. An engagement ring. Emerald cut. Huge. Two diamonds flanking the center stone glistened in the palm of his hand. He slipped the ring on her finger. It nestled against her wedding band, a crowning glory to the vows they'd taken.

"When I told you I loved you, I did not lie. I will love you until the day I die. Now I need to know. Do you love me and will you stay wed through richer or poorer, sickness and health until death do us part?"

The tears that filled her eyes were like a baptism for them both. She wrapped her arms around his neck, pressing her body as close to his as she could possibly get. With every ounce of love and willpower she could muster she met his gaze. He could see it in her eyes.

"I don't need this most precious gift from you to promise my love, trust and fidelity through any goddamn test the good Lord should choose to send us, but I accept this ring with gratitude. I am honored to hold your love. You have brought me happiness I never believed would come for me."

The most beautiful smile he'd ever seen curved her mouth as she reached down and unfastened his shorts. When they dropped to the ground, she smiled at the effect she'd had on his body. Leading him to the bed, she pulled him down next to her, her skin like silk as they entwined arms and legs. She kissed his mouth with a tenderness that touched him right down to his soul. He rolled her over, the magic of this woman, this place and her promise setting him on fire.

Kelly sighed her satisfaction as he trailed kisses down her neck. She answered by using her hands to wreak havoc on his body. Bringing her lips close to his ear, she whispered, "I love you now, Evan McKenna, and will love you through eternity. These words, my sweetest Irish heart, are no lie."

* * * * *

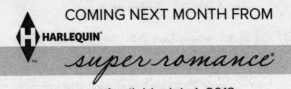

COMING NEXT MONTH FROM

HARLEQUIN®

super romance®

Available July 1, 2013

#1860 BETTING ON THE COWBOY
The Sisters of Bell River Ranch • by Kathleen O'Brien

Brianna Wright has ventured to the Bell River Ranch to make peace with her sister. She's *not* here to be romanced by Grayson Harper—no matter how good-looking he is. But working together on the ranch proves he's more determined than she guessed, and he just might win...her!

#1861 A TEXAS HERO • *Willow Creek, Texas*
by Linda Warren

Abby Bauman has found her ultimate hero. Detective Ethan James brought her through a terrifying kidnapping, but will he be there for her in the days that follow—when she needs him most?

#1862 ONE-NIGHT ALIBI • *Project Justice*
by Kara Lennox

A disgraced cop. An heiress. A night of passion and a murder. Now top suspects Hudson Vale and Elizabeth Downey must fight their attraction *and* work together to prove their innocence by finding the real killer.

#1863 OUT OF HIS LEAGUE
by Cathryn Parry

Professional athlete Jon Farell is the nurturing type, and there's no one he'd rather have lean on him than Dr. Elizabeth LaValley. Though she seems to enjoy their kisses, she wants her well-ordered life back. Well, Jon will just have to show her how much fun a little chaos can be!

#1864 THE RANCH SOLUTION
by Julianna Morris

Mariah Weston keeps her distance from the city dwellers who visit her working ranch. Then she meets single dad Jacob O'Donnell and his troubled teenage daughter. Try as she might, Mariah can't get Jacob out of her thoughts, no matter how wrong for her he might be....

#1865 NAVY ORDERS • *Whidbey Island*
by Geri Krotow

Chief warrant officer Miles Mikowski fell for lieutenant commander Roanna Brandywine the first time he met her—but she's repeatedly turned him down. Now a sailor's unexplained death draws them both into an undercover investigation. And that means working together. *Closely* together...

YOU CAN FIND MORE INFORMATION ON UPCOMING HARLEQUIN® TITLES FREE EXCERPTS AND MORE AT WWW.HARLEQUIN.COM.

HSRCNM06

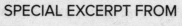

Navy Orders

By Geri Krotow

On sale July 2013

Chief Warrant Officer Miles Mikowski fell for
Lieutenant Commander Roanna Brandywine
the day he rescued her mother's cat. Too bad
she's always turned him down. But now they're
working together investigating a sailor's death
and the attraction is growing. Then, one night to
avoid detection, Miles kisses Ro...
Read on for an exciting sneak preview!

"That was a surprise." Ro's voice was soft but Miles heard steel
in its tone.

He traced her cheek with his fingers. "I'm not sorry I had
to kiss you."

"You did it to keep the wing staff from seeing us, didn't you?"

"Yes."

"Is this how you usually run an explosive ordinance op,
Warrant?"

"Out in the field, the guys and I don't do much kissing." He
saw her lips twitch but no way in hell would she let him see
her grin. Ro was so damned strong. He knew it killed her to

let go of her professional demeanor, even in civvies.

"No wonder, because it would prove way too distracting. I hope you don't plan a repeat maneuver like that, Warrant."

"I do whatever duty calls for, ma'am."

She glared at him. She didn't usually show this kind of heat, and it took all his control not to haul her onto the bike and take off for his place.

"What we're doing will not call for that kind of tactic again, get it?"

"Got it," he replied. She'd enjoyed it as much as he had, he was sure of it. But this discussion was for another occasion, if at all. "It's time to get to work, Commander."

Will this *really* be the last time for that kind of tactic? Or will circumstances keep pulling Miles and Ro together? Find out in NAVY ORDERS by Geri Krotow, available July 2013 from Harlequin® Superromance®. And be sure to look for other books in Geri's WHIDBEY ISLAND series.

REQUEST YOUR FREE BOOKS!
2 FREE NOVELS PLUS 2 FREE GIFTS!

HARLEQUIN®

super romance®

More Story...More Romance

YES! Please send me 2 FREE Harlequin® Superromance® novels and my 2 FREE gifts (gifts are worth about $10). After receiving them, if I don't wish to receive any more books, I can return the shipping statement marked "cancel." If I don't cancel, I will receive 6 brand-new novels every month and be billed just $4.94 per book in the U.S. or $5.24 per book in Canada. That's a savings of at least 14% off the cover price! It's quite a bargain! Shipping and handling is just 50¢ per book in the U.S. and 75¢ per book in Canada.* I understand that accepting the 2 free books and gifts places me under no obligation to buy anything. I can always return a shipment and cancel at any time. Even if I never buy another book, the two free books and gifts are mine to keep forever.

135/336 HDN F46N

Name _____ (PLEASE PRINT) _____

Address _____ Apt. # _____

City _____ State/Prov. _____ Zip/Postal Code _____

Signature (if under 18, a parent or guardian must sign)

Mail to the **Harlequin® Reader Service:**
IN U.S.A.: P.O. Box 1867, Buffalo, NY 14240-1867
IN CANADA: P.O. Box 609, Fort Erie, Ontario L2A 5X3

Are you a current subscriber to Harlequin Superromance books
and want to receive the larger-print edition?
Call 1-800-873-8635 or visit www.ReaderService.com.

* Terms and prices subject to change without notice. Prices do not include applicable taxes. Sales tax applicable in N.Y. Canadian residents will be charged applicable taxes. Offer not valid in Quebec. This offer is limited to one order per household. Not valid for current subscribers to Harlequin Superromance books. All orders subject to credit approval. Credit or debit balances in a customer's account(s) may be offset by any other outstanding balance owed by or to the customer. Please allow 4 to 6 weeks for delivery. Offer available while quantities last.

Your Privacy—The Harlequin® Reader Service is committed to protecting your privacy. Our Privacy Policy is available online at www.ReaderService.com or upon request from the Harlequin Reader Service.

We make a portion of our mailing list available to reputable third parties that offer products we believe may interest you. If you prefer that we not exchange your name with third parties, or if you wish to clarify or modify your communication preferences, please visit us at www.ReaderService.com/consumerschoice or write to us at Harlequin Reader Service Preference Service, P.O. Box 9062, Buffalo, NY 14269. Include your complete name and address.